*Also By Jancee Dunn*

But Enough About Me:
A Jersey Girl's Unlikely Adventures
Among the Absurdly Famous

# Don't You
# Forget About Me

Jancee Dunn

Don't You
Forget About Me

*a novel*

Villard  Ⓥ  *New York*

*Don't You Forget About Me* is a work of fiction.
Names, characters, places, and incidents are the products
of the author's imagination or are used fictitiously.
Any resemblance to actual events, locales, or persons,
living or dead, is entirely coincidental.

Copyright © 2008 by Jancee Dunn

Published in the United States by Villard Books,
an imprint of The Random House Publishing Group,
a division of Random House, Inc., New York.

VILLARD and "V" CIRCLED Design are registered
trademarks of Random House, Inc.

LIBRARY OF CONGRESS CATALOGING-IN-PUBLICATION DATA
Dunn, Jancee.
Don't you forget about me: a novel / Jancee Dunn.
p.   cm.
ISBN 978-0-345-50190-5
1. Adult children—Fiction.   2. Class reunions—Fiction.
3. Domestic fiction.   I. Title.
PS3604.U5577D66   2008
813'.6—dc22        2008006068

Printed in the United States of America on acid-free paper

www.villard.com

2   4   6   8   9   7   5   3   1

First Edition

Book design by Laurie Jewell

# Don't You
# Forget About Me

Join us for our "Totally Awesome" 20-year Reunion of Bethel Memorial High School Class of 1988!!!! (Now it's James J. Florio High School, but it'll always be Bethel to us!!! Right, gang?)

*Where:* the Hamilton Park Hotel & Conference Center

*When:* November 28–29. Business/Festive attire.
For those who are arriving on Friday night, there is an informal get-together at Playmaker's Bar & Grille starting at 5:30 p.m. Although not an "official reunion event," we agreed that it might be fun.

*Saturday's Schedule:* Bethel Rams homecoming game, Welcome Cocktail Hour, 5:00. Buffet dinner at 7:00. Activities at 8:00: Door prizes, slide show. Music provided by DJ Noyz—lots of 80s tunes!!!! And to our "missing" classmates who have signed on to our website— Thanks, guys!!! But we are still having trouble locating 31 classmates, so please let Patti Choi (now Patricia C. Bradford) know if you have a way to contact them.

*Wanted:* photos for our slide show and pics of your kids for our special Family Bulletin Board! E-mail Randy "Flem" Fleming at Darklordwarrior@jmail.com. This night should prove to be unforgettable. SEE YOU THERE!

*chapter one*

"Lillian!" Vi caroled from her dressing room. "Can you come in here? We need your opinion."

"Coming," I called. I already knew what I was going to see. The same scene replayed itself every week or so.

Vi stood in the middle of the room, hands on hips. She was wearing one of her usual ensembles: a mint-green pantsuit in what she called a "fine-grain" polyester, a red and green scarf knotted at her throat, colossal red glasses, and shiny white enamel earrings the size of half-dollars. Vi's wardrobe assistant, Keysha, threw me a pleading glance.

"Keysha says this suit makes me look old," Vi said with mock anger.

Keysha sighed. "Mint green is not a good look on anyone. Not on hospital workers, and not on you." She adjusted Vi's lapels. "Could you just break it up with a different pair of pants?"

"It's pistachio, not mint green, first of all." Vi turned and regarded me. "Lillian, does this make me look old?" Whenever Vi showed me an outfit, she thrust her foot forward in a ninety-degree angle, like a fifties fashion model.

It was probably not the time to remind her that she was seventy-four. I took in the entire getup and found myself smiling. I loved Vi's cheery fruit-salad outfits, even when they were slightly demented, but then I always preferred the "before" entry in makeover shows. What was so wrong with piling on accessories and wearing colors not found in nature?

"You look terrific," I said. *Terrific* was one of Vi's favorite words. I had adopted it over the years, along with *marvelous*, *nifty*, and *spectacular*. If any particular day was not spectacular, Vi would will it into being so.

Keysha sighed in defeat. "Tell makeup to put a little more rouge on you, at least, so your skin doesn't look green," she told Vi. *Rouge* was another word that we all had picked up.

I followed Vi into the makeup room to go over the day's schedule. Usually she had two guests on *Tell Me Everything! With Vi Barbour*, but this morning she had landed one of the fifties' biggest names, Gene Murphy, so he had the full hour. Of course, in his heyday, Gene would never have deigned to appear on a minor network chat show with an autumn-years demographic, but these days he was happy to guest on a program where he'd never have to explain who he was to a blank-faced twenty-two-year-old production assistant. On *Tell Me Everything!*, Vi would announce grandly that a man like Gene Murphy needed no introduction.

"Gene will be arriving in fifteen minutes," I said. "His only request is that he wants to talk about a cable documentary he's featured in about the studio system in the forties. Oh, and he says he has a 'cute story' about a contest the studio ran that involved a date with him, so be sure and ask about that."

Vi nodded. "Check, and check," she said. Vi retained everything. Never once did she require notes or a cue card. She grabbed my arm. "And did you find those books that Monte wanted?"

"I sent them yesterday." I had ceased being a mere producer years ago. I was social secretary, shrink, stylist. To my husband Adam's eternal irritation, the phone started ringing at dawn, when Vi awoke to do her "calisthenics," basically a series of swishing movements. Her constant consulting with me maintained a reassuringly bustling level of activity in her life.

A production assistant rushed in. "He's here," she said, panting.

I looked at my watch. Gene was ten minutes early. I had friends who worked at other talk shows in New York—hair splitters would say "more popular prime-time talk shows with millions of viewers"—who exchanged war stories of agonizing waits for rap stars or hungover starlets who insouciantly rolled in thirty seconds before they were due onstage. This was never a problem with guests from the Greatest Generation, who would tell me repeatedly that had they ever been late at MGM, Louis B. Mayer would have thrown them right out the door.

"Where's my girl?" Gene boomed from outside the makeup room door.

"In here, Gene!" Vi trilled. She leapt from the makeup chair as he burst in. No one gave a more enthusiastic welcome than Vi, who told him that he looked spectacular and proclaimed to the younger staffers that they were in the presence of a living legend.

Gene, tall, trim, and straight-backed, was matinée-idol casual in a safari jacket and brown ascot, his wavy toupee perfectly arranged. After giving Vi a kiss on both cheeks, he sat in the makeup chair and crossed his long legs. "Hello, Maria, my dear," he said to our makeup artist. As a repeat guest, he loved being on a first-name basis with all of Vi's staff members. Maria gingerly dabbed foundation on his forehead with a cosmetic sponge. She was famously tactful and discreet, for no one is more insecure than a star in his Lifetime Achievement years. Maria had been with *Tell Me Everything!* since its inception a decade ago, and during that time she had navigated countless cravats, turbans, hairpieces, and hats. She knew to stock a constant supply of Brylcreem and tangerine lipstick. Without changing expression or breaking her easy patter, she took requests to yank up the creased sides of faces and tape them behind ears to achieve temporary tautness, apply hemorrhoid cream to diminish eye bags, pencil in patchy eyebrows, camouflage liver spots, and spackle various crevices. She was not fazed when a famous R&B producer in his seventies asked that she use eyebrow pencil to painstakingly draw curls on his balding head while he chatted on his cell phone.

Gene turned to me. "Hello, Lillian, darling. Still married?"

I smiled. "Still married."

He snapped his fingers. "Drat. Well, you know I'll always be here, waiting, when you come to your senses."

"You rascal, Gene," I said stiltedly. I had zero flirting skills.

He looked at me approvingly. "You know, you really do look a little like Elizabeth Taylor," he said. "Slimmer, especially around the bustline—I don't offend, do I? But you do have the same dark hair, same eyes—a double row of eyelashes, just like she does. I dated her once, you know."

I knew, because Gene dropped it into every conversation. He was soon hustled onto Vi's small stage, which held two fatigued mauve armchairs and a little table. I watched the monitor, my arms folded, but I wasn't worried. Usually each show proceeded soothingly apace. If we featured slapstick comedians, a little controlled wackiness might break out—maybe one would turn the table over or dump his glass of water over his head—but otherwise the hour was filled with G-rated tales of USO tours or the tantrums of a long-dead director.

"Gene, I understand you have a marvelous story for our viewers about working for MGM," Vi began.

He leaned expansively back in his chair. "Well. When I was making pictures in the early fifties, the studio would send me all over the country on tour, you know, to get my name out there." He twinkled at Vi as if to say, *Do you believe my name once needed to get "out there"?* "And I remember one magazine, I think it was *Movie Mirror*, ran a contest to win a whole day with Gene Murphy. So this really lovely housewife in Boise, Idaho, wrote a terrific letter about how she and her kids watched my films together and they felt that I was the sixth member of their family. So what do you know, I get sent to Boise. I had certainly never been there before. The closest I had come was probably Salt Lake City, where I filmed parts of *My Teepee or Yours?* in 1950."

I caught the amused gaze of Frank, my assistant producer, and he rolled his eyes. All our guests acted as if they'd never stepped a velvet-loafered foot outside of Beverly Hills. Gene Murphy, formerly Herman Ehrstrom of Kansas City.

"I can't tell you how much fun we had on *My Teepee or Yours?*, but that's another story." He raised a suggestive eyebrow as Vi chuckled. Clearly he still thought the film, in which white actors wore feather headdresses and made jokes about selling squaws for wampum, was the height of comedy.

"So off I go to Boise, and Betty, that was her name, was so welcoming, a really, really nice lady. She told me that the second-place prize was a Frigidaire." He waited a practiced beat. "Do you know that she confessed to me that what she really wanted was the Frigidaire?"

Vi howled to let him know how outrageous that was.

"Imagine," he continued. "But she and her whole family made me feel wonderful."

After he dusted off a few more stories ("Did you know my first date was with Elizabeth Taylor? I was an extra in *National Velvet*, and . . ."), I cued Vi to wrap it up, bundled Gene into his limo, and sat with her in the makeup room as Maria touched up her face. When a show wraps, most people in front of the camera can't wait to tissue off the pancake makeup, but not Vi. Having been in the limelight for half a century, she felt that she owed it to her fans to look put together at all times.

In New York City, she was still recognized at least a few times a day. Her career began in film, where she was usually cast as the wisecracking best friend and, later, the stern but secretly vulnerable Lady Boss, after which she took a turn on Broadway, most notably in the groundbreaking musical *Mrs. President* ("I know it sounds funny to think about, but it was a completely radical idea at the time"). Then, of course, she became the popular host of the long-running fifties talk show *Let's Chat*, for which she had recently collected an honorary Emmy.

"Give my eyebrows another swipe, won't you, Maria?" she said. Vi was horrified at the sight of young celebrities who slopped around in flip-flops when they were out in public.

From Vi's 1959 autobiography, *It Wasn't Easy:*

I think that looking groomed is a sign of respect to others. My first activity of the day is to put on my "face," even if I'm home alone. If my fans got a gander of me without my "war paint" on, they would faint dead away! So even if I am running out to purchase a quart of milk, I make sure that my outfit and makeup flatter my complexion, and that my hairdo is smooth and up-to-date.

Needless to say, the best way to enhance your looks is to have an upbeat attitude. How many times have you had a friend telephone you and say, "I don't feel well today" or "Isn't this weather terrible?" Well, I don't believe in inflicting your troubles on other people. I always say that Vi is short for vibrant! I keep my telephone voice cheerful and stimulating, and as a result, my phone is ringing off the hook!

Aside from *It Wasn't Easy,* Vi's prodigious literary output included a bestselling 1965 cookbook, *Lights, Camera, Cook! Vi Barbour Shares Fifty Mouthwatering Recipes from the World's Most Glamorous Gals That Will Make You the Leading Lady of Your Next Dinner Party!* and a beauty book (*Is That Really Me?*) before tapering off in the mid-eighties with the follow-up to her memoir, *Who Says There Are No Second Acts?*

Vi, always percolating with new projects and schemes, was probably on her fifth or sixth act. Meanwhile, I was sliding toward thirty-eight, and I was easily more staid than Vi and her geriatric pals.

*chapter two*

"Thank you, Maria, dear," said Vi, rising to leave. "Until to-morrow, Lillian." She gave me a good-bye hug and clicked out the door, trailing a faint scent of face powder and Youth-Dew perfume. I took Vi's tape to the production room, then stopped by my office to check my messages. There was one from the ancient publicist, Sy Rosen, informing me in his gravelly voice of some new senior vitamin supplements that his client Mitzi Taylor was pushing. Mitzi had been a pan-elist with Vi on a long-running game show in the sixties called *You'll Never Guess,* so Sy knew he could call in a favor. Vi was extremely loyal.

"Oh, why not?" I said aloud. "Let's book her."

Next was a message from my mother, her second of the day. They always caught me by surprise. When I was growing up, my mother used the phone strictly for brief exchanges of important information, but since she and my father retired, she had begun to call me with bewildering frequency, often simply to relay various "thoughts." "Hi, honey," she'd begin. "Listen, I had a thought . . ." A simple drive to Wal-Mart could bring forth dozens, sometimes hundreds of thoughts. *Hi, honey, had a thought. I feel like I should save the frog that swims in our pool, because he's slowly turning white from the chlorine and that can't possibly be good for him. But then where do I put him? Hi there. Real quick: You do know that you're supposed to throw out your spices after six months, right? I saw it on the* Today *show. After a few months, they not only lose their flavor but they might be dangerous! Hi, listen, darnedest thing: Your father and I switched to oatmeal for breakfast, and now we don't have our midmorning snack anymore. It's that filling! You should try it, but just make sure it's not the instant kind.*

I never used to return those calls, assuming that once the Thought had been registered, she moved on, but then I would receive anxious follow-up messages. *Did you get my call about throwing out the cotton that comes with aspirin because it might contain bacteria?* I had learned to phone back right away and supply a satisfying reaction. *So the cotton might contain bacteria? Well. That cannot be good.* Then she could provide the additional information that she had been saving for the postmortem: *That's not the half of it. I've read that if the aspirin happens to be expired, it can cause serious irritation of the stomach lining. Mix bacteria in with that stomach trouble, and you've got a major problem. A major problem.*

Today's Thought was *I may do a class on composting this year. It really seems like compost is a hot topic nowadays.* After she retired from her job designing landscapes at office parks all over New Jersey, my mother started teaching weekend gardening classes at County College of Morris. I made a note to phone her back and say, *Oh, composting is huge,* so she could drop whatever bomb she had been harboring (*Do you believe that you can compost dryer lint?*).

I phoned Adam to check in.

"Hey," he said. "How was Gene? Did he hit on you?"

"Of course."

"Same old Gene," he said absently. His voice took on the ghostly tone that meant he was studying his computer. I knew he was scrolling through property listings, which he checked obsessively when he wasn't showing apartments. He made a great pretense of being busy, but he actually wasn't a very successful real estate agent because of his fatal impulse to be truthful. Within five minutes of showing a potential client an apartment, he was sheepishly telling them about the noisy trucks at 5 A.M. and the upstairs neighbor with the flourishing home taxidermy business. I would argue with him: Why rob legions of New Yorkers of the time-honored tradition of finding out an apartment is horrible two weeks after signing the papers? If you didn't have nightmare neighbors and crumbling ceilings, what were you supposed to talk about at cocktail parties?

"How's work?" I asked.

"Mm. Busy today, which is good. In fact, I think I have to go. The boss is heading my way."

"Okay. See you tonight. I'm in a pizza mood."

I phoned him every afternoon to plan dinner. Pizza at home with Adam was my idea of a perfect evening. Adam was more social than I and went out a few nights a week to concerts and parties and basketball games, while my rare nighttime engagements festered on my calendar, looming like annual pelvic exams. I ran from crowds. I flinched at loud noises. I preferred gentle daytime activities: museums that chronicled life in a traveling circus in the 1920s, a botanical garden with an extensive rose collection, a visit to a hat store, afternoon tea at a grand hotel. Adam often said that I was a cross between an old lady and the campier strain of Gay Man.

I just had no interest in contemporary pop culture. The last time I was fully engaged was during my teen and college years in the eighties. After that I seemed to stop, then go backward. Fortunately, during my tenure with Vi, it was easy to forget entirely what decade I was actually living in. Adam and my modest gaggle of friends did not share my more retro interests but tolerated them with good humor, while Vi could have been my more creased twin. Some of my happiest times took place at her capacious house in Connecticut, playing June Christy records on the "hi-fi" and sifting through the piles of jewelry given to her by her three husbands. Her housekeeper would fix us creamed chicken on toast, and we would settle on her mauve floral couch to watch the episodes of *Your Show of Shows* that Vi had glommed from the Museum of Television and Radio.

I was perceived among my contemporaries as charmingly eccentric rather than a weirdo, protected as I was by decent looks and the requisite runner's body of the Upper West Side professional female. It's simple: If you collected old 78 records for phonographs, as I did, good looks provided a handy upgrade from "nutbag" to "interesting." Even so, I had never been able to master the careless ease with which the attractive flitted through life. During the few times that I accompanied Adam to events, he was always surrounded by a horseshoe of chortling people. I was content to laugh along. It was the same way with Vi. I was happy to let her sparkle. I didn't want to be them; I just wanted to be around them.

My co-workers, used to me begging off, stopped inviting me to their shindigs years ago. It didn't bother me. After all, it was my doing. Still, it was painful to discover for myself the two saddest words in the English language: "What party?"

I glanced out my office window. The light was fading and the streets glowed dark blue. I went to the production room to edit Vi's tape, a painless process that took the usual forty-five minutes, and then shut down the equipment. I called out my "See you tomorrows" as I walked down the hallway, in which every inch of wall was covered with photos of Vi and various grinning guests. As I headed for the subway, a rough wind spiraled the trash. Plastic bags lurched and twirled on the street like urban tumbleweeds. I shivered happily in the crisp September air. Vi had been humming "Autumn in New York" for the past week, and now I was too.

The #1 train was crowded but I slid into the one remaining seat. I opened my *New York Post* and glanced at Page Six as a lanky guy with a knapsack wended expertly through the passengers, plying hand-cranked flashlights that ran without batteries. "Better to have and not need than to need and not have," he announced in a deep voice. No takers. "Don't want to be running to the battery store when there's a blackout." One more time. "How are you gonna get to the battery store anyway if you can't see where you're going?" He shrugged and moved to the next car.

One stop later, a pair of sturdy women, chattering loudly and carrying shopping bags, planted themselves in front of me.

"So if *The Lion King* is at eight tomorrow, then we should go to dinner at six," said the taller one with the pink floral purse. Out-of-towners. "Mike likes to eat early, right?"

"Yah. We have to go to Red Lobster in Times Square, it's supposed to be *yuge.*"

The corners of my mouth twitched. *A stupendous idea! Travel hundreds of miles from the suburbs to the culinary capital of North Amer-*

*ica so that you can order the Admiral's Feast and the Fudge Overboard at
Red Lobster, just like you do in your hometown!*

The taller woman shifted her bags and looked around in vain for
a seat. "What's going on next week for you?"

"Well, it's Kaylin's fourth, so we thought we'd get her that swing
set, like the one you got for Taylor. You know, the orange one."

*Ah, yes! Those orange and yellow molded plastic swing sets that sit
forlornly in every suburban backyard! The ones with the depressing,
three-foot slide, right? Hey, question: Have you ever seen a kid playing on
one? Ever? But go ahead and buy it for Kaylin, and after she halfheartedly climbs on it once and then goes inside to watch television, it can
function as a clown-colored memorial to the last time she played outside!*

The women had stopped chatting, their eyes fixed uneasily on
me, and I realized that I was mouthing the words like a crazy person.

After they exited the train at Times Square, I read in silence
until a blond man next to me said loudly, "How are you today?" He
was staring past me at a fixed point, smiling, and I realized that he
was blind. Was he talking to me? He seemed to be taking a gambit
that someone, anyone, would answer.

The other riders were silent. *Oh please, someone speak.* He
waited, smiling vaguely.

After ten seconds of eternity his smile wobbled. I couldn't bear
it. I cleared my throat. "I'm doing all right," I said.

"Well, good," he said, loudly enough to make people look up
from their papers. "Just getting home from work?"

"Yes," I said. Everyone was studiously pretending not to listen to
the spontaneous theater.

I jumped up abruptly as the train slowed. "That's my stop," I
said overcheerfully, as I made my escape. "Have a good night."

I blinked confusedly at the sign above the platform. In my haste to escape, I had gotten off two stops early. Well, it served me right to have to walk the extra ten blocks. Why couldn't I just talk to the guy? That bit of conversation might have been his only chance for social interaction before retreating to his apartment. Or maybe the people on the train were this man's way of passing the time, his Page Six. I was still rattled as I climbed the stairs to our third-floor walk-up. I needed to get right into my robe and my Socks to Stay Home In, an actual brand name of socks that my mother gave to me every Christmas. They were the sock equivalent of I-give-up elastic-waist sweatpants—fuzzy and comfortable, in fashion-forward colors like pea green and fuchsia-and-black stripe. Petroleum-based Socks to Stay Home In did not contain a particle of anything found in nature, so during the colder months I kept my feet well away from our fireplace because those highly flammable socks could easily catch fire and the chemical ooze would weld them permanently to my feet.

Fortunately, Adam rarely noticed what I wore (the trade-off being that he would only comment on a nice outfit if prompted), so my Socks got quite the workout. Tonight: fuchsia and black. *Oh yes.*

I always made it home before Adam, who liked to have a post-work wind-down with his realtor cronies at a pub below the office. I planned to flip through the pile of magazines that teetered on the coffee table. Were there any gingersnaps left in the pantry? I had hidden the box from Adam, behind the mugs, but sometimes he found my stash anyway.

I frowned as I fumbled for my keys. Was that the squeak of shoes on the kitchen floor? Somebody was already home.

*chapter three*

I was slightly miffed to open the door and find Adam standing in the kitchen. He didn't appear to be doing anything. His arms hung at his sides as he stared at me.

"Hi," I said. "What are you doing home?"

He swallowed. "I have something to tell you."

I smiled, but my heart lurched and began to pound. I didn't like the expression on his face.

I put my bag down. "Sure." I hesitated. *Come on,* I told myself, *this is the guy that children climb all over at parties, the one who does funny dances in public places to embarrass me.*

He took a breath. "I can't do this anymore."

I stared at him. "What do you mean, 'this'?"

"I think . . ." He struggled for composure. "I think we need a break from each other."

I sat down on a kitchen chair, slowly, gently.

"I know this is a shock, and I'm sorry to do it this way, but I've been trying to tell you for weeks," he said in a rush.

"Can't we . . ." I cleared my throat. "Can't we at least go back to counseling?" Last year we had seen a couples therapist after our marriage hit one of our "rough patches." It's not that we had been arguing. We rarely did. We were, as always, respectful of each other. We had just stopped having sex for a month, which stretched into two, and then four. Sometimes when we were both home we could spend the whole evening not exchanging a word—a situation not helped by Adam's newfound habit of wearing an iPod in the apartment—but I always felt that we didn't need meaningless chatter to feel connected.

He sighed. "All counseling told me was that we're great friends. I knew that already."

"But isn't that the basis for a good marriage?"

"I have plenty of friends. I want something more. I want to be excited to see you, Lillian. And I'm not. We barely have sex—"

"We've been together for fifteen years! Show me one married couple that has a ton of sex when they've been together for as long as we have."

"A ton? How about once a season? We don't even look at each other anymore. We don't do anything together on the weekends. Every so often, we make these big plans to improve our relationship, but then we get caught up in work and friends and . . . and dentist appointments, and nothing ever changes."

"But we love each other," I said dumbly.

He softened. "It's not the same as being in love. We're comfortable around each other, but that's not enough, at least for me. I'm going to move out. Just to step back."

When I was a junior in college, I had been in a car accident, and I felt the same numb panic now that I did before slamming into an embankment. I said the first inane thing that popped into my head. "But we're seeing Chris and Elaine's new baby on Saturday." As if our brunch plans would make Adam change his mind. As if Adam would say, *Oh, right. You know what? Never mind about the whole moving-out thing.*

He didn't answer.

I just sat there, gaping at him. I tried to talk, but my face didn't seem to work.

He raked his hands through his hair. "I'm bored by our life," he said quietly.

"I thought you liked our little routines," I said, trying to keep a querulous note out of my voice. Every Sunday I looked forward to our noon matinée; one week I picked the movie, the next week, he did. Every Tuesday, Adam made pizza because he said that Tuesday was the dullest day of the week.

He sighed. "It's more than that."

"It's the kid thing, right?" I said. His face wavered glassily as tears filled my eyes. When we got married right out of college, I made it clear that I was not interested in having children. At the time, he said he loved me so much that he was willing to accept it, but I knew he assumed I would eventually soften. I didn't.

"It has more to do with your reasons," he said. "You never wanted kids because you always say that things are fine the way they are. I'm tired of fine." His voice rose. "I'm fucking *tired of fine*, Lillian. It's like you picked a place and just want to stay there forever—

no risk, no change. I've never understood what you're so afraid of. You don't want to meet anyone new, you aren't interested in—"

"What about all the traveling we do?" I broke in. We had recently returned from Palm Springs, where we stayed at a hotel that Vi had told me about, a favorite of Sammy Davis, Jr.

"We were the youngest people there, as usual, and I think the old guy behind the desk was getting more than I was. Didn't you notice that I wasn't having fun? I couldn't wait to get home. And that trip just ate into our savings once again. We're in this holding pattern where we're still renting an apartment, we're in our mid-thirties and we don't own a thing, and I'm in the business—" He stopped himself. "But I want to be clear. This isn't about money, or the sex. This isn't about kids. And this isn't about someone else. It's about us, right now. This is just not working, and the fact that you look so shocked tells me we're even more disconnected than I thought."

The still-rational white space in my mind offered up one last question before it winked out entirely. "So what do we do now?"

"I'm going to stay at Jason's, so you can live here for a while. I know the lease is up in a few months, and I'll pay for my half until then. After that, I'm sure I can find you a cheap rental." He had planned this. He had been planning this for a while.

After he left, hardening himself to my frantic pleading, I lay on the bed and stared at the ceiling with blank eyes until the cold morning sun slanted across the dresser and crept over the rug. When I could focus my cotton-wrapped mind at all, it returned, over and over, to our first anniversary.


*Good morning, honey. Did you have a nice sleep? Happy anniversary. What's the traditional gift for one year together? I believe that it's paper, but I thought this might be nicer. Yes, open it now! You always look so confused when you wake up. It's very endearing. Do you like it? I know you love bracelets. You are so pretty in the morning. That's the true test of beauty, you know. Do you believe a year has gone by? It has been the best one of my life. I mean it. Even better than the year I met you.*

*Now I am going to make you some anniversary pancakes, and serve them to you in bed, if I can find a tray. With blueberries? I think that can be arranged.*

*I can't stop kissing you.*

*chapter four*

When I stepped off the train in Morristown, New Jersey, I saw the slight figure of my father waving cheerily—no, it was more like frantically—as he waited in the car. "Hello, sunshine," he called gaily, jumping out of the driver's seat to take my bags and enveloping me in a crushing hug. His pale, slightly watery blue eyes scanned my face intently before he reaffixed his cheerful expression. "We need to fatten you up," he said heartily, opening the car door for me. He was wearing his usual post-retirement uniform of "dungarees," black sneakers, and a plaid shirt with the sleeves a precise three folds up his arms.

When my father was worried, he patted my arm a lot.

"Got your room all fixed up," he declared. Pat pat pat. "There's a new coffee place in town, we'll drive by, I know how you like the coffee." Pat pat pat. As he drove, he snuck looks at me. I knew I had lost too much weight. After Adam left, my regimen had consisted of one bowl of cereal in the morning and another when I returned home from work. A week would pass and I would run out of cereal bowls before the dishwasher was filled, so that I ended up washing the ten bowls—that's what we received as a wedding present, ten place settings—and starting anew. For some reason, that bare dishwasher depressed me more than anything. Until, that is, Adam called me and haltingly said he wanted a divorce. I had actually believed that he wanted to "step back for a while," conveniently forgetting that Adam had a ravenous need to be liked, even when he was divorcing someone. So he cut me loose in manageable stages.

One day rolled blearily into the next. If I slept at all, I woke well before dawn, then sat on the edge of the bed for half an hour until I could commit to standing up. At night, friends came over and clucked over my spotty bathing habits, suggesting therapists and antidepressants and trips upstate. I waited for them to leave so I could resume my dead-eyed television watching. My folks called me every day. I think they took the news even harder than I did. They loved their charming, gregarious son-in-law, who insisted on cooking them elaborate dinners whenever we would visit and readily helped my father with his never-ending landscaping projects.

It was alarmingly easy to sleepwalk through work, until one afternoon when Vi announced that she could stand it no longer. "I'm giving you some time off," she said, standing in the door of my office. When I protested that work was helping me, she cut me off. "Lillian, I must tell you frankly that you look like death warmed over. It's depressing me. Please, take a vacation."

I passed a hand wearily over my eyes. "I don't want to take a vacation."

"Well, then, why don't you stay with your parents? Haven't they invited you, over and over? Take a break, put your things in storage, and go home to your mother and dad. There's no shame in picking yourself up and dusting yourself off! You can get an apartment later." She was in take-charge mode, hands planted on hips. "And don't you worry about me, I'll be just fine. Frank can produce; he has enough experience."

She sat nimbly in the chair opposite my desk. Her bright, quick movements reminded me of a sparrow, or a squirrel. "You know, when Morty died, I felt old for the first time in my life," she said. "I thought that no man would ever want to take me out. I can put myself together, but Rita Hayworth I'm not. I thought that nobody would ever hire me again. And of course I felt guilty that I was alive while Morty was dead. I realized that I was grieving, and there was no way around it, over it, or under it. I just had to face it. You, my girl, are not facing it."

She leaned forward. "You know, Lillian, it took years before I discovered some of the simple pleasures of being on my own. But now I can eat chocolate chip cookies in bed at midnight if I want to! I can watch my programs and gab on the telephone all I want. You know how men hate the telephone! I'm not making light of my loss. Or yours. But go home to your parents." She took off her glasses to dab at her eyes. "Oh, what I would have given to have Mother with me after Morty passed! What a comfort she would have been."

She patted my hand. "Go. Frank has been itching for more responsibility, and the show almost runs itself at this point. After ten years, I think you're entitled to some time off. In fact, let's call it a sabbatical."

And so my father was driving me home to the town in New Jersey where I had grown up. I relaxed instinctively as we passed one nail salon after another, their names familiar friends: Sharyn's Touch of Class Nail Creations, Fingerz and Toez, Unique Nail Design by Camille, Who Does Your Nails. Every one of them was jammed. New Jerseyans love their nail salons. And their tanning salons: Bronze Age, Life's A Beach, the unfortunately titled Sun Spot. And, of course, nail-and-tanning salons: Pretty Feet and Hands Plus Tanning II.

As my father hunched over the steering wheel, he gave me his customary update of our town. He jabbed a finger at a half-built complex on the left. "You know what's going in there, don't you?"

To his obvious joy, I did not. "A senior living center, one hundred and seventy-five units. It's the same model as that famous center in Tampa, you know, by that developer. He was in *Time* magazine." My father frequently remarked that he had no use for books because the newspaper and *Time* provided everything that a man needed to know. "Ah, Jesus, what is that fellow's name? Anyhow, I'm on the board. Who knows, I might end up in that senior center myself. Might as well get on their good side."

We passed a hulking brick version of a French château, done Jersey-style with multicolored bricks, glass windows etched with decorative filigrees, and three garage doors. "See that house? Two lawyers bought the old place, a great little cottage, knocked the whole thing down, and built that monstrosity," he said. "Takes up more than three quarters of the lot, which is a total violation of village guidelines. I heard they put an elevator inside. Why, when the place only has two floors? People should get off their big fat behinds." My dad maintained a perpetual state of outrage, in defiance of the doctor's warnings about his rising blood pressure. I suspected he felt that the vinegar coursing through his veins acted as a kind of preservative that maintained his youth.

He braked so I could observe the McConahys' house. "A deer," he said disgustedly. "Right on the McConahys' front lawn, just as casual as you please, doo-de-doo. They're bringing the deer hunt back this year. Some animal groups were protesting, but they obviously don't have deer eating up all their flowers like it's a g.d. salad bar."

He was clutching the wheel a little too tightly. I knew part of the reason he was talking so much was that he was praying to Jesus I would hold it together emotionally until we got home and my mother could handle everything. When we pulled into the driveway, he practically jumped out of the car and speed-walked up the driveway. The house, I noted with satisfaction, hadn't changed much since my last visit, aside from the shutters, which had been painted a cheery shade of blue, and the "fun flag" with a pumpkin on it that snapped and fluttered over the front door.

For my father's sake, I managed not to cry until I was in their hallway and my mother ran over with a teary *Oh, honey.* He grabbed a newspaper and fled to the den while the two of us sniffled.

"You look terrible," she said, her sharp gaze darting from my face to my neck to my spindly arms. "You're even thinner than you were when we saw you at your apartment, and that was, what, two weeks ago."

"I know," I said damply. "Oh, Mom. You shouldn't have to take care of your grown daughter at this stage in your life."

"Now, stop it. How many times have we offered? A change of scenery will do you good."

"This is the exact opposite of a change of scenery. I grew up here."

"You know what I mean. Now, come on, let's take that stuff to your room." We trooped upstairs and she pushed open the door. "And here it is, just as you left it. Except this time it's clean." She swept her hand across the room in an oddly formal gesture.

"Okay, Ma. Thanks." She continued to stand there, so I pretended to look in my wallet for a tip, to make her laugh. I wanted to signal to her that I wouldn't always be moping.

"Funny stuff," she said. She looked at one of my bags and frowned. "What's that?" she said, pointing to a furry ear sticking out of my luggage.

"Oh," I said, embarrassed. "It's a stuffed elephant that Adam and I picked out for my friends Chris and Elaine. You know how they had a new baby? I don't know. I just couldn't give it away."

My mother saw my stricken face. "No, no, no, don't cry again," she said quickly. "Oh, what is wrong with me?" Her eyes flicked around the room for an effective distraction, as though I were a fussing toddler. "Here's something that will cheer you up," she said suddenly. "Dinner will be ready in just twenty minutes, and your father is making your favorite."

I snuffled. "Chicken in a bag?"

"Chicken in a bag," she said triumphantly. This news actually did give me a lift. My dad, the sole cook in the family, was obsessed with convenience, so his favorite entrée was a slab of meat in a plastic roasting bag. The only problem was that the cooking aromas remain tightly encased inside, so my mother learned long ago to make a verbal advance announcement to build anticipation.

"I'll be down to help in a second," I said. First I had to make my ritualistic room inspection. Because of my vigilance, my bedroom was never in serious danger of being transformed into a guest room or my mother's fleeting scheme of a crafting center. Over the years I had always looked crestfallen when they hesitantly proposed various ideas, so my room remained as carefully preserved as Graceland. When my older sister, Ginny, had left home two days after graduating college, she gave our mother her blessing to turn her bedroom into a scrapbooking station, which has since evolved into an eBay-packaging-and-shipping room (one of my father's retirement gigs was flipping local garage-sale merchandise).

I shut the door and flopped luxuriously down on my old bed. Dinner was in twenty minutes! I felt a flash of shame at being so gleeful, remembering Ginny's ten seconds of silence when I informed her that I was moving back home.

"Wow," she had said finally. Ginny had about seven ways to utter the word *wow,* all with varying degrees of condescension. Ginny, a psychology professor at the University of Wisconsin at Madison, had never lived alone. She married Raymond, an endocrinologist, right out of grad school and promptly produced two kids. Ginny had never faced Sunday at 4:30 P.M., the worst part of the week for a recently single person. No friend wants to meet on Sundays at 4:30. It's too early for dinner. The museums are closing. There is nothing on television.

On some weekends, I wanted to tell Ginny, I didn't receive a single phone call. Most of my friends had retreated into family life, toting their young children to birthday parties and playdates. On weekends, the bustling quotidian activities that move the day forward would slow and catch. I was steeped in lonesomeness. My pride wouldn't allow me to tell Ginny that I was foolishly, absurdly glad to go to sleep knowing that there were other people breathing quietly in a room down the hall.

I surveyed my bedroom. The branches of the tulip tree I used to wake up to every morning still tapped gently at the window. Had my mother changed anything? I scanned the faded lilac walls for my familiar artifacts: to the left, the black-and-white Soloflex poster of a guy pulling a white tank top over his denuded chest; to the right, the mandatory Robert Doisneau shot of the French couple kissing; behind me, the poster for the Squeeze *Singles* album that Molly Ringwald had hung in her bedroom in *Sixteen Candles*. On the wall above my desk hung the collage that my friend Sandy Swartz had made for one of my birthdays, a medley of blurry party photos, pictures of Sandy looking better than me, and phrases cut out from magazines, some of which made sense ("when you need a friend," "Spice up your life," "rad body") and others that did not ("Come to flavor country," "There's only one Capri Sun").

My mom had managed to take over my closet and filled it with her summer clothes, but the contents of my dresser were intact, the bottles of Anaïs Anaïs and Giorgio still resting reassuringly on the dresser top. I opened a drawer with leisurely anticipation. I knew what was inside, having inspected it dozens of times, but it had been a year and I was banking on my evaporating memory to yield a surprise or two. The drawer slid open with a jingle of caps from the beer bottles and berry-flavored wine coolers I had saved to commemorate when something noteworthy occurred at a party.

I couldn't bear to throw out a thing; not the barrettes with pastel satin ribbons woven in, nor the cards from my late grandma, with ancient pieces of cracked Beech-Nut Fruit Stripe gum taped inside (one with a note that read, "I'm so proud you're turning 18. You're a special young lady now"). Amid the flotsam at the bottom of the drawer were brown bits of dried carnation that had flaked off of a prom corsage, three black rubber bracelets, *The Official Preppy Handbook*, blue novelty shoelaces with tiny rainbow prints, and high school notes folded to the size and density of bullets for easy passing in class.

I carefully unpleated one note with the precision of an origami craftsman for correct refolding later. It was from Lynn Casey, one of my three best friends in high school. On the front she had scribbled, "for your eyes only." For added security protection, we had devised nicknames—mine was Lulu, hers was Mimi.

*Lulu,*

  *Howya doing? I'm in Earth Science right now, almost over, thank god. Twelve minutes left! I'm totally dreading field hockey, I think Miss Chestnut is going to make us run the two mile. I would ditch it if we didn't have a game on Friday. Hey do you want to go to the mall on Saturday, I swear I only have three pairs of shoes, I need some new Mias. I saw K__ this morning in the hall and he said hi to me, and then after lunch, again. We're practically going out, ha ha. T.T.L.C. right?*

K__ was her crush, Kurt Sebalius. For triple protection, Lynn and I only used initials for key phrases. T.T.L.C.—what could that be? It was something boy-related. I couldn't remember.

  *Sue is wearing her black fringed boots again, UGH, I can't take it anymore. Talk to ya later, Mimi.*

Lynn wrote me a note every single day, all with recurrent themes of seeing K__, feeling totally fat or, at the very least, bloated, teacher bashing, the gossip of the day, and field hockey practice dread. The point wasn't the actual messages. It was about being seen by others as we gave and received notes.

  I unwrapped another, this one sloppily folded. It was from Christian, my senior-year boyfriend. Christian Somers, the star soccer player who drove a battered black Jeep and only drank Dos Equis, his "signature" beer! He rarely spoke or smiled, which of course only burnished his allure. A gaggle of followers slavishly copied his every move, collecting Christian-sanctioned albums from the Clash and the Smiths and joining him for midnight screenings of *Eraserhead*, never daring to admit that they'd much rather just go to the multiplex and see *The Breakfast Club* at seven-thirty.

After Christian boldly wore black Girbaud jeans to a Friday-night basement party, his acolytes couldn't race to Bloomingdale's fast enough. When he abruptly decided to stop eating lunch at the school cafeteria to spend the hour under a knot of trees behind the track field, reading, each day another devotee would be seated beside him, trying to look engrossed in a copy of *A Confederacy of Dunces*. Even Mr. Kast, the soccer coach, twenty-two and fresh out of Rutgers University, cultivated a friendship with him. On Friday nights, the two would kick a soccer ball back and forth in the twilight, while those not lucky enough to play checked their watches anxiously in the parking lot near the field, waiting for them to finish so the night could begin.

Christian's mystique trailed him through college, when he spent a semester in London and impulsively decided to stay. His friends were wounded when he dropped away entirely. Hadn't he had a great time in school like they did? Eventually, as the years passed without a word from him, he was dismissed, Jersey-style, as a "total douche."

I opened the note, my heart thumping painfully. On a piece of wrinkled notebook paper he had written "THIS IS SO FUCKIN BORING." At the bottom corner was a doodle of a bomb with a long fuse that ran the length of the page. "This letter will self-destruct in thirty seconds," it said. On the opposite corner, I had marked "Social Studies class, May 20, 1988" with the precision of a museum curator.

I had saved that thing for twenty years.

*chapter five*

"Lillian!" my mother called. "We're just about ready. Do you want iced tea? It's caffeine-free, so you can drink it at night." I speed-folded the note, stashed it in the drawer, and ran downstairs.

My father was hacking open the chicken bag. "Want to set the table?" he said. On the counter sat three plates, three napkins, three forks, and three vinyl "rattan-like" place mats. The real rattan was tucked away for company.

My father had changed into his favorite navy V-neck sweater for dinner. "It goes with everything," he explained. "Since I retired, I only have about six outfits. That's what retirees do. We whittle it down to a few favorites, and we wear them until we die. Right, Sharon?"

My mother winced. She was in the same size 8 Liz Claiborne jeans she had worn for a decade and a yellow cable-knit sweater with a daisy pin. When she was younger, her hair had been as dark as mine, but after she read in a magazine that women should lighten their color every five years, she had gradually upgraded from Medium Golden to Ash Blonde to her current incarnation of Winsome Wheat.

My parents were very capable, involved-in-the-community types, and the way that we expressed familial affection was to find methods to make one another's lives more comfortable and efficient. We weren't huggers, but my father always did my taxes. He never told us he loved us, but if my sister drove to visit them, he was up at dawn, taking her car to the car wash. Whenever Adam and I moved into one of our many new rental apartments in the city, my mother showed up and descended on the bathroom, bucket and bleach in hand. I, in turn, set up my parents' computer and programmed their remote control. It never felt like a chore, because we all prized more than anything crossing a task satisfyingly off a list.

I watched with bemusement as my dad put together dinner and my mom briskly swabbed the counter with a sponge. Then I brought the plates and place mats to the coffee table in front of the television in the den. "Lily, can you toss the salad?" called my father from the kitchen. He had placed a bag of prewashed greens next to a bowl.

I stared at it. "Isn't it already tossed?"

He sawed off the top of a bag of microwavable Rice-A-Roni and dumped it into a bowl. "Take a look. There's a bag inside of the bag that contains two bags, one of Asian dressing and one of crispy noodles. You see? Open them all up and toss." When my father went grocery shopping, anything that came in a pouch or required little cleanup went right into his cart.

As I sorted out the bags, I saw my parents exchange a brief look and then my mother cleared her throat. "So, do you still talk to Adam fairly regularly?" she asked.

"Yes," I said shortly. "About once a week." Adam still wanted to be buddies, so he was exceedingly upbeat during our hurried exchanges, mostly about paperwork and stray possessions. Détente was achievable as long as our chats did not exceed seven minutes in length.

Adam used to phone me and use funny voices, like Grover from *Sesame Street,* or he'd sing my name. Now he began each conversation with a jovial *Hey, you,* which acknowledged our shared past without being too intimate. This was often followed with the more ludicrous *I gotta go* ("Listen, I gotta go, but how are you?")—Adam, suddenly so busy-busy-busy. After he moved out, he had gotten a new job at a glitzy real estate company that peddled trendy "lifestyle" apartments.

My mom regarded me. "Lillian. I know how much pain you're in. I say that you should have a good wallow." She squeezed my arm. "Even when you were a baby, you weren't much of a crier. I used to forget you were there, you were so quiet. You were always—what's the word I'm looking for, Don?"

"Quiet," he said over his shoulder as he wrestled with the chicken.

"I already said she was quiet. Honest to God, do you listen to me at all?" She studied me. "I think the word is *watchful.* Ginny was a nonstop talker, but you were a very watchful child."

Her concerned gaze caused my chest to start hitching, so to head off more tears I announced, "Who's hungry?"

I helped my dad carry the platters into the den, and we automatically took the same places in front of the television that we had when I was a kid. At my spot on the couch, Mom had placed an afghan. Each member of the family had his or her own ratty afghan, knitted by my great-aunt Ruth during the seventies. Mine was orange, Mom's was avocado and gold, Dad's a manly brown and tan. When Ginny and I left home, our afghans awaited our return in the hall closet. I spread the disintegrating orange web on my lap, taking a luxurious sniff of its familiar aroma: sour wool with a dash of corn chips. Every suburban home has at least one item that smells like corn chips—a rug or a reclining chair or an old blanket—even if it's a family of strict potato chip eaters.

As we sat down, the lights on the deck adjoining the den clicked on right at seven o'clock. My father had rigged every bulb in the house, inside and out, on timers.

He fished around inside the remote-control holder that hung off his chair—a Christmas gift of Ginny's to make life easier—and turned on the TV. "Sharon, I taped a good movie," he announced to my mother.

She sighed.

"It's called . . ." He consulted a pad and paper also kept by the chair. "I believe it's called *A War Worth Fighting*."

My mother took a bite of chicken. "Five minutes."

"Your mother is the eternal movie pessimist," said my father. He turned to her. "If you recall, you're the one who mentioned you wanted to see this."

"When did I say that?"

"You probably saw a preview and then asked me to write it down. How else would I know the title?"

"Don, you don't know the title." She picked up the tape. "It says *Enemy Down*. Do you even know who's in it?"

"That young kid. You've seen him before. He was in that TV show, about the people who had a nuclear winter, and whatnot." He turned to me conspiratorially. "I can't remember names. Then again, neither can your mother."

"I'm better than you are," she said. My mom didn't appreciate his "senior moment" jokes.

"I remember faces."

"Oh, no you don't," she said, throwing her frayed afghan over her lap. "Five minutes," she repeated. I sighed happily. This was much better. Their bickering about movie taping was utterly unchanged since my childhood.

Fifteen minutes later, my mother wandered away to her room to page through gardening catalogs. Right after dinner, she usually stopped talking entirely, to "recharge." My mother was the eldest of six demanding siblings, and her butterfly attention had always fluttered in all directions, from friends to members of her various clubs to my father to the students she taught part-time at the community college. All of us received a maddeningly equal sliver and no more.

She was the only one who could tease my father, and her needling made him less intimidating to us. He was the blustery star, she his affable but perpetually distracted manager. When I would ask her too many personal questions, she would wave me off ("Honestly, you're the most inquisitive person, it's not *healthy*") so that her inner life was a complete mystery to me—and, I presumed, to my father, who regarded her with muted awe.

I glanced over at him. His lids were drooping as he sprawled on his easy chair. Sometimes he slept with his eyes open. You could never tell, because his gaze was always trained on the TV whether he was awake or not. Ah. He was snoring. I wanted to change the channel, but he had a death clutch on the remote and I didn't want to wake him.

He dozed through anything except the faint clinking of a spoon on an ice cream bowl, at which time he would snap awake like a snoozing dog who hears a can opener. When I was a kid, he and I had a tacit agreement that when my mother left the TV room to peruse her catalogs, I was to steal into the kitchen to fix him a bowl of ice cream. ("Your mother has got us on a low-sugar diet again," he would mournfully prompt.) I got up, tiptoed into the kitchen, and opened the freezer. Jammed in among the foil-wrapped parcels that required carbon 14 dating to determine their age and jumbo bags of frozen vegetable medleys ("now with mini-butter pats inside!") was a lone container of vanilla ice cream, an oasis of sugar among the Healthy Choices.

I made us each a bowl and, for a festive touch, sprinkled on some walnuts. He was awake, of course. "Thanks, honey," said my father as I handed it to him. Suddenly he heard my mother on the stairs and in one swift motion shoved the bowl underneath his chair.

My mother poked her head into the room. "Has anyone seen my seed catalog?" We both shook our heads.

She looked sharply at the television. "Don, do you even know what you're watching? Weren't you just sleeping?"

"My eyes were closed, but I could hear it."

"How could you hear it over your snoring?" He didn't say anything and she drifted away. He smiled at me. "That was a close one, eh, kid?"

I grinned back. "That was a close one." Had I ever gone to college? Had I ever left home, traveled to China after graduation, gotten a job? Had I ever been married at the New York Botanical Garden, squeezing Adam's hand as a flamboyant justice of the peace named Frankee Love read our carefully nondenominational vows?

As I headed upstairs to bed (stopping first in the kitchen, where three small piles of senior supplement vitamins and three cups of water were lined up on the counter), I remembered I had to phone Vi. She had instructed me to call and let her know I was fine, but the real reason was her need to include me in everything she did. I dialed her private line.

"Grand Central Station, good evening," Vi sang. "Oh, hello, Lillian. It is just chaotic here!" There was no audible background noise, but Vi thrived on commotion. "Mrs. P and I are getting ready for a card party tomorrow with the girls." Vi had trouble pronouncing the name of her Portuguese cook, Mrs. Postiga ("Posh-TEE-ga," the cook kept correcting), so eventually she shortened it. "Mrs. P is making hot tamale pie, a big salad, a rice ring—you know, with the bits of pepper—and what did we decide on dessert, Mrs. P? Right, your marvelous chocolate frosted brownies. Arlene is trying to reduce and she wanted something low-calorie, but I told her absolutely not. She'll end up licking the plate, like she always does."

Vi, a comfortable size 12 after years of dieting for *Tell Me Everything!*, ate with evangelical enthusiasm. "I'd rather have some unfashionable padding than be a sour-face like Arlene," she said. "You know what I think, Lillian? Self-denial leads to a meanness of spirit. You know me, I gain weight just looking at a Betty Crocker commercial!" She waited a beat for me to laugh. "But I have to have a small dessert every night, or honestly, I wouldn't want to get up in the morning."

Ah, the well-polished "joie de vivre" speech.

From *Is That Really Me?*, Vi's 1957 book of beauty:

There's a certain sort of person who will calmly announce, "Why, I was so busy that I forgot to eat lunch today." Well, that's the sort of person I don't care to be around. If I ever skipped a meal, paramedics would have to rush me right to the hospital! More to the point, I feel that people who like the good things in life, who are generous and welcoming and hospitable, are simply more fun. I recently attended a dinner with a woman who was as slim as a pipe cleaner who announced, "I never eat starches." Well! I can tell you that I won't be breaking bread with her again. Not that she would eat it in the first place. And she may have been svelte, but her face looked worn and drawn. That's because a little plumpness around the face keeps you looking youthful.

Of course, if your girdle is making you gasp for air, simply avoid heavy desserts and say "no thank you" to cream-based sauces. But please don't bore those around you with details about your latest all-asparagus "fad diet," which I can guarantee you was invented by a secretary at a doctor's office who weighs 190 pounds.

"So who's coming tomorrow?" I asked. I liked most of Vi's friends, many of whom she had collected after they were guests on her show. This time around, she was hosting my absolute favorite, Millicent, a brusque former reporter for Associated Press who had once shouted down Henry Kissinger, as well as a fashion designer, an interior decorator for two First Ladies, and a "lady doctor" who used to dispense health tips on the show every Wednesday. And, of course, puppy-eyed, bucktoothed Arlene, best known as the dead-pan sidekick to Bob Schackman in *The Consolidated Oil Comedy Hour.*

Vi was waiting for me to ask her what she was wearing to her shindig, so I dutifully did. "Oh, my apricot pantsuit, with that silk blouse that you like, with the dachshunds on it," she said. "And maybe the white enamel bracelet that Morty gave me. Do you know the one I'm talking about?"

I knew. "What about the glasses?" I said. "I'm thinking the brown frames with the apricot-tinted lenses." Vi had dozens of pairs, something to match every outfit.

"Oh, Lillian, you know me so well!" She laughed. "So, are you adjusting well to life at home?" She didn't wait for an answer. "I really think that a good rest will be the best thing for you. And of course your parents will take wonderful care of you. Oh! And are you still thinking of guests for December? Doris keeps pestering me, she's doing *Steel Magnolias* at the Palm Beach Playhouse, but I don't know. Oh, what the heck, she's a good old broad. And did you ever get those invitations out for me before you left, the ones for the chili cook-off? It's for sick kids. Leukemia, I think, but I must confess that I'm not sure."

I told her I sent the invites, wished her luck, and hung up. Then I climbed into bed, pulled my old blue floral Laura Ashley bedspread up to my chin, and opened a book with a sigh. After a few hours, my head was nodding and I turned off the lamp. A crack of yellow light from the hallway still shone through the door. Then, abruptly, it winked out. *Must be eleven o'clock*, I thought drowsily. *That's when the timers click off.* Then I turned over and went to sleep.

*chapter six*

The next morning I woke up and wandered down to the kitchen. It was eight-thirty and my parents were long gone. A note on the counter read, "Went to Costco, etc. Help yourself to breakfast!!!" Next to the note sat a bowl, a spoon, a carton of orange juice, and a Tupperware container of the cereal that my parents bought in bulk. Every variety had a brand name that was familiar but a tiny bit off, like Frosted Flecks or Rice Krinkles.

They hadn't written when they were going to be home, so I consulted the calendar hanging on the kitchen bulletin board. Every day was black with markings. Today's agenda:

Glass recycle. United Way dinner committee. Oil change. Leaf blower and bags. Pantry duty.

Some welcome home. And what was pantry duty? I distractedly ate some Flecks and wandered upstairs to their office and turned on their computer. The screen saver was a photo of Ginny's children, Blake and Jordan, dressed in crisp blue and white outfits posing barefoot on a sand dune. The tousle-haired kids grinned at the camera, Jordan's arms around her younger brother. They looked like they just alighted from a boat.

Blake was named at the last minute, after months of agony on the part of Ginny. I didn't ease the process when she would call me to sound out her latest name choice, but what was I to do when her journey to Blake traveled through ancient Greece and the pages of Shakespeare? "I was thinking about Nestor," she would say casually. "He was king of Pylos in the *Iliad.*"

"Huh," I'd say. "Nestor's kind of a fat-butt name, isn't it?"

"You think?" I could hear instant doubt in her voice. For all of her gold-plated degrees, I was still able to undo Ginny just by sounding coolly emphatic when I made my insane, baseless pronouncements. I had never met a Nestor, let alone one with a giant behind. But Ginny rarely demanded proof, she just accepted without question that if she named her son Nestor, he would be cursed with a jiggly, womanish rear end.

"What about Menas? From *Antony and Cleopatra*? The character was a pirate, but I love the way it sounds, and—"

I cut her off. "That name says 'bad breath' to me. 'Can somebody give Menas a mint?'" This made no sense, but her hesitant silence told me that the idea had been effectively squelched. Who wants to confer a lifetime of halitosis on an innocent baby? Her unusual submissiveness was so satisfying that I became addicted to vetoing names, and I did so by the dozens as the birth date neared. When she was researching old family names, I became positively dictatorial.

Arthur? "Mm," I said absently. "Hairy ears."

"Name me an Arthur with hairy ears."

"Arthur Miller," I said smoothly. "Art Garfunkel, Arthur Schopenhauer, Arthur Conan Doyle." Being the bratty younger sister had the most rejuvenating effect on me.

"How do you know Arthur Conan Doyle had hairy ears?" She tried to sound challenging, but I could sense her enthusiasm already waning.

"From photographs," I said. Truthfully, I mistily recalled a handlebar mustache, but no hairy ears.

Everett? Dandruff. Leon? Drifter. Boris? Bushy eyebrows with one rogue two-inch-long hair that waved crazily like an antenna.

"Do any names have positive connotations?" she said miserably after one fraught conversation. "What about your own name? It's a family name, too."

I considered for a moment. "My name makes me think of a dish of dusty hard candy that has congealed into a loaf. But for me, that's a positive image."

Eventually I drove her away. In retrospect, I should have approved of a few to keep the game going, Still, I saved Blake from being called Alexey, which I dismissed as something you'd name your rottweiler.

I sighed and clicked onto my high school reunion website. When Adam left me, I had decided not to go. I had lost touch with most people, aside from Lynn, who had become a private-school teacher and lived in Richmond with her husband and son. But lately, just for kicks, I had begun to check the website daily to see who was attending and to scan through Classmate News for fresh posts.

There was a uniformity to most of the updates—many references to kids ("I have two beautiful boys, Shayne and Taylor, who keep me on the go all the time—soccer, tai kwon do, etc.") and unfathomable job titles. What was a systems analyst? Or a logistics manager? How about an associate technical fellow for the Boeing Company working in the area of computational fluid dynamics? Still, there were some gems to be had. Todd Bevan, a slightly unhinged loner with lank, greasy hair who sometimes threw chairs in class, was a clean-cut fireman with three kids. In his picture now, grinning in his uniform, he seemed like a handsome, well-adjusted catch.

Uh-oh. Our class president, Hugh Futterman, seemed to have lost his footing:

I am "between jobs" right now but I have been having a blast with a society that reenacts WWII battles (link to our website is below). Just trying to have fun because life is short. I also raise ferrets in my spare time. Love my little guys! Still into cars & vehicles.

If one has to point out that one is "having a blast," is one actually having a blast? And I always associated ferret ownership with meth labs and matted shag carpeting and drunken parties where the ferret emerges around midnight, crawling around on the shoulders of some kid who should be in bed.

Moving on, Lynn's erstwhile crush, Kurt Sebalius, was doing well for himself:

Took my first job after college as a stockbroker in NYC but got disillusioned. Married a great lady named Cindy and we have two kids, Matteo and Michaela. Last year my wife and I started a home organization company called Clarity Begins at Home and we are kicking ass! Psyched for the reunion. Jonesy, I can still drink you under the table so get ready.

There was, unsurprisingly, no update from Christian, but my heart lurched at the sight of a post from Charlotta Janssen, a tall, arty girl with angular features who was inevitably described as "striking" or "interesting-looking," the sort of person who parents noticed immediately but classmates passed over.

Moved to San Francisco and opened an art gallery. . . . I have traveled all over the world in search of new artists . . . Kenya, Iceland, Thailand, to name a few places. . . . Saw Christian Somers in Paris, he is doing great.

Charlotta saw Christian? He probably never said two words to her in school. And he had lived in London, not Paris. Did they run into each other on the street on a random weekend?

It was maddening.

I checked the RSVPs. Christian hadn't said yes, but then, he hadn't said no, either.

The phone rang. I heard Ginny's voice on the machine. "Lillian, I know you're there. Pick up."

I grabbed the phone. "Here I am."

"How's it going? Are you settled in?"

"I am, pretty much."

"Let me guess. They're out, right?"

"Right. They had something on the calendar about pantry duty, whatever that is."

"Yes. They go to the women's shelter in Newton and fill the pantry with donated goods."

"What? Since when?"

"Lillian, they've been doing it for over a year. So, what are you up to?"

"Since you asked," I said, "I'm reading updates on my class-reunion website. Here's a good one. Do you remember Derek Szymanski, the burnout?

"Derek. Derek. No."

"Remember? They called him Scum-anski?"

"Oh, Scum-anski, right, right."

"Well, now he's a born-again Christian living in Montana. Listen to this: 'and yes, I am enjoying church attendance, and serving God in whatever ways I am able.'"

"Am I correct in assuming you've decided to go to the reunion?"

I paused. "You know what? I think I will."

"Good for you. I had no interest in going to mine. You had a better class than I did, anyway. I haven't thought of any of those people in years."

"Oh, come on. There has to be somebody who crosses your mind occasionally."

Ginny was silent for a minute. "Well. There was this one guy. He wasn't very popular, but I always thought he was so cute."

I sat up. "Really? Who was it?"

"Do you remember Jon Burke?"

"No." I nimbly Googled his name. There were acres of Jon Burkes, but locating people online was a special skill of mine, honed from years of tracking down Vi's cronies to book them on her show. Usually I was armed with only a name and some erroneous detail like *I could swear he was a panelist on* What's My Line?

"Jon moved to our school during my sophomore year," said Ginny. "Normally I would never have talked to him, but we did *Pippin* together. He was in the drama department. I always thought he was very handsome in that classic kind of square-jawed way, but I never saw him at parties. He was just too shy. And you know me; I went out with the jocks. But I always did wonder about him."

Hm. A would-be actor. I tried a few different searches while she reminisced. Nothing. Then I went on the Internet Movie Database, my favorite source for Vi's more obscure actor pals.

Ah. There he was, although he now went by Jonathan Burke. "If I could dig up something, would you be interested?" I asked casually.

"Sure, I guess."

"Well, I have his head shot and résumé right in front of me."

"You do not. You do not!" Her voice rose. "Oh my God. What does he look like? What does he do? Does he still have his hair?"

I could hear a toddler's voice in the background. "What's wrong, Mommy?" Blake piped.

"Blake, honey, go play in the other room," she said absently. "Oh my God. I'm going on my computer right now. Stay there." Ginny never said *Oh my God.*

She gasped. "He looks good," she said quietly. "It's a black-and-white picture so you can't tell, but he had the most beautiful blue eyes. They're the exact color of Windex. Huh. He lives in Los Angeles. Good for him. I wonder if he's married. Wow, he really is cute."

I scanned the bottom of his résumé, after Additional Skills (Southern and Irish Dialect, Driver's License, Red Belt Karate, Billiards, Tennis), and saw that he was "engaged to fellow thespian Lindze Stevens."

"Look at the bottom of the résumé," I said.

"Where? Oh, right, right." She was quiet again. "His résumé is pretty long. He's done well. Look, he starred in some film called *Highway Justice.*"

I called up *Highway Justice.* "It says here that it was only released overseas."

"Oh. Right. Hm. When you really scan through his credits, most of them aren't starring roles," she said. "See? 'Waiter.' 'Agitated salesclerk in store.'"

"Look at the eighth one down. 'Man Eating Apple.' And see the next one? He played a teacher's aide in *Summer School Slaughter.*"

"Well, he's working steadily and that's what actors want to do, I suppose." Then she snickered. "*Summer School Slaughter!* Oh, Lillian." She laughed harder and then let out a snorting noise, kind of like *snoik.* I knew that she was clapping her hand over her mouth. When we used to get into laughing fits, I would goad her until I heard the *snoik*ing noise.

"Let's find out how well he's doing, shall we?" I said. I located his name and address on the White Pages and typed it into the home valuation website that Adam had once showed me, all the while humming fake elevator music to keep Ginny amused. "Aha. So he lives in downtown L.A. in a six-hundred-square-foot apartment. It says here that he paid $229,000 for it two years ago."

"All of this information is available to the public? Is that ethical? Six hundred square feet. That's the size of my garage. And where is the fiancée supposed to live?" She paused. "Well, I wish him luck." In five minutes we had transformed our envy into pity, which was much more manageable.

"He might need some luck. I don't see any parts in the last year. I definitely—"

"Hang on," she said. "Blake, Mommy's talking. What did I tell you about respecting my private time? You can either go watch cartoons or have a cookie. Your decision." Ginny believed in providing her children with a choice between two things, which gave them freedom but allowed her control. Her every action was supported by a theory and multiple footnotes.

"Cartoons or a cookie," I repeated, just loud enough for her to hear. "*Sophie's Choice.* You're a real disciplinarian."

"Wait until you have children." Blake began to wail. "That's my cue. See you."

I meandered downstairs, the beige wall-to-wall carpeting muffling my footsteps. The house was utterly still. My parents preferred to keep the doors and windows shut at all times so that no sounds of a lawn mower or a barking dog ever made their way inside the sanctum. I inspected a pile of books on the kitchen counter that my mother had gotten from the library. *Tai Chi for Beginners.* Which one of them was learning tai chi? *European Travel for Spirited Seniors. Kabbalah and the Power of Self-Transformation.* They had never been interested in religion.

I sat down at the kitchen table and leafed through their recent mail. The only arrival that was the least bit compelling was a J. Crew catalog. I realized I was still in my pajamas and it was nearly lunchtime. Pajamas were my at-home attire in New York, no matter what the hour, but they might look strange in front of my mother, who applied lipstick upon arising, and my father, who always wore shoes in the house. I decided I should order some sort of formal leisure wear and dialed the number at J. Crew.

"Hello-welcome-to-J.-Crew-my-name-is-Trish-how-can-I-help-you-today."

"I'd like to place an order," I said.

"Wonderful. And could I just have the nine-digit customer

number that you'll find on the upper right-hand corner of your catalog's mailing label?"

"Oh, sure." I flipped the catalog over. The label had been carefully scissored away. My father immediately did this to all incoming catalogs and magazines to thwart would-be identity thieves. "Uh, sorry, that page is missing."

"No problem. Okay, then. What is your first item number?" After giving her the style number of my cotton hoodie and drawstring pants in 'Bright Sherbet,' I automatically recited my New York address for shipping. "Ninety-five West Seventy-fifth Street, apartment 3D. Oops. Wait, no. Scratch that. I live with my parents in New Jersey now."

As I heard her typing in their address, I filled the silence by saying, "I'm also going to be thirty-eight years old."

"Huh." She dropped her professional veneer. "Well, it happens. My kid lived with me when she got out of school. I says to her, 'You got one year, and then you gotta go.' And she did. A year to the day, almost."

"Yes, but she wasn't thirty-eight and divorced very soon."

"Ma'am, I don't know you, but you know what? Maybe this could be an opportunity. My mother passed, let's see, three years and six months ago. Lung cancer. You know what I'd give for one more day with her? Do you want to hear about our sale items today?"

"Oh, ah, no, thanks."

"My husband is Italian. In Italy they all live at home until they get married. He had a couple of cousins in their forties still at home. So it's kinda different everywhere. In Italy, no one would bat an eye at you. Think of it that way."

"I don't know, Trish," I said, opening the fridge and rooting through it. "A few of my friends have made snotty remarks."

She snorted. "Some friends. Do you want standard shipping?"

"Yes, please."

"Okay, you'll receive your hoodie and pants in five to seven business days. And I hope you don't mind me saying so, but you should enjoy being with your folks, and don't listen to anybody else."

"Well, thanks. I appreciate it."

I hung up, strangely cheered.

*chapter seven*

The afternoon stretched luxuriantly before me. I started by pulling some leftover chicken in a bag out of the fridge to make a sandwich. Maybe I would watch *General Hospital*, like I used to after school. I could fish out my old Ithaca College sweatshirt and sprawl on the couch. Or I could attempt to find my high school journal. I used to rotate its hiding places to evade Ginny's snooping, but I had done it so well that now I couldn't locate it anywhere. I had thoroughly searched my closet, under my mattress, even a spot behind an old air-conditioning unit in the attic where I had stashed it during a particularly paranoid time. I had looked half-heartedly under the bed but only found a large Tupperware box of wrapping paper, tape, and ribbons. The "wrapping station," a typical first-year project of the recently retired female, along with Finally Getting That Laundry Room in Order.

After changing out of my pajamas, I took a sandwich into the TV room and flopped down with a satisfied sigh. I had stopped watching *General Hospital* years ago, but perhaps there was a chance I could still pick it up. The theme song was the same, if a little jazzier and with extra guitar thrown in to make it "contemporary." I preferred the original. I liked show openers to stay exactly the way they were. At least the producers of *Days of Our Lives* had the good sense to keep the sands in the hourglass right where they belonged.

The show opened on a spray-tanned blonde who was pacing back and forth—agitated, it soon emerged, about whether or not she should go ahead with plans to have a baby. "Sweetheart," said her graying but hip father. "You have to make the decision based on how you *feel.*"

"Good Lord," I said aloud to no one. Her father was Tony Geary, otherwise known as Luke Spencer. Luke! Along with most of America, I had watched his wedding to Laura in 1981. My friends Kimmy Marino, Lynn, and Sandy Swartz raced home from school with me, and the three of us piled onto the same couch I was slumped on at the moment (with new beige slipcovers over the original brown plaid).

And look, there was Jackie Zehman as the scheming Bobbie Spencer, teen prostitute turned head nurse! Back in the eighties, when the other characters would describe poor Bobbie, they would inevitably mention that she was a former call girl from—lower your tone here—*Florida*. As though that explained it. *Florida. Uh-huh. Say no more.*

Bobbie was holding up nicely, too. If you watched the show with the shades drawn, it would seem that no time had passed at all, although Bobbie had to be on her fourth or fifth kidnapping at this point. It was easy to pick up the soothingly familiar plot lines—philandering, blackmailing, tense conversations at the fifth-floor nurses station. The best part of all was the program's final scene. Rick Springfield had returned as Dr. Noah Drake, now a hollow-eyed alcoholic who had drunkenly fricasseed his wife on the operating table.

"I think I need to go on his website," I announced to no one. "He must have a website, right?"

*Who's supposed to answer me? Maybe I should take off one of my socks and use it as a hand puppet. "Right!" it could squeak. "You're my best friend in the whole world!"*

A few hours of channel surfing later, I heard a commotion at the front door as my parents burst in. Good. At least we could all eat dinner together. I had a request ready for one of my father's specialties that I had grown, somehow, to love: teriyaki-marinated filet mignon in a bag. As the meat cooked, it slowly shrank from eight inches to three, while the teriyaki marinade condensed to form an intensely salty, lacquered brown crust. It was strangely satisfying, even if my heart beat a little more heavily after I ate it as my sodium levels spiked.

I turned off the television and jumped up. "Hi, honey," my mom said, panting and tossing her purse onto a chair. "Listen, we're not staying, we have a fund-raiser dinner at United Way. Sorry about that." She and my father dashed upstairs to change.

"Did you have a good day?" I called.

"We did," hollered my dad. "Listen, there's a Stouffer's French bread pizza in the freezer. Pepperoni. Three hundred fifty degrees for twenty minutes." They whirled through the house, and then, before I could preheat the oven, they were gone.

I hadn't had a French bread pizza in years. I used to love them. I shoved it into the oven and went up to my bedroom in search of my Rick Springfield tape. Had I loaned it to Kimmy? I rummaged through various drawers, looking beneath carefully folded piles of Original Jams shorts and striped Esprit tops. There it was. I grabbed a Culture Club tape for good measure.

Now for a tape player. I didn't have my boom box anymore. My father took it outside when he worked in the yard, and eventually it had given out. Was there still a tape player in my folks' spare car, the ancient Honda Prelude? I thumped down the stairs to the garage. *Yes!* I wolfed my pizza, grabbed the keys that always hung on a nail near the door, and slid into the front seat.

It was just getting dark. The night sky was clear, and the bracing October air smelled of wood smoke and fallen leaves. Was there anything better than driving alone in the suburbs at night with the music blasting? I wasn't in a city amid the honking or overwhelmed by the chaos of a highway, so the songs were even more immediate, more satisfying. In the suburbs, sometimes you get the whole road to yourself.

I popped in the tape and pulled out of the driveway. Rick's voice instantly conjured the sweet, wild feeling of high school anticipation. And being in the car—the windows were down, the car was moving forward, and I was right back in high school on a crisp autumn night that carried the very scent of possibility. I was dressed for a party in my new fall clothes, slightly nervous but excited, singing along with the music as I headed to my friends' houses to pick them up.

On a Friday night in the suburbs after a certain hour, I always marveled that it was as if the kids took over the roads. The parents went to sleep and disappeared and you passed other kids in their parents' cars. My friends and I would shout along to Rick Spring-field until we neared the party, then we fished out the cassette that we'd rather the guys heard when we pulled up. Where was Bob Mar-ley? Quick! And then, as you walked in the door, that giddy, sick-making anticipation: Anything could happen!

I cranked the volume and sped faster, singing as loudly as I wanted. Why was it, I wondered, that when you loved a song, the feelings it evoked were so profoundly personal? Pop music always reached me in such a specific, hidden place, and my reaction to cer-tain songs was so unthinking, so visceral, that it was almost sexual. Linear thought vanished completely, replaced by images and moods that I could never rationally discuss even with close friends. Hearing "Jessie's Girl" made me think, simultaneously, of hearing it late at night for the first time on the cheap clock radio by my bed, of watch-ing Michael Garrett put his arm around Lynn during study hall and feeling covetous, and of the video in which a keyed-up Rick smashes his guitar into his bathroom mirror. This was mixed with prickles of elation, the queasy fear of the "make-out room" at parties, unspec-ified longing, and the vivid recollection of one fall afternoon in which I returned home from a victorious Bethel Rams game, shuf-fling through the flame-colored leaves on our front lawn and bounding up the stairs of the porch where a fat pumpkin rested by the door. In the kitchen, a Crock-Pot bubbled with the chili that my dad had made earlier. Why this memory was tied to Rick Springfield, I don't know.

Without even realizing it, I was nearly at Christian's house. I had driven past it approximately three thousand times and had honed the formula years ago. His house was located on a side street, so I used to cruise by first on the main road to ascertain if his black Jeep was in the driveway. If it was, I would double back, turn down his street, and nonchalantly drive by, my eyes carefully forward but not missing the smallest peripheral detail. I dreaded seeing him, yet I craved a sighting of him—preferably through a window or raking in the backyard, just not in the driveway where I would be caught.

Spotting a family member of Christian's was almost as exhilarating, particularly his scarily hip older brothers, Marc and Geordie, or his rarely seen workaholic dad. The most prized sighting of all would be to discover—from afar—the three carelessly good-looking Somers boys raking the lawn together. The appearance of his mom was a bit more mundane but still provided insight. Even a glimpse of the dog was a bonus, or a package resting on the porch. Basically any sign of life to the house was significant, down to the new holiday decorations outside, because it got you to wondering: Was Christian involved in the purchase of the decorations? Was he embarrassed by them? Or did he even notice them?

For years as a teenager, I would take the long way to the grocery store or post office so that I could swivel my neck whenever I drove past that house on Linden Lane, but I had learned to be more discreet after an incident involving Kip Williams, a mild crush of mine that had flared up when Christian seemed especially unreachable. I was seventeen, in recent possession of my driver's license, and was sailing past Kip's house, using one hand to man the steering wheel because I thought it looked cooler. I was so absorbed in the fleeting sight of someone's profile in the kitchen window that with a sudden, mortifying crunch, I hit a parked car in front of Kip's house.

The noise brought six women running out of the split-level next door to Kip's. I realized with awakening horror that they were all my teachers. Who knew that my homeroom teacher lived next to Kip? In my teenage mind, teachers disappeared inside the classroom's coat closet and hung themselves up on a hanger until the next school day.

But there they were, apparently conducting some sort of meeting. Ever sensible, they had quickly called an ambulance, and within two minutes, one came screeching to the curb. Out jumped a woman who looked vaguely familiar. It was Mrs. Garrett, mother of my third-string crush, Michael Garrett. Mrs. Garrett worked as an EMT? I never knew, or cared, what anybody's parents did for a living. They were just a vague presence, there to answer doors and exchange awkward pleasantries before I fled with relief to friends' bedrooms.

My head was throbbing from a hard crack on the windshield, but even if it had been dangling from my neck by a gore-spattered skin strip, there was no way I was going to be publicly bundled into an ambulance, so Mrs. Garrett wrapped a silver blanket around me.

Drawn by the commotion, Kip appeared on his front porch with Brian Miller (known as "Mildew") to idly watch the action. They were rewarded by the sight of my dad driving by, on his way home from work. When he was halfway down the street, his brake lights blazed. Then he jumped out of the car and ran toward me. "Goddammit, you could have been killed," he said, choking, and grabbing me in a rough hug. Mildew snickered and I gazed with envy at a squashed squirrel corpse on the side of the road.

*chapter eight*

I neared Christian's street and recklessly took a left without doing the investigative drive-by first. I peered at the Somerses' house. Still the same white aluminum siding and black shutters. Two planters still stood sentry on either side of the front door. In the summer they were filled with red geraniums, but in the fall his mother replaced them with coleus. The mailbox, as always, featured three ducks flying over a lake and the words THE SOMERS FAMILY. An unfamiliar blue sedan was parked in the driveway.

Why had Christian chosen me, all those years ago? I never dared to ask. I did have a good look in those days— dark glossy hair against a deep eighties Bain de Soleil tan, and I was toned from field hockey drills. Adam always went crazy over my dark sheet of hair. Who knows? Maybe I had a certain mystique of my own. I giggled and chattered around girls but was more composed around the boys, more from shyness than an effort to cultivate an alluring detachment.

The moment Christian had started lingering by my locker at the end of my junior year, I shot from the periphery of popularity to being the girl everyone imitated. During that annus mirabilis of Christian's interest, when we were all seniors, all the elements of my life had woven seamlessly together. It reached a pinnacle on one gold-flecked June morning when I persuaded a few of the class luminaries—including, in a coup, the new pet of the elites, an Australian exchange student named Spencer—to cut class and drive directly down to the shore.

Nine of us had piled into cars (*I am making this happen!* I exulted), stopping first at Chippy's Deli, where Christian's older brother Marc was working and able to slip us a few cases of beer. Then off we went to Jenkinson's Beach—called "Jenks" by those in the know. As I bounced along in the front seat of Christian's Jeep, my hair whipping in the salt breeze, he grinned at me as he turned up "Boys Don't Cry" on the radio and I concentrated so hard on freezing the moment forever that my head ached.

When we returned in the late afternoon, tipsy and sunburned, Christian dropped off everyone but me. "You're coming over to my house," he said. "Everyone's at some lacrosse dinner for Marc." Geordie, meanwhile, was off at college.

I had been officially "hanging out with" Christian for a few weeks, but I had yet to graduate to girlfriend status and so had never been inside the Somers home. With trembling legs, I made my way between the planters of the front door. The hallway was dark and I blinked, trying to get my bearings. Every house has a scent, and theirs was a mélange of dog, dryer sheets, and traces of dinner from the night before, which smelled vaguely Asian. Was it takeout, or did his mom actually cook ethnic meals? They probably used chopsticks. All the cool families used chopsticks.

His dog, a husky named Rufus, trotted over, tail wagging. *Hi, boy! Who's a good lil' doggie! If you stick your nose in my privates, so help me I will stomp your head in!*

Christian saw my expression and laughed. "I'll put him in the basement," he said with a mock sigh.

I looked around greedily. I had always pictured his house as light and airy, but it was comfortingly dank, just like my house. The living room was overwhelmingly brown: leather couches, lifeless plaid curtains, the dog bed in the corner, the pocked coffee table. Family pictures were arrayed on every available surface. Somehow I assumed they would be tastefully housed in matching frames and hung on a pristine eggshell-colored wall.

There was just too much to take in. I picked up a photo of Christian as a laughing toddler holding a red ball and committed it to memory. *This is what our child will look like.* When Christian came back into the room, I now had something to talk about. I could look up and wryly say, *And who is this?*

Where was he? Maybe he was feeding the dog? I held the edge of the frame, waiting to pick it up as he walked into the room, and readied my amused expression. The minutes ticked by.

"What are you doing?" he said as he came back in, holding an Echo and the Bunnymen tape and putting it into a player.

"Who's this?" I said, raising an eyebrow.

"Oh, that's Geordie." I put the photo down.

"How about this?" I said, picking up another.

"Put that back," he said, mock wrestling with me while he grabbed the frame. *We're having a playful moment!* "Come here," he said, sitting on the very couch upon which the mysterious Somers boys draped themselves as they watched television. If only I had a brother who gulped milk out of the carton in his boxer shorts, I would not be as awed by boys. Instead, I had fastidious Ginny, who once told me she shut the door to go to the bathroom even when she was alone in her house.

Christian reached up and tucked a lock of hair behind my ear. Then he leaned in to kiss me. *I am on Christian Somers's couch, and we are making out for the fourth time—four and a half, if you count that day in the parking lot. I may be the only girl who has kissed Christian in his actual home. It can never undo itself. No matter what happens after this, I have officially kissed Christian, on his couch, in his house. He smells like soap, and salt water, and beer.*

I didn't even ask when his parents would be back. *What if they burst in?* The dog was whining and scratching the basement door. *What if it got out? Remember to hold in your stomach, even if your outfit is mercifully loose:* a purple T-shirt with the neck hacked, *Flashdance*-style, a green tank top underneath, and Esprit shorts with a nice, forgiving paper-bag waist. Did I want it to go further? Not if the parents might come home. *Okay, then: don't lie down. Stay sitting up, no matter what.*

He pulled back for a moment and gazed at me with a sleepy grin and soft eyes. Was I supposed to say something? Five seconds crawled by. My left knee was jumping crazily, and I shifted to make it stop. I leaned forward and kissed him again to break the spell.

*He is an expert kisser, and I am kissing him back in the right way. We are meant to be together! Why do boys always seem to know what they're doing? Please, please, Christian, tell just one friend that this has happened! Then it will get around the entire school!*

He pulled away again. Was he finished? It was too intense when he looked at me like that. Some of his top front teeth were slightly crooked. It didn't look bad; it gave him character. My hands were trembling slightly, but I don't think he noticed.

"Hey," he said softly. What did I say back? The "hey" seemed to have some sort of significance.

Once I had quizzed Ginny on what to say after you'd been kissing someone for a while. She thought for a minute and said, "How about 'More, please'?" When she said it, it seemed saucy and self-assured.

"More, please," I said, assuming what I hoped was a devilish expression.

He pulled back, his brow furrowed. "What?"

Did he misunderstand or not think it was funny? Both were horrible options. "Oh, nothing," I said.

The dog began howling and slamming its body against the basement door, and Christian leapt up, irritated. *Thank you, Rufus.*

Is there a greater high in the world than being seventeen and kissing someone you have loved from afar? In college, it just wasn't the same. There may have been a thousand people to choose from, but their history was a blank; there was none of that sweet buildup from longingly studying a boy for months or years and compulsively archiving everything he did. In high school, you catalogued a boy's full wardrobe: He purchased a new shirt; it was noted and banked.

In high school, I saw the boys in class, and at parties, but then they vanished into their homes for the more mundane activities of video games and dinner. In dorms, that crucial distance disappeared. Everyone ate together in the cafeterias, and I knew the color of my crush's bedspread because there it was in his dorm room (a predictably "masculine" navy or dark green). When he returned from the shower in flip-flops, holding his bucket of shampoo and soap with a rank towel wrapped around his waist and a livid red pimple on his back, I knew what brand of antiperspirant he used because there it was, sitting on the television in his room with the cap off and a thick underarm hair clinging to the applicator. And why was there a box of tissues by his bed?

Even when I met Adam in senior year and was so infatuated with him that I couldn't sleep for weeks, when we finally kissed, standing on the steps of my dorm on a snowy night, I was able to coolly assess his skill (solid) and capacity for sensitivity (points for rubbing my shoulders). I was charmed that he was stuttering slightly as he talked to me between kisses, and that he wrapped his scarf around me "in case, you know, we wouldn't, wouldn't want you to get cold." But my hands were steady and my smile was calm.

In some way, I had probably been chasing that high school make-out feeling for the past two decades. Nothing, but nothing matched it. Some of my friends told me that having a baby reproduced the sensation, that it was like having a constant crush, but I had never felt a maternal tug stronger than a mild curiosity to see my physical traits reproduced in another. Adam had always wanted a boisterous houseful, having grown up with four siblings. "We're only twenty-three," he had said soothingly after we were married. "Of course you don't want kids now. But trust me, you will. My sisters say that, boom, all of a sudden it happens."

"What if it doesn't?"

He kissed me on the forehead. "I'm willing to gamble," he said grandly.

For the first few years, we didn't even discuss children, but by the time I reached thirty, Adam had begun a gentle but never-ending campaign. I kept waiting for my magical transformation, but my resistance increased when friends with babies would say, *I never really knew how selfish I was until I had kids* and *I haven't left the house in a year, but I've never been happier.* Our hurried socializing was confined to endless first-birthday parties, as I stood around awkwardly, holding a paper plate with a cupcake on it while other people's children played.

After Adam left, I wondered many times if I had gotten so caught up in passionately taking a stand and proving Adam wrong that I hadn't actually examined in any great depth how I actually felt about the issue.

No husband. No house. No kids. No car. No career plan. I had barely ever been on a date. Some nights, I woke with a crawling fear that it was entirely possible I would never be kissed again. Ginny suggested online dating, but who, exactly, would jump at my profile? Even if people say that they seek someone unusual, I suspected that they do not. No one wants an eccentric.

Let's see: *Shy television producer; irritable, set in ways. Interests include bird-watching, office-supply stores, and the films of Joan Crawford. Just wants people to "behave themselves." Bursts into sentimental tears upon hearing Kate Smith's version of "God Bless America."* What liver-spotted swain would reply to that ad? Then again, older men might be my only alternative.

I flashed to Adam, red-faced and shouting, "Lillian, how could you not see that I was bored out of my *fucking* mind? Sitting around in the living room like my parents did, like we were *embalmed.* What is wrong with you? Don't you want more out of life?" I gaped at him, dumbfounded, because the answer had been no.

My shock seemed to enrage him—Adam, who never raised his voice. "I needed oxygen; your world is as narrow as a closet, you and that old lady, collecting stuff together—"

"You always said that it was charming, all of my quirks," I said.

The wildness drained a little from his eyes, and his shoulders dropped. "Look, I'm sorry," he muttered, seeing my face. He moved to hug me. As his arms encircled me, I could feel the pads of his fingers on my back. He was cupping his hands so he didn't have to fully touch me. For months, he hadn't been able to stand me, and I had not seen it.

*Surely you knew it was coming,* Ginny ventured gently when I told her. *You must have seen the signs.*

"I didn't see it coming," I said aloud. "I didn't see it coming at all." Tears rose in my throat, and I pulled the car over. "Why didn't I see? Why didn't you tell me, or warn me, or . . ." I searched clumsily for tissues in the glove compartment. I unearthed a spare hanky that my dad had stashed in there, and it made me cry harder. My father always had a crisp white handkerchief in his pocket, which had dried both of his daughters' tears many times. Soon the generation of men who carried handkerchiefs would die out completely. I put my face in my hands and sobbed.

A maroon minivan passed me and slowed. A plump blond woman on a cell phone gawped at me, concerned, and I waved her on with a weak smile. After a few minutes, I heaved a long, shaky sigh and dabbed my face with my father's soaked hanky. Then I rolled down the windows and slowly pulled away from the curb. Rick Springfield would cheer me up. I looked at the clock. Almost nine. My parents would be home by now.

*I'll drive for one more hour,* I thought. It was a little too soon to return to the present. I wiped the last of my tears with the back of my hand and drove away.

*chapter nine*

I decided I would establish a routine by running in the park in the morning. It was the same place I had spent countless Saturdays as a kid, so flashbacks would ambush me as I rounded each corner of the paved path: a grove of picnic tables where we had family birthday parties, a patch of grass that was the site of my first Old Milwaukee beer after the Bethel Rams lost a football game.

Exercise is so much easier when you've been dumped. You're so preoccupied that it barely registers if your legs are moving. An hour and a half whizzes by, and suddenly you find that you're sitting on a kid's swing in the playground area, panting and sweating, without the faintest recollection of how you got there.

Adam had gone on a date. A friend of mine had seen him with a woman at a Mexican restaurant we used to frequent. She reported that she was a brunette about twenty-five years old, smiled a lot, and wore a clingy brown wrap dress with high-heeled boots. Then I didn't want to hear any more.

Absently, I pushed myself forward on the swing with one foot. I had to assume that Adam had not been cheating on me, that he had probably met someone at his new job. And what did it matter? He had moved on. I disinterestedly examined the wood shavings under the swing and hummed an old tune by Nat King Cole that Vi thought was upbeat and I found unbearably sad. *Pretend you're happy when you're blue. It isn't very hard to do.* . . .

My thoughts were broken by a grinning boy with leaves in his hair and a goatee of chocolate who was streaking toward me. "Mommy!" he hollered, panting. "Mommy, look at me. Look at me, Mommy!" He hurled himself into an adjoining swing. "Mommy look at me, look at me!"

I threw him a freezing glance before it could register with Mommy. Six swings and he picked the one right next to me. *Didn't you ever hear about "stranger danger"? How about some boundaries?*

"Coming, Kade!" called a voice. "Hang on, buddy."

*Kade.* I jumped up, feeling in my pockets for my car keys.

"Is he bugging you?" asked the mother apologetically. She had a blond bob and a sunny, open face with a sprinkling of freckles on her nose. Her outfit was Moneyed Suburbanite: yoga pants and sneakers for errands, designer purse, and assertive but not vulgar diamond studs.

"No, no, I was just heading—"

She looked at me brightly, her nose crinkling. "Lillian?"

I froze.

She beamed. "It's me, Dawn."

I squinted at her. It was my old classmate, Dawn Shulman, un-recognizable at first with a blond dye job and twenty extra pounds.

"How are you?" she squealed, enveloping me in a tight hug. "You look amazing! God, you haven't changed at all." She pulled away and looked me over appreciatively. "Look at your little tiny waist!"

I beamed back at her as two emotions wrestled within me for dominance: genuine pleasure in seeing her and the enduring guilt that arose whenever I remembered my earlier treatment of her.

In middle school, Dawn and I had the sort of hysterically intense friendship peculiar to prehormonal ten-year-old girls. We spent every afternoon together, broke briefly for dinner, and directly afterward resumed our conversation on the phone, gossiping and planning our matching outfits down to the Bermuda bags. Weekends were for sleepovers and their strict rituals: Every Friday was spent at the Twin Theater for repeated viewings of favorite movies (we saw *The Breakfast Club* a record eight weeks in a row, each time spending the rest of the night trying to replicate the way that Molly Ringwald's character, Clare, danced in the library). Every Saturday found us at Friendly's in front of a Reese's Pieces sundae (chocolate ice cream for me, vanilla, in a rare show of independence, for her). Ceremony was extremely important, especially at the onset of puberty when we lost any semblance of control over our awakening glands.

Dawn, with her limp red curls and pudgy frame, was the classic shy child who flowered among people she trusted, becoming bois-terous and funny. I was more outgoing, my awkward stage less en-during, and when my braces came off the first month of freshman year in high school, I began to attract the notice of Lynn Casey and

Kimmy Marino, two glossy racehorse girls who owned alligator shirts in sugar-almond colors for every day of the week. We people on the pavement looked hungrily at them, with their swinging walk, their clean, tanned limbs, as they chatted in conspiratorial tones on their way to lacrosse practice, cleats slung carelessly over their shoulders. Their white shirts were tucked perfectly in and then pulled out just the right amount in a way that I could never duplicate. Kimmy and Lynn looked just as crisply pulled together at lacrosse practice as they did on a Friday night in full dress. Even their blindingly white scrunch socks were pushed down perfectly on their slim legs.

Lynn was my reluctant science-lab partner, but after a few days, I made her laugh with an imitation of Mrs. Davis's adenoidal drone. Soon I had parlayed the laughs into an invitation from Kimmy and Lynn to walk to the drugstore to buy a bag of lollipops and then watch the boys' soccer practice on the bleachers. Somehow, post–middle school, lollipops had lost their innocence, and Kimmy and Lynn knew it.

Dawn drew into herself when I told her. "How could you hang out with those bitches?" she said finally, her eyes on the ground.

"It's nothing," I said. "It's one afternoon." But it wasn't, and as the weeks rolled on in a thrilling blur, Kimmy and Lynn made it clear to me that Dawn and I were not a package deal. So I avoided Dawn's phone calls and ducked her entreating looks in the hallway at school.

But Dawn Shulman would not conveniently withdraw. She dared not approach when I was with Lynn and Kimmy but waited until she found me alone one afternoon in the girls' bathroom.

"Why won't you talk to me?" she said, her voice unnaturally high and loud. Her round face went red, filling me with both pity and revulsion. How could I tell her the truth? *Because I want to ride around with Kimmy in Dr. Marino's navy blue Mercedes. Because I want to go out with Michael Garrett, or Christian Somers, and it will never happen, despite the plots of John Hughes movies in which a shy girl triumphs, unless I'm in the boys' sight line next to girls like Lynn. Because behind your back, people call you "Dawn Dyke-man." Because given the opportunity, you would do the same thing to me. At least I think you would.*

I glanced hurriedly toward the bathroom door. "Look, Dawn," I said. "I can't be late for class again. Okay? I'll call you tonight, all right?"

She sniffled. A shiny trail oozed from her left nostril. "Really?" she said timidly.

"Yes. Yes. After dinner. I promise."

I did not call her after dinner, or the next night, and eventually she stopped looking my way in the halls.

"So, are you visiting your parents?" Dawn asked, jarring me back to the present. "I see them every once in a while around town." I scanned her face for any sign of animosity, but there was only calm, open friendliness. Did I detect a trace of admiration? She was probably aware that I was a television producer.

"I heard you were living in New York. God. I can't imagine that kind of pace. I just read the average apartment there is almost a million dollars."

Kade ran over and tried to climb Dawn like she was a tree. "I'm looking for an apartment now," I said. "Renting, not buying. I just got divorced." I waved away her concerned look. "Long story," I said. There was really no need to share last Tuesday's little scene, in which I took the train into New York with my mother, holding her hand the whole way, to see Adam in divorce court for "dissolution of marriage with no children and without property." I wanted the grounds to be "irreconcilable differences" or "incompatibility," but New York divorce laws didn't permit the use of any of those benign terms, so we settled on "abandonment." Then my mother waited in the hallway as Adam and I, flanked by our lawyers, signed the final papers. He and I were both crying, but when it was over, he hugged me and told me to take care. Then he turned and left the room.

Dawn was peering at me. Had I been standing there in a trance? "How about you?" I said brightly. "Do you still live here?"

"No, we live in Belleville, so my husband, Dave, can take the train in. He's a civil engineer for the city, in the bridge and tunnel division." She tried unsuccessfully to fend off Kade, who kept slamming his head into her crotch. "I've got another one in school. Her name's Kelsey. She's seven and already so picky about her clothes. She and her friends know more about designer clothes than I do. God forbid they wear matching outfits, like we did."

My jaw tensed. Did she mean "we" as a generation, or was she referring to the two of us? Was she going there, so soon?

"So are you visiting your folks?" she asked, her face impassive.

"Yes, for a few weeks," I said smoothly. "My job can wear me down, and I needed a break." I didn't want to link the divorce and my trip home.

"You must meet so many interesting people at work. I feel like I never have a conversation with anyone over the first grade. I used to be in finance—I met Dave at Penn—but now I guess that correcting math homework is about as deep as it gets." She laughed. "Do you have little ones?"

*I had crabs once,* I thought. *Does that count?* I shook my head. "Not yet," I said.

Dawn nodded absently and checked her watch. "You know what? I have to get Kade to a playdate before I pick the other one up at school." He yanked forcefully at her arm as she serenely ignored him. "Hey," she added. "I don't know if you have plans while you're here, but if you want to slip away and get a cup of coffee, I could use the break." At this point, Kade was nearly horizontal as he hung from her arm. Wasn't Dawn worried? I could barely focus because the kid was three seconds away from a gaping head wound.

"Sure," I said quickly. Anything to get the kid to stop. "You probably don't remember my home number, but it's—"

She grinned. "555-2084." She colored. "Remember, I'm good with numbers."

I sat in the car for a moment after waving good-bye to Dawn's retreating minivan. When we were kids, we concocted elaborate biographies for our grown-up selves, usually along the lines of a marine biologist or a fashion designer who lived in a SoHo loft and traveled to Antarctica and Paris. Now Dawn lived one town over and had married a guy named Dave. Did that mean she had never left Bethel? And why go through all of that schooling and then give it up to hang out at a park?

I found myself smiling. Her admiring gaze made me sit up a little straighter. If she called me, I would definitely meet for coffee. Why not?

On the way home I passed two teenage boys in a black sedan who craned their necks to get a better look at me. *Oh, yes! Lillian Curtis has still got it!* Admittedly, my face was a blur because I was driving twenty miles over the speed limit. And I was wearing sunglasses. Still, they looked.

I was so distracted that I almost missed my turnoff into the CVS parking lot to pick up my dad's heartburn medication—with strict instructions from my parents to buy the store-brand knockoff—and I had to return a DVD of *Some Kind of Wonderful* to the tiny rental store next door. I had been working my way through old John Hughes movies and was pleased to find that they held up nicely.

My parents' endless round of suburban errands made me chafe, but I never needed coercion to go to CVS. It baffled Vi that I could have a strong emotional connection to a drugstore chain. She would shake her head sadly when I explained that the tangy, chemical aroma of strawberry Bonne Bell Lip Smackers sent me dreamily back to childhood. "You know what takes me back to growing up in Kansas?" she would say, clucking. "The scent of hay. Or burning leaves, or even cow manure, which, to me, was never unpleasant. But that junk doesn't even smell like a proper strawberry."

How could I fully explain to Vi the wonder and magic of CVS? It was my Tiffany's, where nothing bad could happen to you. The welcoming automatic doors, the cheery red shopping baskets, the tender, womblike embrace of the industrial gray carpeting, so much more lavish than the cold linoleum of your inferior chain drugstore! Ginny claimed that volatile organic compounds lurked in the rug and increased my risk of infertility, but I didn't care. CVS! All had stayed reassuringly the same since I was a child: the squat red logo, the vests worn by beleaguered but friendly teen employees, the Hall and Oates songs playing over the speakers. My world would have crumbled had the perfume cabinet not stood by the doorway as always, inexplicably locked and housing colognes unchanged since the Carter administration: Jean Naté, Love's Baby Soft, Brut, L'Air du Temps, Charlie.

During my first, homesick year of college, I spent hours drifting through the aisles of the local CVS in Ithaca, lingering over every section. What other store carried three rows of Lip Smackers? Three-packs, six-packs, pocket-sized, jumbo, Lip Smackers with string to wear around your neck, holiday flavors like gingerbread or candy cane, glitter-studded, scented like candy (bubble gum, chocolate) or soda (Dr Pepper). But they all smelled the same, really. The gingerbread smelled kind of like the root beer. Which was not a bad thing.

I made my way to the candy aisle. One side of it always displayed wonderfully dubious confections in cloudy cellophane bags—Circus Peanuts, Maple Nut Goodies, caramel bull's-eyes—while the other side rolled out seasonal candy four months in advance. On to the school supplies: twenty varieties of folders, daily planners, fat pens with six different kinds of ink. I inspected everything with satisfaction. No matter how broke you were, there was always something you could afford in CVS.

As I rounded a display of body wipes to study the skin-care products, I stopped abruptly. The middle-aged woman on my left— the one opening a bottle of lotion and sniffing cautiously—looked familiar. I turned my face away, pretending to be absorbed in the overnight foot cream, and sneaked a look at her. She was tall and slim, with short reddish hair souffléd into a bob. Was she a teacher? No. Wait a minute. That mole on her cheek.

It was Christian's mother.

My heart pounded sickeningly. *Steady now,* I told myself. *Steady as she goes. She's not looking your way, and even if she was, there is scant chance that she would recognize you, as you have only met her twice in your entire life. For Christ's sake, get a hold of yourself.*

But I could not. Blindly, I groped for a tube of antibacterial hand wash and pretended to read the ingredients while craning my neck ever so slightly to inventory the red shopping basket at her feet. Lightbulbs. Pet vitamins. Was Christian's dog Rufus still alive? He would be at least twenty by now. Did dogs live to twenty? Some sort of lozenges to . . . looks like . . . yes, to quit smoking. Who was smoking?

. It was unthinkable that I should stroll over and inquire about her son. She replaced the lotion, glanced my way, and frowned slightly. I tossed the antibacterial hand wash back into the bin as if it were crawling with fire ants and blundered into the next aisle, lingering among the saline solution until I was certain she had gone.

I rocketed the car out of the parking lot, turning on the radio with one hand while turning heedlessly into traffic with the other. "Just Like Heaven" by the Cure was playing. It was Christian's favorite band. When Ginny and I were teenagers, we were convinced that certain songs on the radio carried prophetic messages. One of Duran Duran's rarer tracks—"Rio," perhaps, which had never cracked the Top Ten—was a signal from the great beyond that a hookup was imminent. Clearly Robert Smith was trying to tell me the same thing.

*chapter ten*

"I'm home!" I yelled, opening the front door.

My mother was putting away some dishes in the side-board. She stood up. "Hi, Lillian," she said, peering at me. "Why are you so flushed? Are you feeling okay?"

"Yes, yes, I'm fine." I threw my purse onto a chair.

"Hell-*o*," she said. "That's not where it goes." At least she didn't add "young lady," as she used to.

"Sorry," I said, picking it up.

I tossed it into my room, shut myself in my parents' tiny home office, and turned on their cold-war-era computer to check my e-mail. First I touched down—so very briefly—on Rick Springfield's website, because I had some questions.

Ah, yes—he was still touring, and he had a live DVD, too. Still married as well. The dog that adorned the cover of his 1981 album, *Working Class Dog*, had long since croaked, but apparently he had a new one, named Gomer. Just a few peeks at his Photo Gallery and I would move on.

Then I clicked onto Adam's real estate firm, the Havilland Group, for a quick look-see. Hm. I had to allow that his new photo looked good. It nicely showcased the deep dimple on his right cheek. Peeking out from his charcoal-colored suit was a shirt in a groovy violet hue, a shade that might as well have been called Newly Single Guy Purple. Claiming that he had "fifteen years' experience" in his bio was pushing it, but no matter. It seemed that Adam was in charge of selling units from the Platinum, Water Street's Preeminent Luxury Building.

> *Distinctive. Original. The Platinum's expansive menu of unique amenities includes a sparkling-water concierge and a fleet of telescopes on the roof to spy on naughty neighbors. What's your pleasure? A club room with billiard table and plasma TV, an authentic Turkish hammam? A state-of-the-art golf simulation area, a stretching room with bamboo flooring? Enjoy your morning cappuccino in our luxury club lounge. Have our concierge phone you a limo as you wait in the lobby by our indoor birch forest, and contemplate our collection of world-renowned art. See the latest film in our screening room with complimentary popcorn. It's all here.*

Adam and I used to laugh at these sorts of descriptions—the humid, semi-pornographic lingo, the painful wording ("for the truly unique individual"). Maybe I could call him and tease him about it, a lighthearted interlude after our last strained exchange. I dialed his new work number.

"Adam Sheffield's office," a voice said crisply.

"Oh. Hi. I didn't realize he had a secretary."

"Assistant," she corrected. "May I help you?"

"This is Lillian."

Her voice lightened. "Lily from Yeager Realty?"

"No, Lillian the ex-wife."

She didn't laugh. "One moment, please," she said, putting me on hold before I could thank her.

"Hey, you," he said. He sounded friendly, even eager. We could do this.

"Oh, my," I said. "A secretary. As we say in the Garden State, fa-fa-*fa.*" New Jerseyites—and Long Islanders—say this with a posh accent while pantomiming the holding of a porcelain teacup with their pinky in the air.

"Carly's great," he said. "I don't know what I'd do without her."

"I was just looking at the website for the Platinum. It offers everything but a chocolate fountain."

This would normally elicit a chuckle. I could hear the sound of shuffling paper.

"So, what's going on?"

I realized I needed an agenda. It wasn't enough simply to call him anymore. "You didn't happen to find my address book, did you?" I said quickly.

"No," he said. "As a matter of fact I couldn't even find mine after the move. I just bought a new one."

"Have you been writing any new numbers in it?" I tried to sound playful.

A pause. "I thought we weren't going to talk about that."

"But we're friends now," I said, my voice rising ever so slightly. "That's what friends talk about."

Another pause. "This is too weird for me. I'm sorry. Maybe it's too soon for us to be casual friends." Mercifully, he changed the subject. "But it's good to hear from you!" he said brightly. "How has it been, being at your folks' house?"

I told him some funny stories, but his uh-huhs grew fainter as the tapping on the computer became more audible.

"You're obviously busy," I said, hoping he would contradict me.

"Yeah, I really should go," he said. "Say hi to your parents."

I hung up, my cheeks ablaze. Adam had never even mentioned me to Carly, a woman who organized his life, a woman who took calls from people I did not know and would likely never meet. I had been married to Adam for over a decade, but somehow, during the entire livelong day, he had never brought me up to Carly. *Carly's great.*

Tears of embarrassment slid from my eyes down my nose and splotched onto the keyboard. Four months after we split, and I was still crying in the shower so my parents wouldn't hear. In the meantime, Adam had sidestepped my question about seeing someone.

My New York friends who knew us as a couple periodically called and wrote with messages of support, but I sensed that most of them had gravitated toward Adam, a handsome single male in New York with a flashy new job who cheerfully waived his broker's fee for apartment-hunting pals. Meanwhile I lived with my parents in the suburbs and got a charge out of going to CVS. My New York friends weren't unkind, but I wasn't a subway ride away anymore, and their lives barreled onward.

I wiped my eyes and sighed. A friend had suggested making a list of Adam's annoying habits to make the split easier. He couldn't fix anything, for starters. He never flossed, despite my warnings that gum disease could lead to heart trouble. Never once did I observe that man floss, and in my mind, plaque had spackled his teeth into one single curved unit on the bottom and one on the top. Also, when some of his friends would call—fellow nice Jewish boys who grew up with him in Westchester—he'd lapse into the most mortifying homie-speak. *What up? Nuh-in!*

Not to mention that every single day of our marriage, he shed his socks by the side of the bed, two pungent snake skins waiting for me to deposit them into the hamper. When he would put on a CD, he'd whistle along in the most piercingly tuneless way. When I would remind him that the purpose of putting on music was to actually hear it, he'd laugh and promise to refrain.

More tears. *Oh Lord.* Because my little list wasn't that damning. The truth was that Adam was a human golden retriever, sloppy and energetic and so affable that he sometimes smiled in his sleep. He said I grounded him. Or was it that I kept him down?

I briskly closed the computer. Vi would be ashamed at my sniveling. I meandered downstairs to root through my parents' refrigerator. It comforted me to see all of their condiments. To me, a fridge stuffed full of ketchup and lite salad dressing and mayonnaise and jars of pickles—albeit ones so ancient and the fluid so cloudy that it resembled a specimen jar—meant festivity and birthday parties and barbecues.

My parents, like Adam, had always been much more social than I. Every weekend a loop of their friends made their way noisily through the house. As a teenager I would slouch down at noon on a Saturday morning in my pajamas to the shrieking delight of my parents' cronies, already on their second Bloody Mary as they clustered around the stove to judge the chili cook-off. At first, I would shrug into some decent clothes and swipe on some lipstick before I descended the stairs. Then I realized that my pajamas and sleep-puffed eyes were part of the shtick, so that my father could cry, "Gangway! Here it comes! Don't make it mad!"

I liked people, in theory. How I wished I could be some sort of benevolent old Italian man whose dozens of grandchildren ran in and out of his villa, crashing with a giggle into the groups of friends who were constantly arriving to nibble on the antipasti arrayed hospitably on the sideboard, the sort of open-hearted patriarch who mock complained that he never had enough chairs for everyone and that the house was never properly clean, but *eh*, it's not about that, is it? Clean house, empty heart! More grappa? *Salute!*

Instead I had to stop myself from hiding under the kitchen table when the intercom buzzed in my apartment. It wasn't just that I was usually wearing some inappropriate outfit like Adam's boxers rolled at the waist, threadbare Socks to Stay Home In, and one of the many promotional T-shirts I received from Vi's advertisers that touted blood-pressure monitors or orthopedic supports. It was also that I was unable to relax, even in my own apartment, so afraid was I that my drop-ins were not having the time of their lives. As my mother said, I have always been watchful.

No luck in the refrigerator. On to the pantry: crackers with added fiber, "fiber-rich" cereal bars, high-fiber hot chocolate. No, no, and no. I poked around on the second shelf where my father reliably stashed his bag of Chips Ahoy! What was this? Whole Grain Chips Ahoy! Every snack that they had resembled some sort of kindling: twiglike cereal, flaxseed chips, bran crispbread. How much fiber did seniors require? It was a wonder my parents hadn't hired a circus attendant to walk behind them with a shovel. And didn't they have an additional arsenal of products in their bathroom cabinet with names like Mount Vesuvius Psyllium Capsules and Super Colon Blast?

I finally excavated a generic version of Doritos called Dos Titos, which sounded like Spanish for "two breasts," but at least it was nonfibrous. I grabbed the bag and ran up to my bedroom. I felt safer there than I did anywhere else in the world, even in my last apartment with Adam, which was undeniably cozy but infested with roaches. There were no roaches in my parents' suburban house.

I glanced around the room, seeking to eradicate the memory of my clumsy conversation with Adam. I could always reread the note I got from Christian—my only written artifact from him, aside from two letters sent during our first few months of college in freshman year before he cut me off completely. I still had not fully explored my dresser, which I vowed to do in increments in order to harvest forgotten treasures such as the Swatch watch I recently found.

I fished it out of the third drawer and held it up. It was called the Osiris, with the Eye of Horus stamped on the top of its pink face and hieroglyphics inscribed along its bottom. One band was gray and the other was that particularly hideous shade of eighties mustard. It was in perfect condition, although I had gotten it in 1986 along with Lynn, Kimmy, and Sandy. We had collectively decided that the Egyptian design was more worldly and arty than, say, an abstract pattern of pink and aqua diamonds, and so we wore them as a group to express our individuality. Lynn's signature look was two Swatches on one wrist and one on the other, while Kimmy wore one, daringly, to tie back her hair.

Gingerly I took out a note. From Christian? No, it was from Lynn.

*Lillian, do you want to sleep over tonight? My mom is getting mad
at me because I never do anything anymore. Kimmy might come
too. If you come over we probably won't eat anything because I'm
on this massive diet. Sorry, my pen just ran out. Okay I found a
pencil. As I was saying. I only eat like one meal a day usually
when I come home from school. It consists of:*

> *½ ham and cheese sandwich*
> *1 orange*
> *2 swallows of diet soda*

*Sounds good huh. I started yesterday. So we won't be eating
much o.k. If you want, you can bring your own stuff. Look at me,
I'm talking like you said you could come over. You probably have to
babysit or something or don't want to come. I understand. I'm too
ugly & boring for you. It's o.k., maybe some other time. No seriously you can come if you want.*

> *Got to go, class is almost over.*

> > *Bye! Lynn*

Lynn never did get over her eating issues. After the birth of her
son she lost the baby weight in three weeks with a maniacal schedule
of marathon training. I scrabbled around the drawer some more
until I found the note from Christian. Although I was alone in the
room I blushed slightly as I flopped onto my bed and opened it yet
again. I could remember every detail of that May morning when he
passed that note to me. The class was restless as Mr. Clifford droned
on about classical conditioning. Behind his back, he had been chris-
tened "Mr. Clit-ford" by students whose apex of creativity in life was
devising names for unpopular teachers. They clung precipitously to a
D average but could handily turn Mr. Bodem into "Mr. Scrotum."

Christian had made out with me, miraculously, at a basement party the weekend before. I was coming out of the bathroom, and there he stood, to my astonishment, grinning and blocking the door with his arm. I had had no idea he was even attracted to me, and the mystery continued the following Monday, when he had simply waved at me in the hallway and mouthed, *What's up?* Still, I enjoyed a decidedly more enthusiastic welcome at the popular table in the cafeteria.

Beautiful Christian, with the shock of black hair tumbling over his eyes like Johnny Marr from the Smiths! I never fidgeted in social studies because he sat three rows up from me and the back of his head was directly in range for an extravagant forty-five minutes. Making brief eye contact with Mr. Clifford bought me extra time to linger on Christian as he shifted in his seat, his left leg—always the left—jiggling constantly. I missed nothing, making mental notes every two minutes as if I were creating a captain's log. When Mr. Clifford rummaged in his desk for more chalk, I observed that Christian wore his black Chuck Taylors, maroon corduroys, a Ramones T-shirt, and the green army jacket that he had worn the previous Tuesday. Look, he was writing something directly on his social studies book! I would never deface a book. His pen slashed back and forth. Was he crossing something out? Or maybe it was a drawing of a lightning bolt.

His eyes looked a little puffy. I pictured him in his dark bedroom listening to a Clash album past midnight. Or maybe it was the English Beat, whose name I saw him scribble on a desk last week, along with SPECIAL BEAT SERVICE in capital letters. Were the bedroom walls painted black? Did he make his bed, or was it always messy? I couldn't imagine him doing anything as mundane as brushing his teeth. I only saw him as I did movie stars, moving from one significant scene to the next. On the lower left quadrant of his head were two loose curls of hair that he kept tucking behind his ear. When we had made out I made a point of hesitantly touching the curls that I had stared at fixedly, Monday through Friday, for a year.

He bent over his desk, rapidly writing something in his notebook. Then he ripped off the page—a few kids jerked awake from the noise—and folded it into a tiny package. It was probably for his toady, Lance, who sat two rows over and was constantly trying to catch Christian's eye and make him laugh with obscene gestures. Christian twisted in his seat and I hurriedly glanced down. "Lily!" he whispered. "Hey!"

A current shot through the class as twenty-four pairs of eyes flicked in my direction. I looked up and in one smooth movement Christian threw the note at me. I stopped breathing, having attempted to catch many a note only to have them ricochet out of my hands, but it landed lightly on my desk. I opened it, keeping my face carefully neutral except for the slightest conspiratorial lip curl, as if this was only the latest dispatch from Christian Somers. I opened it up and read it: "THIS IS SO FUCKIN BORING."

*What to do what to do what to do. Do I write back? What would I say? How about "WHEN WILL THIS END"? No. No. More forceful. Maybe "KILL ME NOW." But oh, Lord, what if I wrote back, threw it, and missed?* He turned around and I smiled at him, then rolled my eyes in what I hoped was a THIS IS SO FUCKIN BORING way.

I lay back on my bed and sighed. *Oh, please, Christian, don't be too hip to attend the reunion. And if you do go, and you have male pattern baldness, may it start at the crown rather than the hairline. That's all I'm asking.*

*chapter eleven*

"Lillian!" my father called from the hallway. "Want to go for a ride? I could use the company." My dad always liked for me to join him on his Saturday errands. I was perfectly content staying in my room, but a sense of obligation compelled me to grab my coat. I was still a guest, after all.

"Sure, Dad," I said hurriedly. When my ex-army-captain father wanted us to do something, we responded quickly. I bounded down the stairs and he was already at the door, impatiently jingling his keys and scowling. His temper, always robust, had grown strangely worse after his retirement. Usually he was one malfunctioning remote control away from liftoff. His tirades were more flash than heat, but when they started, we duly fled the room in what I imagined was a satisfying way. His explosions, at least, were brief, unlike his rants, which were excruciating not just for their length but because I had to carefully stifle a laugh at some of his expressions. If he commenced with *You know what cheeses me off?* I could barely listen to the rest, so intent was I on composing my face into a sympathetic mask. If he detected even a flicker of amusement, rant would surge to rage.

I suspected that his rants were his way of keeping himself tethered to the larger world after his retirement, although it was mostly my mother who had to endure them. He would buttonhole her as she tried to read the morning paper or, worse, would follow her around the house as she emptied wastebaskets or put away laundry, talking nonstop as she nodded absently.

Some complaints were local, such as the Neighbor's Goddamn Dog, Yap, Yap, Yap, All the Livelong Day, but most of his rage was reserved for society's general decline. His greatest hits included the following:

- *The phone companies:* Press one to speak English. Why should you have to press anything to speak English, for shit's sake?
- *Those commercials at the movies now:* The movie says two o'clock, but there's fifteen minutes of commercials and what have you. Then you get some human garbage talking in front of you for the entire movie, and you can't get a manager to make them stop because nobody works there, it's all automated. Computers run the world now.
- *Fixed-price menus for $19.95:* But then they charge you ten dollars for a glass of wine. Half the price of the stinkin' meal!

- *Kids blaring music in their cars:* They're all going to be deaf by the time they're fifty, and you know what? Good.
- *Tipping:* It's the business owner's responsibility to pay waiters. You don't tip at department stores. It's a ridiculous custom. It's extortion, is what it is.
- *Human garbage on their cell phones:* I thought all the nuts were in New York City with the cell phones, but now we got 'em everywhere.
- *Bottled water:* Everybody under thirty has to carry around a bottle of water with them like they're dying of thirst. It costs more than Scotch!

Sometimes my mother would whirl on him and say, "Don, stop it. You're working yourself up so much that I'm afraid you're going to have a heart attack."

This was just the sort of feisty give-and-take he wanted. "You get mad at me when I hold things in, you get mad at me when I let things out. So what do you want me to do?"

Then she would sigh and continue to empty the wastebasket as he resumed his denouncement of separate medical plans for Congress.

In his gruff way, my father loved us. His motto was "Fix it." There was nothing he hated worse than inaction (or, as he put it, "jackin' around"). If he passed a stranded motorist, he stopped, brought out his jumper cables, and had them back on the road in ten minutes.

One spring Saturday as we pulled up at an automotive-parts store, we saw a small crowd gathered around a middle-aged man sprawled on the ground. His breath came in ragged gasps as his panicked eyes darted from one person to another.

"Heart attack, probably," my father muttered, pushing his way to the man as he whipped off his coat, balled it up, and put it under the man's head.

"An ambulance is on its way," said a guy in mechanic's overalls.

The murmuring people fell silent, watching my dad. He looked up sharply and glared at everybody. "If you're not being useful, go about your business," he barked. Most of them scattered.

"Can you hear me?" he asked the man, who nodded but could not speak. "I'm no doctor, but it could be that you're having a mild heart attack. I want you to try and calm down and get your breathing regular." To my astonishment, he took the man's hand. "I had a heart attack," he said, looking intently at him. "I lived. I'm here. See how strong I look? My daughter might disagree, but I'm telling you I'm as strong as a horse." The man's breathing slowed and he nodded, his lips even twitching into a grimace of a smile. We could hear sirens blaring in the distance.

My father smiled. "I'm just fine. Okay? You hear me? You'll be fine too."

We watched as the man was bundled into an ambulance. As it drove away, I said, "Dad, you never had a heart attack."

"No. But I imagine if you're in that position, you want to see a person who did, who is walking and talking and getting his oil changed on a Saturday. His heart was going like a jackhammer, and if we didn't do something, another attack might have finished that poor sucker off." Then he strode off to talk to a mechanic about his car.

On errand days we mostly drove in companionable silence as we listened to the oldies station on the radio. "Now, *that's* music," he would say, turning up the Drifters or Sam Cooke. The Saturday destinations were rarely exciting, so I braced myself for our latest excursion as I followed him into the garage and got into the car. "I have to go get a plunge router," he muttered, and then his need for moral support became clear. He hated going to the hardware superstore that had hastened his retirement and derailed plans to sell his own store, Center Street Hardware (slogan: "Yes, we have it!"). It had been a neighborhood institution since he opened it in the early seventies, but it was no match for the new twenty-aisle supercenter and he had reluctantly closed it last year and sold the building. Its new owner was a Korean manicure place called Confetti of Nail.

My father avoided the new store for months, but given that he was forever fixing up the house, he grudgingly broke down one morning and grimly marched in to purchase some plastic sheeting. Each subsequent visit culminated with him storming out of the store, cursing under his breath and furiously whipping his plastic bag into the backseat.

"Come on, Dad," I said heartily as we drove to the supercenter. "We'll have some laughs."

We passed Dunkin' Donuts (hilariously dubbed "Drunken Donuts" when I was a teen), our local diner, the Nautilus (aka "the Nauseous"), and Friendly's ("Unfriendly's," where we'd get a "Reese's Feces" sundae). A young guy with a tattooed arm hanging out of the window zoomed past us, gunning his souped-up engine. "Look at this shit," my father said sourly. "What's he in such a hurry to get to? Obviously not the barbershop." He muttered curse words for a few minutes, unable to let it go. Then we caught up to him at a stoplight and my father glowered at him, unblinking. The kid met his eyes and quickly looked down.

"Speed demon," barked my father, still aiming his furious laser-beam gaze at the kid, who was staring with great concentration at the light. "Big hurry. And here we are at the same light. Well, you picked up fifty feet."

The kid sped away and we pulled into the parking lot.

My father stopped the car and looked at me. "You're coming in, right?"

I nodded. He got out first and walked ahead of me. With his skinny arms thrown back, his sharp chin thrust forward, and his quick movements, he looked like a grackle getting ready to quarrel over a scrap of bread. He never wore a jacket unless the temperature was subarctic, so even though it was a chilly October day he was clad in his usual "dungarees" and plaid flannel shirt.

He liked to do advance surveillance of a situation, even if I was only five paces behind him, so that he could deliver bulletins over his shoulder. "Look at the trash out front," he called back at me disgustedly. "They haven't emptied this can in days. First thing a customer sees when he walks up to the entrance."

I used to help him in his store as a stand-in son, and I was inevitably enlisted to hold the ladder when he cleaned the gutters on the roof, or to pick up tree branches and rocks while he mowed the lawn. Ginny, with her more delicate build and frequent migraines, used to beg off so frequently that my father had stopped asking her to help.

"You know, I bought some crown molding here once that didn't match," said my father, striding into the entrance so quickly that I was almost running next to him, "and they wouldn't let me return it because it had been eight days, and they have a cockamamie policy where you have to return it within the week. At my store, we took things back that were years old. They didn't even need a receipt. I knew all my customers. Here, it's a different high school kid every week." He stopped in front of a pimply teenage boy wearing a red smock.

"Hi, son. I need a plunge router. There's one that's preset with three plunge depths; that's the one I need."

The kid stared at him, his wet mouth slightly open. "Well, is it, like, something to cut wood, or, like—"

"You know what?" my father interrupted. "I'll find it." I thought of my dad behind the counter at Center Street in his neat sweater vest and white shirt, saying, "Follow me, sir," and disappearing down the cramped aisles.

"Look at this," he muttered, picking up paintbrushes and replacing them on their hooks. "Stock all over the g.d. floor. Do you know I've been in here dozens of times and not once have I seen the owner? It's not a career anymore. It's an eight-dollar-an-hour stopover."

"I know everyone misses you, Dad."

"Hell, I run into my old customers all the time. They actually stop and ask *me* questions. I should be getting a commission. Christ. At least I know a thing or two about a thing or two." He strode off to inquire about renting a power washer while I inspected some drawer pulls. Because of my childhood in my father's store, I could lose myself for hours among plumbing parts and hooks and nails. I was even moderately handy—thanks to my dad, I could work a drill and build a birdhouse. I headed for the paint colors and examined them for a while, enjoying the poetic names. Turkish Coffee. Purple Twilight. Serengeti.

I looked up. "Dad?" Was he outside? "Dad?"

"Over here!"

I scanned the aisles but all I saw was the top of an old man's head, bald except for a few patches of downy white fuzz. My heart had contracted as the stranger looked up and smiled. "Ready to go?" asked my dad.

chapter twelve

As the reunion approached, every morning brought new e-mails from seemingly every classmate except Christian. It was nice, at least, to hear from Sandy.

*Hey hon! Remember me? Haven't talked to you in forever. How have you been? You know I'm in still in Phoenix, right? Family is good, driving me crazy as usual. I just had number three! Me, who hated babysitting! Heard from Lynn—you know she's coming to the reunion. I'm leaving the kids with Ryan—see ya! Maybe I'll stay an extra week, ha ha. Hey my parents are going to be at the*

*shore so we can even have a pre-party at my house (I can't believe I*
*just wrote that!)*

I became friendly with Sandy in sophomore year of high school, after Kimmy, Lynn, and I had fused into a trio. Sandy and I were early arrivals at school each morning. I had coerced my father into dropping me off at school on his way to work, even though it was a full hour before school began, because I didn't want my carefully sculpted perm to frizz as I walked to school. After spending half an hour carefully blow-drying it with a diffuser and dousing it with Aussie Sprunch Spray, I couldn't take the chance of any humidity wreaking havoc on my poufy creation.

Sandy also hitched an early ride with her dad, because she needed a large coffee in the morning and her mother wouldn't let her have any at home because it would stunt her growth. I had noticed her in the empty hallways, joking around with Doug the janitor, but I was too bashful to approach. One morning she strolled by me as I studied for a math test and called, "Want some coffee? I have a connection."

She told me to follow her and led me to the very back of the closed cafeteria. "Aren't we going to get in trouble?" I whispered, but she ignored me.

"Hey, *chicas!*" she said to a gaggle of cafeteria ladies, one of whom was hastily moving to stub out a cigarette until she saw that it was Sandy.

"Morning, Sandy," said one. "Guess you'll be wanting your coffee. And who's this? You're Lillian, right?"

I realized I had never exchanged a single word with any of them beyond "hello." I smiled and nodded.

"Could we have a bagel?" Sandy wheedled. "Just one? We'll split it."

The huskiest of the women said, "We're not supposed to be giving you bagels."

"And you're not supposed to be smoking, either," Sandy returned as the women cackled. One of them heaved herself up with a groan to get Sandy a bagel with extra cream cheese. From that day forward, Sandy dragged me everywhere she went. I basked in her preternatural confidence.

It took a while to convince Kimmy and Lynn to admit Sandy into the group. Sandy had a big mouth, bigger boobs (later she had a breast reduction), and was incapable of being intimidated. Her unruly hair was a little too curly, and her clothes were a tad too bright, even for the eighties. Her favorite skirt was covered in neon yellow taxicabs, which she wore with her older brother's scissored black T-shirt and black penny loafers. She cheerfully pulled it off because yellow taxicabs matched her outsized personality. Kimmy and Lynn warmed to Sandy when they learned that her parents had a house at the Jersey shore that was nearly always empty.

Sandy was my favorite among all those girls, and we had many late-night drunken conversations in which we dissected the meaning of life while inwardly congratulating ourselves on our extraordinary depth. Over the years those conversations had thinned until our only communication was her annual Christmas card, and a few e-mailed pictures of her kids, which I eagerly opened because they always made me laugh. Sandy never liked to send conventional shots of children grinning at Disney World. Instead she forwarded pictures of her kids behaving badly—screaming, red-faced, in the bathtub, angrily pulling off a Halloween princess costume, or, for the holidays, crying and flailing on Santa's knee.

Sandy had been an elementary school teacher for a few years but had stopped when the kids came along. I hesitated as I wrote a reply.

*San-DEE! I can't wait to see you. Did you know that I'm a single girl now? Adam and I got a divorce.*

Too devil-may-care. "As it happens, Adam and I got a divorce." Strangely worded. "Remember you called Adam 'the perfect man'? It turns out that he wasn't." Too bitter.

Mercifully, the phone rang. "I'll get it, Don," I heard my mother call. "Oh, hi, Ginny!" She never got that sprightly tone in her voice when I called, but then again, Ginny only phoned every two weeks or so. I heard my father run to pick up the phone in the den. "What? Why, sure," said my mother. "Well, of course we'd love to have you."

*Have her where?* I got up and crept across the upstairs hall to my parents' bedroom, expertly avoiding the spots where the floor creaked, a practice I had honed years ago when I would arrive home late, bombed on berry wine coolers. I was filled with unreasonable excitement as I stealthily approached the phone.

The trick to listening in on the extension was to pick up the headset while holding the latch. Then ease the latch up slowly. No heavy breathing; it must be shallow both through the mouth and nose. Many a phone spy has been caught by unmodified nose breathing. *Slowly. Slowly.*

". . . the decent hotels in Princeton were already booked, so you're sure it's okay?" Ginny was saying. "I promise to stay for only a few days."

They all laughed merrily at my expense.

"Of course," said my mother.

"I'll miss the kids but it'll be nice to get away. It's that APA conference I go to every year. I'm chairing a panel on heuristic biases. You remember I told you about heuristics? It's basically decisions based on emotion, often against the person's best interests. Anyway, this session is on the contagion heuristic, which is the more extreme form that you often see during wartime or in cases of mob violence."

My parents made approving noises, but I could tell they didn't know what the hell she was talking about.

"And how are my grandchildren?" my mother asked.

"Oh, they're fine. We're having a bit of a battle about the television. The kids are screaming and yelling because we only allow television on weekends."

*Well, that left the kids more time to play with their hand-hewn blocks made of reclaimed wood and solvent-free organic paint.*

"What was that?" asked Ginny. *Whoops.* I must have snorted at my own witticism. I carefully eased down the latch and tiptoed back into my bedroom, just in time to hear my mother yelling up that Ginny wanted to talk to me. I ran noisily back to the phone in my folks' bedroom and picked it up.

"Hi, Lillian," she said. "I just wanted to tell you that I'm coming to stay for a few days, and it would be so great if we could really catch up. I feel like I haven't been as supportive as I should be, and I . . . well, I want to be there for you."

I fought back sudden tears. Ginny could be sanctimonious, but she had always been kind and protective of me. "I would love to," I said, my voice breaking. "I miss you, Ginny."

"Now you're going to make me cry," she said, snuffling. "I miss you, too. I'm sorry you're going through such a hard time." I could hear a woman's voice in the background, then silence.

"Lillian," Ginny said in a low voice. "Okay. Can you hear me?"

"Barely."

"My nanny just walked in. Remember Irina? You met her once. She does the same thing every day: At nine in the morning, she walks in, takes her cell phone, and then goes to the bathroom for fifteen or twenty minutes. Can you hear her in there?" She put the phone near the door and I heard loud laughter.

"Is she . . . is she . . ."

"Number two? Oh yes, indeed."

"Can't she do her business before she gets there?" I whispered. I didn't know why I was talking quietly, too.

"And how would I tell her to do that?"

"Oh, Lord. You're a germ freak, too."

"I run in there afterward with bleach spray. Hold on. My kid's banging on the bathroom door. Jordan, honey? Irina's having her private time. Go play."

"Maybe Irina needs some reading material. Why don't you give her the paper?"

"I just heard a flush. Here she comes." Irina's muffled voice. "Did you hear that?" Ginny said.

"No."

"She just patted her belly and said, 'I feel ten pounds lighter.' I'm going to go open a window. See you soon."

I hung up and sighed. No one, not my mother, not even Adam, could elicit in me the sort of complex emotions that Ginny could—a frustrated tenderness, an admiring hostility. I wondered what sort of emotions I brought out in her, but assuming it would be some variation of pity, I didn't really want the answer.

*chapter thirteen*

The following afternoon, I was hunched over my old boom box in my bedroom, playing some cassette tapes I had rescued from a box wedged in the back of my closet. I used to tape tunes off the radio, so the whole cassette was a series of song snippets of varying volume and clarity. If I had actually managed to tape a song from the beginning, a deejay ruined the introduction with chatter. "Aannd right now we have Echo and the Bunnymen with 'Lips Like Sugar.' Folks, an interesting note: Echo is supposedly the name of the band's drum machine. Beautiful fall day, and comin' up, we'll be getting the Led out for Zep-tember, so stay with your friends at WDHA, the Rock of North Jersey, Lips! Like! Sugar! Mmm, sounds good to me."

This nattering that continued right up until the moment when Ian McCulloch began to sing once enraged me, but now I found that I liked the sound of the deejay's friendly voice. When I used to play that song, I would wait by my bedroom door and when the chorus dramatically kicked in, I'd pantomime that I was bursting in the door to a high school party. I'd be rushed and excited and pretending not to notice that all eyes were on me as I made my way to the bar—make that the keg—as hands reached out to detain me, voices called to me, Fuzzy Navel drinks were passed to me. I must have rehearsed this moment hundreds of times, even though my actual entrance to parties usually involved trooping awkwardly into a living room enveloped by a gaggle of girls. I never would have dared to enter a high school party by myself.

I fast-forwarded the tape past "Lips Like Sugar." A tinny pastiche of songs followed, mixed with more deejay chatter and chirpy themes of long-dead local radio stations. Radio tapings differed from the carefully cultivated mix tapes made to show off your admirably quirky musical taste to friends. They were for your ears alone—the Whitesnake and Foreigner power ballads, the lite R&B from Ray Parker, Jr., and Billy Ocean. I had just turned up a muffled version of Billy's "Get Outta My Dreams, Get into My Car" when I heard my mother's voice hollering up the stairs.

I shut off my boom box. "What?"

"Dawn's on the phone!" she yelled, just as she had twenty years ago.

"Got it!" I yelled back, even though she was three yards away. I had dragged out my Princess phone festooned with peeling rainbow stickers and reinstalled it in my bedroom.

"Hang up, Mom!" I hollered. "Mom, did you hang up?"

"Bye, Dawn, honey," said my mother. "It was so nice talking to you. Come over one night for dinner."

"Hey, Lillian, want to go get coffee?" asked Dawn, dispensing with opening chitchat. "I have a babysitter. There's a hip new place that opened on Route 10 called Cuppa Joe. Hip for our town, I mean. Why don't I pick you up?"

I felt a little sheepish that I was so available. Then again, I had nothing else to do, so in ten minutes I found myself waiting outside in my parents' driveway for Dawn to pick me up in an enormous red SUV. "Just push all that stuff aside," she said cheerfully. "There's no point in trying to keep the car clean with two kids. If you want a snack, there're some squashed Cheerios on the floor. I've got raisins, too. Hey, you could make trail mix."

There looked to be a forty-ounce cup of coffee already wedged into her SUV's cup holder. "Did you already have something to drink?" I asked. "We could go somewhere else."

"Oh, no," she said, laughing. "That was a couple of hours ago. It's worn off already." She sighed. "It is so nice to get away from those kids. You know what my oldest did this morning? I put out a bowl of strawberries, and he took a bite out of each one. I had turned my back for a second. It's like they invent ways to make you lose your mind. So I cut away the bitten parts and made the biggest strawberry smoothie you ever saw."

Cuppa Joe had mismatched chairs and a few deliberately worn couches. We ordered some lattes and took a seat.

Dawn leaned forward. "Lillian. You're going to the reunion, right?"

"I think I am." Of course I was going. "Are you?"

"Absolutely. I wouldn't miss it! Everyone's coming!" I thought about her small group of friends who seemed to gravitate toward one another out of necessity. They were always having boisterous fun in a conspicuous way that struck me as slightly defensive. "I just can't wait to see what everyone looks like. I run into a couple of people who live nearby, but that's about it." She brightened. "Have you kept in touch with Christian?"

I fluttered my hand vaguely. "No, we lost contact years ago."

"Well, you know he's going, right? You remember my older brother Jim? He works at the same investment firm as Geordie. They're both in finance. Geordie said that Christian is moving back from London and he's definitely going."

I felt as if I had downed my latte in one gulp. If I took one sip of coffee, I'd be sick.

"London, huh?" I let it hang there. I couldn't believe I was getting my information from Dawn.

"I guess he was working for an ad agency?" she said, wrinkling her brow. "No, wait, I think it's a branding agency. I'm not really sure what it was, but Jim says it keeps getting into trouble because they're sort of avant-garde. I don't know."

I assembled my face into a casually disinterested look. "Does he have kids?" That way I could find out if he had a wife without asking outright.

"No, he never got married." She slurped her coffee. "He was engaged, apparently, but they broke it off. Her name was Saskia, I think." Dawn went on, chattering about various classmates, but I wasn't listening. I had not seen him in eighteen years. He was single. *Saskia.* I had never met an unattractive woman named Saskia. Actually I had never met a Saskia. People like me do not have friends named Saskia. I pictured Christian and Saskia living in some cute flat in Clerkenwell. She probably rode her bike to her job at an art gallery. I imagined them walking their Shiba Inu together in Regent's Park.

Dawn was staring at me. "Lillian? Are you okay? Listen, I had an idea. We should go to the reunion together! We could get a drink beforehand. Or maybe a couple of drinks! What do they call it? Dutch courage?"

I snapped into focus. "Great idea," I said automatically. "I don't know what the deal is, I mean, Sandy's coming to town and I'm not sure what her plans are, but I think that sounds good."

Halfway through my cagey speech, she was already nodding energetically. "Sure, yeah, of course. I might have to go with Barbara Karpinski anyway."

"No, no," I said. "Let's go together, sure." I wanted to talk more about Christian. "You know," I said quietly, leaning forward, "to tell you the truth, I'm really looking forward to seeing Christian. He was the last intense relationship I had before I met my husband."

She grinned. "And now you both are single! Lillian, I'm not kidding, you look better now than when we were in high school. It's totally sick." On safer ground, we chatted and laughed for a while, and then Dawn looked at her watch.

"I should go. I have to pick up my son at preschool. Or as he calls it, 'pweschool.'" She sighed. "I used to make fun of kids like that, before I had one."

Dawn actually had a good sense of humor. I felt a rush of affection for her. "Hey, Dawn," I said impulsively as we walked to her car. "Do you ever go running?"

"You mean like jogging?" She smiled sheepishly. "Not really. How come?"

"Well, I'm always at the high school track around nine, so I thought you might want to join me. But no big deal."

She smiled. "I'm normally eating my breakfast burrito around then, but okay, why not? Running. I'll give it a try. You'll be there to-morrow?" With the reunion looming, I most certainly would.

That evening, I was too jittery to sleep. I lay in the darkness, staring at the outline of the tulip tree at my bedroom window. In the past few days I had barely given Adam a thought. After a restive hour I sat up and flicked on the light, startled for a moment by my image in the dressing-table mirror. I was wearing my old faded blue flan-nel Lanz nightgown that I had once saved my babysitting money to get, and my hair was in a ponytail. Why were those sexless granny gowns so popular in the eighties? I peered at the mirror. Dawn was right: I hadn't changed, really. My once chubby cheeks had sunken, which was essentially a good thing because it lent the illusion of cheekbones. In the eighties my bushy eyebrows resembled two pieces of duct tape and would have humbled Leonid Brezhnev, but with pared brows my face looked more delicate. Yes, the naso-labial folds were beginning to droop, but I didn't yet have full-on "monkey mouth," as Kimmy called it.

I sat at my desk and opened the lower left-hand drawer, the last one to be inspected. I picked up a navy Bermuda bag cover, and then some sort of brown, fuzzy item. I examined it, puzzled. It was a tiny braid of hair. Of course Steve DiBenedetto had grown it, 'Til Tuesday style, and then had ceremoniously cut it off one night at a party as we surrounded him and chanted. At the end of the night I had filched it and slipped it into my purse.

At the time, I remember wishing mightily that I had the nerve to grow a similar tiny braid. What cultural forces had conspired to make me think it ever looked hip? I shuddered, tossed the mangy wisp into the trash, and commenced rummaging. Surely there was something else I could excavate. I pulled the drawer out of the dresser and sat cross-legged on the floor.

A crumpled letter: one of only two that Christian had sent me from Boston College. I smoothed it out carefully.

> *Everything is great here except my living situation. One of my roommates is cool but the other is having trouble with his girlfriend and he talks about it nonstop. Typical conversation: Dork: "Christian, I need your advice, should I be mad at her? Why do I feel this way?" Me: "I don't know, man." Dork: "Should I wait to call her? Should I play it cool, or . . ."*
>
> *AAHH, I'm gonna flip out! Thank God I know some cool kids, even if they are not completely my style. None of them make me laugh the way that Mildew and those guys did but we've been having a good time and they're definitely different. This guy Greg had a bottle of ether at a party and I tried it. You inhale it. It's sort of medicinal. This other dude, Basilio, that I play soccer with asked me to join his band.*

In short order, Christian managed to assemble an international cast of hipsters around him. Meanwhile at Ithaca I had three friends named Jen and two Cindis.

> *And I've been taking a lot of photos, remember that old camera that I have of my dad's, and I met this girl who works in a gallery and she says I have a shot at exhibiting a few things so that would be cool.*

My heart still twisted when I read that, imagining a pale art chick with an asymmetrical haircut and electric-blue eyeliner.

*Saw Lloyd Cole at this great dive called the Basement, also the Cult.*
*You can do so much here in one weekend: see some African art or*
*there's this old theater that shows European films from the 50s*
*and 60s, I just feel like I will never catch up, you know? And I like*
*having no real obligations to anyone, and ordering out at 2 a.m.*
*Maybe I could come see you at some point.*

He never did. He came home the first summer but spent each successive one working in Boston. I had heard that he was a bartender at the Basement during his senior summer. I could picture him behind the bar, with his arms folded, his face unreadable, jerking his chin slightly in lieu of saying "What can I get you"? He would look slightly bored, as if he would rather be anywhere else than behind this bar where hordes of silky-haired girls competed to coax from him one of his rare smiles. Then he would close down the bar and walk home alone.

Of course, he wouldn't be alone. Even my relentlessly inventive imagination couldn't conjure that last part.

I was bursting to talk to someone about Christian. Vi? She would just dispense old-fashioned advice about stalking off in a huff if Christian "got fresh." ("Get up immediately," I imagined her saying, "and tell him, 'You obviously misinterpreted the sort of girl I am. Good *night*, sir.'") And Ginny never understood my fascination with Christian. Nor could I consult any of my New York friends, who would hector me to complete my "mourning process." What I needed was someone who wouldn't use the term *process*, as either a noun or a verb. I was tired of crying in the shower, and if this reunion got me over my divorce, so be it.

My parents were long gone, on their way to a remote garden-supply store near the Pennsylvania border that carried the latest squirrel-proof bird feeder. The drive was an hour and twenty minutes each way, so they had packed sandwiches the night before for the journey. My parents had unsuccessfully battled squirrels with weight-activated feeders, feeders that emitted ultraviolet light, squirrel spinners, and dome-topped feeders. This new one, my father excitedly told me, delivered a powerful electric current that fried any creature over six ounces. By next week, if all went well, there would be a neat pile of crisped squirrel corpses beneath the feeder.

There must be someone I could talk to about Christian. I felt a crazy impulse to call Trish at J. Crew. Trish wouldn't judge. I grabbed a catalog from my mother's catalog basket. After she retired, baskets began sprouting up all over the house in little groups like crocus flowers: baskets of remote controls, baskets for slippers, decorative baskets full of decorative stone balls.

I dialed the number and in a businesslike voice asked for Trish, explaining that I had a customer-service question.

"Hello-welcome-to-J.-Crew-my-name-is-Trish-how-can-I-help-you-today."

"Oh, hi, Trish." I cleared my throat. "This is Lillian Curtis. I placed an order last week, and—"

"I'd-be-happy-to-help-you-what-was-the-order-number."

"I don't know if you remember, but I was the one who moved back home, and I'm turning thirty-eight, and—"

"Oh, yeah! I remember," she said, suddenly casual. "How are you?"

I warmed to the enthusiasm in her voice. "Doing fine, except my high school reunion is coming up soon and I don't know what to wear." The truth was that I was going to pull out some of my New York designer clothes, but I needed a hook.

"Well, we have a great black dress with an A-line skirt, it fits everybody real well because it's simple, but the fabric is heavy, a nice silk satin, fully lined. It flies out of here."

"Mm. Uh-huh," I said, pretending to consider.

"Is it formal, or semiformal, or what? You can do separates, like a stretch chino skirt in black with our new ruffle cardigan. Always black, right? Shaves off the pounds."

"I'm definitely going to need to look good," I said. "My old boyfriend is going to be there, the one that I pined after for years. And he's single now."

She snorted. "Listen, I went to my reunion a few years ago, and you never saw so many big stomachs and bald heads. Prepare yourself, is all I'm saying."

"No, I have it on good authority that he looks great." I hesitated. "I'm a little embarrassed by how excited I am. I keep thinking he's the one that got away, but I was a teenager, for God's sake. He was perfect for me then, but I was a different person."

"I married my high school sweetheart. We met junior year." I pictured her living in a house in Lynchburg, Virginia, near J. Crew's headquarters. I wanted to ask her if she had a long commute to 1 Ivy Crescent but reconsidered, thinking it might give her the creeps.

". . . and are you really a different person, deep down?" she was saying. "You're always yourself, inside, don't you think? I still feel like I did when I was ten years old, in a way. Sometimes I forget, and then I look in the mirror and I see a tired old hag and I can't believe it." She lowered her voice. "Supervisor's coming." Then she resumed her chipper demeanor. "Would you like to open a J. Crew credit card? You get ten percent off your first purchase." Then she resumed her normal voice. "I don't get it. So what's the problem?"

"I feel like people are going to think I'm regressing. Like it's a step down. Or more like a step back."

"Who is this jury of people?" she said indignantly. "You know what? When I think of what 'they' will say, I always try not to bunch them in a big group. Makes me anxious. Who are you really thinking of? To me, it's less scary if you break it down to actual human beings instead of a big gang of people."

I thought of two friends from New York who tended to be harsh: Jina, my old neighbor, a cynical yoga teacher who dispelled the beatific yogi image, and Nate, my fellow producer on Vi's show. I knew exactly what Nate would say: *Honey, the day I left high school in Leavenworth was the happiest day of my life. I haven't thought of those people in years, until I saw* Children of the Corn *and it brought me right back.*

"Well, there are two people," I said.

"That's it? Two? Who are these two people whose opinions mean so much to you?" I thought of Jina's estrangement from her family and of Nate's daily morning announcement when he arrived at work: *God, I loathe everyone.*

"Girlfriend," she began. I cringed a little at that. "There are only three people whose opinions matter to me, and that's me, myself, and I. Trust me, I've learned the hard way. Think about all the bad decisions you would have made if you had listened to the bozos around you, giving out their free advice. Which, by the way, they probably don't even take themselves." She laughed sharply.

Gratitude flooded me. "Thank you, Trish. And I'll think about the dress."

"Okay, then. And if you decide on something else to wear, let me know how the reunion went, anyhow. Call me next Tuesday, when our cashmere cable crewnecks are on sale."

*chapter fourteen*

Vi had done it again. Somehow the woman had persuaded me to take a three-hour train ride to visit her, laughingly dismissing my protests that I had a lot of prep work to do for the reunion.

"You can't spare one evening? What, you don't miss your old chum? There's a noon train tomorrow. I'll have the housekeeper freshen up the guest room, and Mrs. P can make that tuna noodle casserole you like, with the crushed potato chips on top. And how about some of her heavenly butterscotch pudding? Isn't that one of your favorites?"

So there I was, obediently taking the noon train to the immaculate, moneyed village in Litchfield County, Connecticut, where Vi had moved with her third husband, Morty, during the Reagan administration. When he died, she decided to stay, even though she claimed she would always be a "city girl." Some of its more buttoned-up residents regularly left Vi anonymous notes in her mailbox, scolding her for the excessive holiday decorations on her lawn, the explosion of orange and yellow gladiolas that lined her driveway, the show tunes she blasted on Saturday mornings. She would just shrug it off with a laugh.

I hadn't seen Vi in over a month, and I found, suddenly, that I missed my old chum very much indeed, and when a taxi deposited me at the foot of her long driveway and I saw a tiny figure on the porch with outstretched arms, I nearly broke into a stumbling run.

"Lillian!" she cried, bustling me into the house as her two fat corgi dogs yapped in circles around my feet and Mrs. P emerged from the kitchen, wiping her hands on her apron and smiling. "We have your room all ready," she announced, leading me into the spare bedroom where I habitually stayed for our "pajama parties," as Vi termed them. A set of crisp pink pajamas lay on the bed, a pair of new terry slippers on the rug. Vi liked to provide everything to spare me the indignity of lugging a big suitcase. On the bedside table the housekeeper had placed a small vase of white roses and a dish of pastel Jordan almonds.

"When I'm a guest, I panic if there's not a little snack around," Vi explained. "Just a little nibble to keep the blood sugar up." She grabbed her middle. "Although I should probably lay off the sweet stuff. No, that's not true. I'm a big-boned girl, and that's that. I think if you carry your clothing well, that's really half the battle."

Today's ensemble was a fluttery dark pink caftan with a starburst pattern (she called it a "hostess robe"), black palazzo pants, and black slippers with rhinestone-encrusted buckles. In the ten years I had known her, I had never seen her bare feet. Her hair was swirled into its customary pouf, and she had pinned a large rhinestone bow in the back.

"I'm so happy to see you, my dear," she said. "Do you like the caftan? Isn't it the exact color of a hibiscus flower? I was in a Caribbean mood." She grabbed my shoulders and began inspecting me. "You're still too thin, but Mrs. P can fatten you up." She squinted at me so closely that I saw my own reflection in her enormous round glasses. "Your eyes are a little brighter. What's going on? Let's dish!"

"I'll tell you over dinner," I said. I knew she was bursting to relay all of the gossip from the show. She led me over to an enormous peach-colored sectional sofa, and we both plopped down on it with a sigh. I loved everything in her house. It was a demented combination of Boca retirement home (shepherdess figurines, silk flower arrangements), Connecticut WASP (needlepoint pillows, chintz, dog prints), and seventies disco (Nagel prints of hollow-cheeked women, gleaming walls of mirror.)

"Morty preferred a more masculine look," she said, looking around contentedly. "He loved his dark furniture and heavy curtains. When he passed, I realized that the décor really wasn't me. So when the fog lifted a little, the first thing I did was have my bedroom painted shell pink—it looks so much like the color of a petit four that my friends swear that just looking at the walls is fattening! And I dusted off my collection of figurines and little objets d'art that Morty couldn't abide, and I put them all over the house." She leaned back on a needlepoint pillow that said FOOL ME ONCE, SHAME ON YOU. FOOL ME TWICE, PREPARE TO DIE, a Klingon proverb (Vi was a closet *Star Trek* fan).

"Now my house is a place of calm and lightness and fun," she said. "It says that I am confident in my own tastes, and if my taste isn't out of *Architectural Digest*, well, too darn bad." Mrs. P hurried in with a big bowl of artichoke dip and a silver tray of crackers. I settled in happily as Vi gave me the rundown on all of the show's goings-on: One well-known old action star had shown up to the set "with a face-lift that was so bad, his ears were practically fastened on top of his head. Lillian, don't *laugh*, I am very serious." And Vi had gotten in a tiff with her friend Arlene, the TV actress whose heyday was in the fifties, when she co-hosted *The Consolidated Oil Comedy Hour*. "It really might be over this time," Vi said with a dismissive wave. "Arlene told me she was going to move to a nursing home, to, as she put it, 'slow down and finish her days in peace.' I told her if she took care of herself and laid off the after-dinner cognac that she likes to drink to excess, she could live another thirty years! That's hardly chump change. Then she tells me that her daughter said it was a good thing to do. The idea! I said to Arlene, 'Is this the same daughter that bought you a funeral plot for your birthday? She's practically pushing you into the coffin!' Well. She didn't like that."

I shook my head. "Jesus, Vi. Do you filter anything?"

"Someone has to tell the truth to these old crows. It's nonsense to shut your ears and live in a world of make-believe. This is not *Fantasy Island*." She placed a fat yellow throw pillow on the coffee table and propped her feet up on it. "Now. Tell me why you have that flush to your cheeks."

I relayed the whole story of Christian, while she nodded intently. Telling Vi any sort of long tale was entertaining because you could see her constant struggle not to break in with her own stories. Her eyes blazed when I talked of my crying jags, and I knew she was itching to supply a corresponding saga of her own divorces, but she admirably held back. Anything that had to do with overcoming adversity reliably produced her own tale of triumph.

When I finished, she said, "Well, why shouldn't you have a fling with this Christian? I say that you should go for it. Hook up with him."

I raised my eyebrows. "How do you know that expression?"

"I know people hook up these days, Lillian. I'm not a fossil."

I couldn't tell her that I wasn't looking for a mere fling, so I cued her to talk about her own dating adventures. She had been divorced twice (Barry, Alvin) and widowed once (Morty) but was unapologetic about wanting a fourth husband.

"Ugh," she said dramatically. "Doris set me up with a man who looked like a plucked chicken. I'm a big woman, Lillian, with a big personality, and frankly, I need a big man. Which I have told Doris repeatedly. This one looked like he had just crawled out of a crypt. He had on an old suit, and he had obviously shrunk since he bought it, so it gapped around him and didn't fit properly. Worst of all, he was unable to converse. I wanted to ask him, 'Did somebody forget to plug you in tonight?'" She shook her head. "I can spot a certain sort of widower a mile off. I can't count the number of men who get older and lose touch with their friends as their wives become their entire world. Then their wives die and they have completely lost their social skills. Well. I raced through dinner, even though it gave me indigestion. Too bad. And he was a physicist, too. You know how I love the sciences."

I had never heard one thing about her love for "the sciences."

"But I persevere. I'm not settling for a man just because he's breathing." She brightened. "Ooh, Mrs. P, you have outdone yourself!" She clapped as Mrs. Postiga grandly set down a huge sterling silver dish that overflowed with tuna casserole and set up two TV trays in front of us. Vi fervently believed that everyone should use good silverware and dishes every day.

From her 1985 autobiography,

*Who Says There Are No Second Acts?*

I know people who have driven shabby cars their whole lives, but when they die, their hearse is a limousine. Why not take a trip in that limousine while you're alive and can enjoy it? Get out the good dishes that you inherited from your grandmother and use them to serve pigs in blankets! Don't deny yourselves for that "rainy day." Open that bottle of champagne this instant! Any day can provide an excuse to be festive. When I watch the Academy Awards, I put on a colorful dress and high heels, even if I am alone.

I'll make a confession. Do you know what else I do sometimes? I run down the driveway in the morning to fetch the newspaper dressed only in my pajamas. It's a little game that I play with myself: I run as fast as I can, hoping the neighbors won't spot me. Then I rush into my house, giggling like a crazy lady. Let them think I'm nuts. I don't care! Better that than a soda pop without the fizz.

Vi popped in a video of *Singin' in the Rain*, our traditional entertainment as we ate dinner on the TV trays. Then, as Mrs. P cleared everything away, Vi and I changed into our pajamas for a little "girl talk." "You know," said Vi, using her lower-octave "candid, confiding" voice, when we had returned to the couch, "the two of us have a lot in common. We're both back on the dating scene. Last week I was talking to my friend Joan—you've met her, the decorator for Lady Bird Johnson? I was telling her about my difficulties in finding a good man, and she said to me, 'Vi, I just can't identify with your troubles. You are beloved by fans all over the globe. You have preserved both your face and your figure. You have a uniformed chauffer to take you wherever you need. You . . .'"

Never had I heard sedate Joan rhapsodize in this manner, and who uses the words "uniformed chauffeur" in normal conversation? I had learned to allow Vi a certain amount of creative license.

". . . But I told Joan that I get anxious just like everyone else."

I watched Vi as she relayed her long conversation with Joan. Vi was a self-described "people person" who surrounded herself with a whirl of friends, staffers, and colleagues, but occasionally I detected currents of loneliness. When we were taping her talk show and were between guests, I would observe her from my perch in a dark corner of the set. When she thought no one was watching, it was fascinating to see her face drop the cheerfulness. Then, the moment the cameraman returned from a smoke break, she resumed her bright, expectant expression, as if she were waiting for the punch line of a particularly good joke.

She never said it outright, but it was clear that she was distant from her two children. Vi portrayed herself as a truth teller whose candid disclosures made her friends gasp in shock, but she was selective in what she chose to reveal. She did admit that both of her kids—from her first husband, Barry—were raised by "nurses" as she energetically pursued her career, and I guessed that the relationships had never fully recovered. I had met Barry Jr. exactly once, and Vi seemed to rarely receive calls from him. He was closer to his father. Vi alluded to an acrimonious divorce from Big Barry, an oil executive whom she had met through her many appearances on *The*

*Consolidated Oil Comedy Hour.* He had assumed that she would stop working once they had a child, and had sued her for abandonment.

Barry Jr. was a tech-industry honcho who lived in Sacramento with his wife, Leah, and their two kids. They made grudging visits to Vi at Christmastime, but most of his contact consisted of sending computer pictures of the grandchildren. He was a colorless lump of a man with square-shaped glasses who chided her in a honking voice to act her age.

Vi's daughter, Pamela, was an artist who lived in Taos. She inherited some of the flamboyance of her mother—the trailing scarves and big jewelry—but what was missing was the Big Personality. Pamela was querulous and needy and drifted from one "creative" job to the next—managing a gallery that sold silver Native American jewelry, making serviceable pottery to sell at trade shows. She had never married but lived with a shadowy jack-of-all-trades named Ozzy, whose distinguishing characteristic was a thick beard the exact texture and rusty brown color of a coir welcome mat.

Pamela did phone Vi frequently, but it was often with requests for money, and Vi dutifully wrote out the checks. At other times she would call after a therapy session to excavate long-buried hurts. Vi would never dream of going to a "headshrinker." She liked to focus on the future.

I knew that Vi thought of me as a surrogate daughter. She was attentive to me in that spotty, offhanded way that well-meaning but self-involved people are, but the effort on her part was touching. Our bond proved to her that she was capable of nurturing, but her remorse stemmed not from her long absences from and early disinterest in her children but the fact that she harbored no real guilt about it.

"... so the next man with whom I am having dinner is a physician named Reed," Vi was saying. "We shall see. He's in his late seventies. He has false teeth, which I think I can live with. I don't think it's a—what do you kids call it? A deal breaker. Am I saying it correctly?"

I nodded. "I have so many deal breakers that I can barely get past a crush." Even when I was with Adam, I rarely harbored even a mild infatuation. My crushes were fragile organisms that withered at the smallest infraction—if I heard a man use a common grammar error such as "between you and I," for instance.

I told Vi about watching in dismay as I sat across from a handsome production assistant in a coffee shop and as he ate, out popped a thick tongue like a Pez dispenser to meet his forkful of potato salad in midair. This was one of my many pet peeves. "For the whole meal, it was as if his tongue was independent from his body and just got impatient," I said as she hooted. "And I just felt like the whole lizard-tongue habit was too much to take on. What if we got married and when it was time to feed him a ceremonial bite of cake, he unfurled that tongue, to be captured on video for eternity? Then years pass, nothing changes, except it's a thinner, dryer tongue that jets out."

"You are outrageous," Vi said, laughing as she wiped her eyes. "Well, then, for me, a deal breaker would be ill-maintained dentures."

"At least you never have to hear the words 'and this tattoo on my back is the Chinese symbol for prosperity.'"

"Better that than hairy ears. Oh, it's hard to be a single girl nowadays." She brightened as Mrs. Postiga reappeared with two bowls of butterscotch pudding crowned with twin frills of whipped cream. "Gorgeous!" she cried, clapping her hands.

After dinner, she put some MGM musical soundtracks on the

"hi-fi" and taught me dance steps from her early days on the Broadway stage. "I was never that great of a dancer," she said, panting just a little as she deftly executed a few twirls. "I never had any solos, let's put it that way. But I worked harder than anyone."

Then we retired to her vast gold and cream mirrored dressing room so she could apply "war paint" to my face. My natural look pained Vi, so I periodically allowed her to make me up in the vain hopes that I might be converted to her way of thinking. She made me take a seat on a pink satin padded chair as she busily arranged an armada of cosmetics on the dressing table.

"I still pinch myself when I look around this room," said Vi. "When Father died in the war, my mother, my sister, Gladys, and I moved from our farm in Council Bluffs, Iowa, to a cold-water flat in Kansas City. Mother had never worked before, but she had to support us children, so she . . . Where is that eyebrow pencil?"

"So she took work as a seamstress," I prompted.

"Oh, yes, I must have told you. So she took work as a seamstress and we never had any money, but once a week Mother would give me a nickel so that I could see a new picture on Friday as soon as it came out." She held an eyebrow pencil up to my brows to perfectly match the color. "I waited all week to go to the pictures! And my favorite scenes were of ladies getting ready for a party in their enormous dressing rooms, with maids scurrying about and flowers arriving. I vowed that when I grew up, I would have a dressing room the size of the entire cold-water flat that I was raised in. Well, lo and behold."

I picked up one of the lipsticks that she had placed carefully on the table and opened it. It was shrunken and dry, liked cracked mud. "How old is this lipstick?" I demanded.

She grabbed it and examined it, adjusting her glasses. "Hm. I don't know. But lipstick doesn't really go bad. In fact, I prefer an older lipstick because the pigment gets richer."

"Vi, what are you talking about?" She ignored me, glancing into the mirror and rearranging her lacquered swirl of reddish hair. "I really must make an appointment," she said absently. Vi had a "girl" in midtown who had maintained her trademark coif for the past three decades. Once I joined Vi on her weekly trip to "Ilsa of New York" and met Ilsa herself—a "girl" of fifty-two. I inquired about Ilsa's additional salons—the "of New York" implied that there were others—in Gstaad, perhaps, or Monte Carlo.

"No others," Ilsa said shortly. "Is only New York." Ilsa had what Vi would call panache.

Vi peered at my face and then applied some bat-wing eyeliner. "You really have beautiful eyes, Lillian. You must emphasize them more. And look at your skin. Dry, dry, dry. You are neglecting yourself."

From Vi's 1967 beauty book, *Is That Really Me?*:

We gals take care of everyone in our lives, but I firmly believe that we should pamper ourselves too. That is why once a month, without fail, I unplug the telephone and have a day just for me. I start by drawing a nice, hot bubble bath. I close my eyes and listen to soothing music. Then I put on a robe and do whatever I please for the whole glorious day—watercolor painting, watching talk shows all morning, making a lavish lunch just for me—including a generous piece of blueberry cheesecake!

Then I treat my skin with a special masque. First I apply

cleansing cream to one of my electric complexion brushes and give my face a thorough scrub. This brings blood to the surface of the skin, essential for a glowing look. While my face is still moist, I apply a masque. Effective beauty treatments needn't be expensive—they can come right from your refrigerator. Luxury is not about cost! Mayonnaise makes a wonderful face masque, as does cod-liver oil (and don't forget your neck). A famous comedienne I know uses a purée of bananas and sour cream, and she has the complexion of a newborn baby.

Vi buzzed around me, vigorously brushing my hair. "It just lies flat on your head," she fretted. "You need volume." As she teased the back of it into an unwieldy pouf, she said casually, "About this Christian. I know you might be anxious about the sex. It's been quite a while since you were intimate with anyone but Adam, after all." She paused, brush in hand. I nodded cautiously and she went on.

"When Morty died—and he really was my one great love affair— I felt that having relations with someone else was betrayal. But I'll be honest. My real worry was letting anyone else see me in dishabille. As you know, I'm comfortable with my body even though I'm not in the bloom of youth, but I kept wondering: *What if my date wants me to do something that I can't bring myself to do? What if some new sexual technique has been invented that's too far out for me?*" She shrugged. "The problems were far more pedestrian, as it turned out." She leaned forward confidentially. "One of my paramours had a problem with impotence," she said, raising her eyebrows. "You know me, Lillian: I tell it like it is. I hope this doesn't shock you."

It did not. Vi's tell-it-like-it-is pronouncements were fairly tame, but I did wonder just how much she got around.

"The point is, you can always confide in me once you become

sexually active again," she said. Her voice was steady but her cheeks were flushed by the attempt to be "modern," and I fought the urge to grab her in a hug. I had a similar impulse when she patted my hand and told me I could extend my sabbatical another month, because it was clear that she was desperate to have me back at work again and managing her every minute.

Later that night, as I drowsed under an old-fashioned pink chenille bedspread in the guest room, I was enveloped by a deep peace. A soft knock at the door roused me. "Thought you might want this," whispered Vi, tiptoeing in and placing a white satin sleep mask on my bedside table. "I can't abide any light. Good night, my dear."

"That's so thoughtful, Vi. Thank you." I knew she wanted to tell me that she loved me but she was too shy. Or maybe that's what I wanted to say.

*chapter fifteen*

Ginny was due to arrive at one, so I waited at my bedroom window, slightly irritated that my eyes were trained to the driveway like a springer spaniel's. She was never late, and sure enough, her white rental car pulled in at 12:55. I watched her from behind a sheer curtain as she pulled her luggage out of the backseat. Her dark hair was cut in a shoulder-length bob that was a bit longer in the front, which for Ginny was very edgy. Her crisp hairstyles never looked dated in family photos—no embarrassing frippery, no perms or orange splotch of Sun-in, no Courtney Love baby barrettes. Hm. Black pants, slim black coat. What was with the high-heeled boots? Why was she in business casual to sit in my parents' den? Even as a kid, she dressed formally, wearing shoes in the house and eschewing jeans. She always looked neat and clean and a little austere. I glanced down at my frayed bedroom slippers, which had spread and flattened from age so that they resembled scuba flippers.       .

Ginny closed the car door and turned to look straight into my eyes. *Hi, Lily,* she mouthed, and waved. I waved back. *How did she see me?*

"Don! She's here!" my mother shouted. I lingered in the hallway as my parents stampeded for the door like there was a Christmas Eve sale at Best Buy.

"How was your flight?" my father cried.

"Completely painless," she said, giving him a hug. Then she turned to me. "Come here, Lily Bear," she said, using the childhood nickname that released unexpected tears as I hugged her. When would I ever stop crying? Ginny was forty-one, but her pale face was unlined except for a small crease between her brows. She studied me with a slight frown as I talked, her gray-blue eyes ranging over me with an intensity that I only got used to around the third day of being with her. Occasionally she stroked my hair or took my hand in hers. I envied the easy way she was so physically demonstrative. I just couldn't sling an arm chummily around someone's shoulders. The most natural move I could make was a sort of clumsy, Lennie Small–style petting.

Lunch, complete with genuine rattan "company" place mats rather than the usual vinyl ones, resembled a small press conference, with Ginny smoothly taking questions from the three of us. From my father: How was Raymond's practice? "He's working so hard," Ginny said with a sigh. Raymond was an endocrinologist and director of the diabetes program at the Dean Medical Center in Madison. "He just implemented an after-school program for kids with diabetes so they can go to the center and get their blood checked, and then hang out, play games, go on computers," she said. My mother glowed; my father nodded approvingly.

My relationship with Raymond was cordial, if distant. In his dealings with me, he was charming but terse, as if there were a patient waiting behind me. If I sat next to him during a long family dinner and our conversation went on a little too long, he would start to nod more vigorously, muttering *uh-huh, uh-huh* as if he were prodding some sort of growth on me. That was my cue to wrap it up, even if we lapsed into silence afterward, Raymond with a pleasant but slightly tight smile on his face. He walked on an invisible street in which each encounter was brief, jocular, and informative, and then he was free to continue down the road.

Another question from the lady in the back: How are my adorable grandkids? Did you tell them Grandma misses them?

My mother kept a rotating series of framed photos of Blake and Jordan on a shelf in the kitchen next to her decorative basket of mail. Until recently there was a photo of Adam and me in front of a pile of pumpkins at a farm stand. He's hugging me too tightly, and I'm laughing. I noticed that my mother had discreetly swapped it out for one of me standing in a field of sunflowers. Adam had taken it during a trip to Italy, so the ghost of him still hovered off-camera.

"Your grandson is looking forward to his fifth birthday," Ginny was saying. "And he told me he wants to learn Chinese! Do you believe it? His friend May is Chinese, and I guess he got it into his head."

I broke in. "Or you inserted it into his head. A five-year-old taking Chinese lessons? Do they really know what they want at that age? When I was five, I wanted to fly."

"I think it's smart," said my father through a mouthful of turkey sandwich. "Gotta get a jump. China has the fourth largest economy in the world. You see that article in *Time* magazine? Pretty soon we'll all need to speak Chinese just to keep up. I'll tell you something, those Chinese aren't afraid of hard work, boy. Unlike kids in this country who can't even be bothered to get after-school jobs anymore."

He was cranking up for Goddamn American Kids Who Think They Can Just Walk Outside and Pluck an iPod Off a Tree, so my mother stepped in with a question about Ginny and Raymond's hunt for a new house. They had "outgrown" their home and were forever forwarding photos of new candidates to my folks, who excitedly dissected each e-mail.

Ginny took a delicate bite of sandwich and swallowed. "Do you remember that last set of photos I sent, of the house built in 1820? We're really serious about it. They've kept a lot of the period detail, but we'd need to reno the kitchen. It's on an acre, which is the minimum that we would want. It borders a conservation easement, so of course that's a major plus. And you saw the six-on-six leaded windows, right?"

Ginny possessed the sort of grown-up knowledge that I had mistakenly assumed I would magically acquire someday. She knew her wines (we always looked beseechingly at her when we were out to dinner and a list was produced). She knew her jazz musicians, her poets, her architects.

My parents' eyes were shining as Ginny went on about the gabled slate roof and the mature plantings in the backyard. Retired parents love to talk about real estate. They love it. They used to come into Manhattan and make a day of looking at Adam's apartment listings.

"All those windows might lose heat," my father gibbered happily. "And didn't you say that it had well water? You'd better get that tested."

My mother hadn't touched her sandwich. "I think you should

keep the original color of the house, white with black shutters. It's a classic."

"A classic!" my father brayed.

Ginny dabbed her lips with a cloth "company" napkin. "Well, before we sign any papers, we'd like you both to come take a look. We'll fly you there because you'd be doing us a favor."

*Oh, for the love of Christ. "We'll fly you there." Which sounds so much better than "We'll pick up the ticket for $198." Champagne wishes and caviar dreams!*

I shook my head to clear it, suddenly ashamed. For as long as I could remember, a parallel dialogue ran in my head when Ginny held forth, followed by self-recrimination. Ginny was entitled to buy a house, and it was generous that she offered to fly my parents to their place and to involve them in a decision she could easily make herself; she was probably humoring them. And she wasn't lording it over me. When she made the offer, her eyes had flicked discreetly, almost imperceptibly, to my face, and I knew she felt a momentary spasm of self-consciousness.

After lunch, Ginny and I did the dishes as my mother pulled out her recipe binder to plan dinner. Because of our special guest, she was making a "fancy" dish. "Ginny, you're not a big fan of meat, right?" my mother said absently as she paged through.

"Not really," said Ginny, drying a bowl. "I mean, I'll do it once a week or so. The kids eat more meat than I do. They love their chicken nuggets, even though Raymond says that there's an average of thirty-six ingredients in addition to the chicken." That Raymond was a one-man party.

My mother put on her reading glasses and scanned one stained clipping. "Well, I was going to make chicken enchiladas, I remember you like them, but—"

Ginny circled her arms around my mother's shoulders. "Oh, Mom. That would be great. Sounds delicious."

Again: Why was I annoyed? She was being polite and enthusiastic. Was it the slightly royal tone? *Ah. Chicken. Mmyesss, poultry will suffice.* But she didn't actually use a royal tone. No, it had to be the once-a-week meat.

I blotted our "good" rattan place mats with a sponge and began unloading glasses from the dishwasher. "Why do you eat meat once a week, anyway?" I asked.

She stopped drying dishes and faced me. "Because it stops me up," she said in a low tone.

My mother looked up sharply from her recipe book. "Do you know, Ginny, meat stops me up, too! The older I get, honest to Pete, the worse it is! I've been using fiber supplements, but somehow they have the opposite effect."

Even Ginny's bowel activities had the power to fascinate, although to be fair, my mother perked up at any mention of fiber.

"I've got a better idea," I said, holding up a glass. "There's enough fiber in these glasses because you pack the dishwasher so tightly that nothing ever gets clean. Look at this." I held it up to the light to show the thick layer of sediment at the bottom. "Just add water and chew."

Ginny grabbed the glass and held it to the light. "Why throw money away on Fiber Choice?" She turned the faucet on, filled it with an inch of water, and handed to me. "Here you go."

"Or you could grow Sea-Monkeys in there," I pointed out.

My mother looked at us over her reading glasses. "You two are horrible to your poor old mother," she said idly, but I knew she was pleased by any show of unity between Ginny and me. Then she frowned. "Rats. We don't have green chiles for the enchiladas. I told your father to pick some up."

"I'll go," I said, grabbing an opportunity to conspicuously prove I was helpful.

Ginny ran to the hall closet to get her coat. "I'll come with you."

We got into my parents' car, and when I turned on the ignition, Ginny jumped, startled, as Siouxsee and the Banshees blasted out of the speakers.

"Lillian!" she gasped over the music. "You're going to ruin your hearing."

"Come on," I teased. "Doesn't it sound good?" She grinned and nodded as we drove to the store. I had gotten back into my old Jersey-girl habit of speeding, and I barreled to the stoplight, stomping hard on the brake at the red light so that Ginny lurched forward.

"You're driving like you did when you were a teenager," she said, but she was giggling.

"Speaking of," I said, eyeing her sideways. "I just have to make a quick stop. I want to go by Christian's house to see if anyone's home. I don't know if he lives here yet or not, but if he's coming from London, he might show up at his folks' house before the reunion."

She folded her arms. "Have you done this before?"

"Are you kidding? Ah, no," I lied scornfully. "But I thought it would be fun with you." I braked and turned the car down Linden Lane before she had a chance to protest. "Come on." I slowed and then parked in front of a neighbor's house a few yards away. "Indulge me." We looked toward the Somers home.

She rolled her eyes. "I feel like we're at a stakeout. I should be wearing a rumpled overcoat and sipping a cup of coffee." She pretended to answer a cell phone. "Yeah. We're still here, chief. No sign of the perps."

I studied the house for signs of life. A black Saab that I didn't recognize sat in the driveway. "That could be Geordie's," I muttered.

"Dawn told me that he lives in Morristown, so he's close enough to come over for dinner. Maybe the whole family has Sunday dinner together."

Ginny raised her eyebrows. "He didn't move to the city?"

"No, but he's raking it in as a hedge-fund manager. He commutes. He married some woman at his firm. I think she stays home now. They have three boys, so they probably need the parents for babysitting duty."

She nodded, then looked at me slyly. "You know that I fooled around with him once."

I pretended to do a spit take with our "coffee." "You *what*? Ginny! Why didn't you ever tell me? I need the details right now." I shook my head wonderingly. "You bagged Geordie Somers? Well."

She shrugged. "At the time, you were mooning over Christian and I didn't want you blabbing to him. We kept it a big secret because our little rendezvous was during my senior year, when, if you remember, he was all hot and heavy with Elizabeth."

"So? What happened?" The house was momentarily forgotten.

"Nothing much. We were at a party. Remember how Brad what's-his-name had those parties in his dad's barn? Well, somehow Geordie's ride left without him and I ended up driving him home." Ginny never had more than a beer or two at parties, while I had thrown up out of many a car window. "So we're talking in his driveway—right over there—as the car was running, and we were having a real conversation. I always thought he was okay, but I never got the whole Somers mystique. He used to call himself 'Geords.' I mean, you shouldn't assign yourself a nickname. And I thought all of those lacrosse players were a bit thuggish."

She thought for a moment. "So he was telling me about how he was a basketball coach at a summer camp and that once a week, he and the other coaches would secretly pick the underdog of the week and manipulate the game so the kid could get the ball and score, to make him look like the jock that he wasn't. Of course, I was impressed. When you're seventeen, that passes for sensitive." She laughed. "And I remember thinking, 'He really is pretty attractive.' He was just wearing jeans and an oxford shirt—it was light blue, and the sleeves were rolled up so you could see his forearms, which were really muscular from all the tennis he played in the summer. And he had the curly hair and the blue eyes, and that big, sexy Roman nose. He had the sort of soft look that teenage boys don't have now. All the girls in my classes go for shaved heads and tattoos."

I flashed to the parking lot at Brendan Byrne Arena where a group of kids from my school had gathered before a Dead show to tailgate. Geordie, wearing an artfully faded yellow polo shirt and perfectly worn-in Levi's with a small tear at the knee, which exposed a smooth, tan expanse of skin, was flipping burgers on a hibachi and laughing. His sun-streaked hair blew around his face. What freedom it was to be a good-looking boy at that age.

"When he stopped telling me about basketball camp," Ginny continued, "he just looked at me, and there was that wonderful moment of tension. And then he kissed me, and it was just . . . I couldn't form a thought. For probably the first time, my mind was completely blank because there was no room for anything but . . . but pleasure." She smiled and sat back in the car seat. "You know, it's funny. I think that when a man looks back on the most erotic moment of his life, it usually involves a deviation from the norm— some sort of druggy three-way he lucked into in college, or the slightly nuts girl that would let him do anything he wanted. But when women think back on that electric, definitive moment, it's never anything particularly kinky. Right? Often it's nothing more than making out on a couch or in somebody's car." She waved her hand absently. "I suppose men are more prone to thrill seeking and would value those moments as episodic frames. It reinforces the idea that you take risks."

"Ginny," I interrupted. "We're not in class here."

She shook her head impatiently. "I know, I know. But I've often wondered about the significance of these memories, if for men it's an artifact of sensation-seeking behavior, the way they put up a sports trophy or a photo of them deep-sea fishing or something." She tented her fingers, which she did when was floating away on a wave of theory. "Whereas women are more inner-directed. Maybe a make-out session satisfies some vision of intimacy on their own terms rather than a socially constructed vision of what constitutes an erotic encounter."

I made snoring noises. "Please," I said, "get back to Geordie. What happened afterward?"

She frowned a little. "You know, nothing, really. At school the next week, he was back with Elizabeth, and our whole encounter was basically forgotten. But it's funny—over the years, I must confess that I've thought about it a lot, that funny little throwaway night. He would hold my eyes a little bit longer when we were all out together, like we shared a private joke. But it's not like I was in love with him. We just had that chemistry, I guess."

I sat up, rigid, and pointed toward the house. "There's some action," I said in a low voice. A toddler had opened the front door. The top of his head was just visible over the windowed storm door, along with two small hands that banged on the glass. Ginny and I watched silently as the child reached repeatedly for the latch. Suddenly he got it open and shot outside, crowing with victory and lurching down the front lawn to the street.

"I can't let this happen," said Ginny, unbuckling her seat belt, but then the door flew open and a harassed-looking man ran after the kid and deftly scooped him up. He was scolding the giggling boy at first, but then he chuckled.

"It's Geordie," I whispered. He was clad in navy track pants and a T-shirt, and his once curly hair had been cropped short to expose a hairline that was in retreat but still holding steady. He was tall and trim and fit, but in the lacquered, overly cut way of a personal trainer. He held the chubby kid easily in one arm.

"He's too slick," she said dismissively.

I whipped around to look at her. "You mean to tell me that your heart isn't beating faster right now?"

She considered. "It is, but it may be more of a reaction of recognition than any sort of romantic feeling. I'm glad he doesn't look terrible, but if I met him right now, I wouldn't be attracted to him. I can just picture him at the strip club with his fellow hedge-fund managers. And then off to a two-hour game of racquetball. 'Work hard, play hard.'" She shrugged. "I don't know. I'd rather have my memory. I don't need to update it."

Meanwhile, my heart was thumping with almost painful force.

Ginny lightly punched my arm. "Okay, you got your sighting. Shall we go? The folks are probably wondering what happened to us."

I just could not seem to pull her in. Sighing, I started the car.

The next morning I was the first one up, so I commandeered the family computer to check our class website. *Aha.* There were a few fresh entries in Classmate Updates. Our resident goth chick, Michelle Brennan, a blank-faced girl with lank black hair and a tattered cape who glided balefully down the halls, had so thoroughly embraced suburban motherhood that her e-mail address was Sippycup3. "My husband and I are the proud new parents of beautiful twin daughters, Madison and Olivia, who join their big sister in keeping me real busy!" she wrote. "Caring for them is a true labor of love. Come and visit me if you ever get to Dallas, y'all!" She had posted a photo of the girls but none of herself.

Why did every other person feel compelled to mention how busy and overbooked they were? And what could I possibly write? *I keep idle with a full roster of daytime television, Internet surfing, and lingering visits to big-box stores to buy nothing in particular. Suddenly I turn around and it's dinnertime!*

Mildew had also weighed in with a terse assessment of his life. "Grad school—got MBA then did a stint at IBM. Five years at Citigroup, then settled in Randolph, NJ. Started adult day-care facility with brother-in-law in PA. Also moved into development two years ago, currently building townhomes in Union County." Well. Mildew was certainly two tons of fun. Christian's giggling sidekick had turned into an adult day-care-facility mogul. No mention of a personal life.

At the end of their postings, many in the class had gamely filled out a multiple-choice quiz provided by the website and designed, apparently, to foster harmony, because every person answered in the same way. *What do you do with your free time?* Dine with friends, go to movies, sports or strenuous activity. *Your favorite type of movie:* Comedy, Action/Adventure. *Your biggest pet peeve:* Sitting in traffic. *If you won $100 million tomorrow, you would:* Quit my job. *Your main source of current events:* TV. *Your dream vacation:* Anywhere warm!!!

I snapped to attention. Kimmy had posted a profile. She and I had kept in sporadic touch, but our last exchange had been a few years back. Kimmy had married a Florida shopping-mall developer and had four children. I inspected her photo. She was sitting in a deck chair at some island resort, or maybe it was her Palm Beach country club, looking tan and rich and wearing spotless white jeans and a brown printed halter top. Her hair was chicly slicked back; her tawny shoulders glowed. She was surrounded by four handsome boys with perfectly tousled haircuts.

Maybe she had written me, too. I checked my e-mail and saw messages from both her and Lynn.

"Hi, Lily," Kimmy wrote. "Can't wait to see you. Do you believe I put that picture up? Look at those wrinkles. Honestly, need to keep out of the sun!!! The bigger question is, how did I get four boys? When did that happen? We must catch up ahead of time. Let's all spend the day together before the reunion. Lynn says she's in, too. Have you talked to Sandy? How is Adam? Are you pregnant yet?"

Kimmy had always tossed around words like *hag* and *whale* when she described herself. I felt a little frisson of jealousy that she and Lynn had already planned to do something beforehand. Did they keep in regular touch? Did their families get together for vacations? Lynn lived in Richmond with her husband and was a horseback-riding instructor.

The irony was that if I'd wanted to, I could have kept in touch with them, too. Whenever I e-mailed Kimmy, I received an enthusiastic note back. So why did I feel jealous? I had already heard from Sandy, and they hadn't. It was the same petty envy that I felt when I used to sneak glances at the calendar that hung on Kimmy's bedroom door. She used to write down all of her social engagements, most of which went on without my knowledge. One Saturday would involve "Mall with Laurie 11 am," "*Eddie and the Cruisers* with Karen @ 2, Susan's house 7 for sleepover, don't forget to bring her Ton Sur

Ton shirt back." I would shrivel with the knowledge that I was the 5 P.M. lacrosse-drill slot, Kimmy's briefest commitment.

I checked Lynn's e-mail. It was written four minutes after Kimmy's, so they had obviously chatted on the phone beforehand. Did they say anything bad about me? Had the word gotten out that I was Taking a Break? There was no reason for me to be uneasy. They were my friends. I could call them right now if I wanted to and they would be genuinely glad to hear from me.

"LIL!" Lynn had written. Lynn was a little looser than the serenely composed Kimmy. "Are you feeling as old as I am? Twenty years ago, we were going to the prom. (Why did you let me wear that hideous black dress?)" Her dress was an elegant sleeveless sheath that she wore with her grandmother's simple diamond pendant, while mine was a peach-colored explosion of puffy sleeves, lace, and enough spangles to shame a rodeo clown.

"Still in Richmond," her note continued. "Michael and I just love it and we're very involved in the community. Still a riding instructor, I have a great crop of kids this year. The parents are a little much, but I can handle it. Remember how I tried to take you riding with me once and how scared you were of the horses? I've attached a pic of me on Senator, I'm madly in love with him. Call me if you want to talk before the reunion, ok? Oh and: no husbands, right? What are you wearing?"

At the bottom of the e-mail there was a photo of Lynn in riding gear perched atop an enormous black horse. She was slim and fit and wore no makeup, her blond hair caught in a smooth low ponytail. Over the years she had sent many photos of herself and Michael rappelling down some mountain range or riding bikes at the bottom of a canyon, interchangeable in their aerodynamic black racing gear, always accompanied by one line that identified the location and another line that mentioned how crazy they were. "Here we are free-climbing Cortina in the Dolomites (some of it completely vertical!) Are we insane or what??!'"

I debated writing a post about myself on Classmate News. Surely Christian would check out the site at least once. Was it uncool to put up a bulletin? Well, Kimmy had done it.

*Hi from New York.* Bold! A lie in the very first line! *I'm on my tenth year as a producer on* Tell Me Everything! *With Vi Barbour, and it continues to be a blast.* No. Revise. I would not lift any words from a beer commercial. Every single classmate post contained the word *blast.* Our entire class was in the midst of a nonstop blast. . . . *and each week is different from the last. I'm enjoying the city (museums, theater) and travel frequently.* Get some culture in there, but don't overdo it. *Just got back from Tulum, Mexico.* Three years ago. *Training for the NY marathon.* I was in decent enough shape that I could fake it. *Single after an amicable divorce.* That seemed sufficiently adult.

Ginny appeared at the door. "Morning," she said in her scratchy just-woken-up voice. "Come have coffee with me." She was wearing crisp white pajamas and soft ballet slippers. Ginny always looked freshly showered. I made a mental note to buy ballet slippers after she left to wear around the house. "Why are you on the computer so early?"

"I'm just looking on our class website," I said, shutting down both her and the computer. We went down to the kitchen and Ginny loaded coffee into my parents' temperamental machine. She took a deep sniff of the grounds. "Don't you love the smell of coffee?" she said. "Even bad coffee, like this stuff." My mother's feeble half-decaf blend kept me in a fugue state all day.

She got out two mugs and placed them neatly by the coffee machine, both handles pointing in the same direction. "So I'm assuming you're excited about the reunion?" she said from over her shoulder.

I grinned. "I kind of am."

She turned around. "Can I ask you something?" Whenever a person requested permission to ask me something, I got tense. It's never a question like *How about some jelly beans?* or *Do you know what your best quality is?* or *Don't you just love puppies?*

She fixed her unblinking stare on me and leaned against the kitchen counter, her arms folded. "I notice that you're romanticizing this time period a little bit," she said. "I don't recall you having this spectacular time in high school. In fact, I remember you crying a lot in your room with the door shut."

I shook my head. "I had a great time. It may have been the best period of my life, in some ways. You know what it was, maybe? The highs were higher than they have ever been since. It's as if I've been trying to capture that first high, the way a crack addict does."

"And if you remember, the lows were suicidally low," she said. "Lillian. When something was bothering you, sometimes you wouldn't talk for a week. Remember?"

I thought for a minute. "You might be right," I admitted. "But I don't understand why *you're* not sentimental about high school. You had a much easier go of it than I did." Ginny was nominated for homecoming queen but had politely refused it, which was interpreted as edgy rather than principled and made her even more popular.

She frowned. The theoretical wheels were turning. "For me, high school was a crude caste system made up of fleeting social ties among hormonally excited teens." Her hand sketched a vague circle in the air. "And why those ties would create anything meaningful twenty years later is beyond me."

I poured some more coffee. "Is that why you didn't go to your reunion?"

"I just wasn't interested in seeing anyone," she said. "I would compare high school to being at a bad job in a dysfunctional company. Instead of being fired, you graduate." She paused. "I don't look back, really," she said thoughtfully, then corrected herself. "Well, I suppose I do, sometimes. But with a reunion, you're re-creating the student body, and you're all supposed to be adults now, but the problem is you haven't acted together as adults, so you're all thrown together in this room, it's like this dress rehearsal for a play." She paced the kitchen as if for a lecture. "It's like everyone went into a cryogenic freezer, and then it was unlocked and everyone crawled out to gather in some conference room with name tags on. My mild curiosity would not have been worth the discomfort."

She looked closely at me again. "I know that people focus on the good things of the past," she said. "Well, that's not entirely true. I've noticed that you dwell on slights. But then when you go to a reunion, you can't control your memories, you don't know what stray recollection will surface. I didn't want to put myself in that position. I'm glad I've forgotten a lot of that time period, and I suppose I prefer to keep it that way."

"But don't you have any unresolved issues?" I persisted. "Don't you want closure on anything?"

She smirked. "What, like Sue Davis figuring out new ways to torture me because she thought I stole her boyfriend? Which I didn't. Would I achieve some sort of closure if she approached me at the reunion and said, 'I'm sorry I wired your locker shut, I'm sorry about the prank calls and the rumors that I spread about you?' Most reunions are so brief that you wouldn't be able to work up to that kind of intimate moment, anyway. Unless she was drunk and became bold, in which case I would discount anything that she said." She shook herself. "Ugh. You see? I don't want to think about how Sue Davis used to call me and whisper 'Slut' and hang up. I saw a picture of her, and it didn't make me happier that she's obese now. I didn't think of it as any kind of justice; it just made me depressed."

I raised an eyebrow. "Sue Davis is obese?"

She shrugged. "I don't know what she could possibly say that would blot out some of those memories. So why bother?" She reached over to pick up a large jug of cheap wine that sat on the table. My parents had made short work of it the prior evening, so it was nearly empty.

She unscrewed the cap and took a cautious sniff. "Did you try any of this last night?" she asked in a low voice.

"No," I whispered.

"Have a sip. Just have yourself a little sip."

To make Ginny laugh, I took a swig out of the jug. Then I ran to the kitchen sink and spit it out. "It's vinegar," I said, gasping. "You could put it on a salad."

"Well, apparently they didn't notice." Making fun of our parents was a hallowed tradition that we faithfully resurrected whenever we got together, even if we occasionally felt a twinge of guilt.

Ginny looked down at my bare feet. "You have the nicest feet," she said admiringly. "I'm the one who got stuck with the huge big toe. Thanks, Dad." She slid a pale foot out of her ballet slipper and inspected it critically. "Look at this thing. It's shaped like a light-bulb. Your feet are in perfect proportion. You're so lucky."

I told myself to just accept the compliment, and tried to quash the suspicion that given my situation, it was the best she could scrounge up.

*chapter sixteen*

For once I was glad that my parents had forgotten my birthday. When I was younger, every birthday was a last-minute scramble culminating in a couple of twenties thrown into a card and some cartons of Chinese takeout (made belatedly festive by exhortations to order from the "Special Dishes" side of the menu, usually forbidden because of the double-digit cost). My parents just weren't the birthday-party type, and they were baffled that I would get so dismayed by their lack of enthusiasm.

As I grew older, their inattention was a blessing. Adam came from a family in which every occasion, from birthdays to Groundhog Day, was rowdily celebrated. If a cake existed in the shape of Punxsutawney Phil, Adam's family would purchase it and throw a Groundhog Day party. Every summer, the group started feverish preparations for Adam's brother Josh's Halloween party, trying to top the previous year's elaborate costumes. During the early years of our marriage, I threw myself into each shindig, buying presents and decorations, thinking up jolly games for my nieces and nephews, and sending around copies of photos marking every occasion.

A few years in, his brothers and sisters started reproducing madly, and between the kids' birthdays and their school events, we never had a spare weekend. His family didn't embrace me so much as engulf me, and if I opted out of a kindergarten graduation party, Adam received a round of inquisitive phone calls. I carefully maintained an attendance rate of 90 percent, knowing that if it dropped below that, my mother-in-law's tone would be slightly cooler to me on the phone, her chitchat briefer before she abruptly asked if Adam happened to be around.

So I grew to appreciate my parents' disinterested approach to holidays, and thus was amazed when the day before I turned thirty-eight my mother brought up the subject of my birthday. Ginny had returned to Madison, so it was just the two of us in the kitchen.

"Isn't it tomorrow?" she asked, consulting her calendar. "One week before Thanksgiving, right?"

"Well, yes," I said, "but let's just follow tradition and let it slide. I'm not feeling particularly celebratory, anyway."

"All the more reason to go out," said my mother firmly. She clapped her hands. "I know. Let's go to Benihana! Your favorite! For dessert, you can get that fried ice cream you like. Don't they roll it in coconut or something?"

I hadn't been to Benihana since the Reagan administration, or maybe the very beginning of the Clinton era.

"I'm going to call right now and make a reservation," said my mother. "We're going tomorrow night at seven, and that's that."

"*Now* you make a big deal?" I said as she grabbed the phone. "Where were you when I was sixteen?" But secretly I was a little pleased, and the next evening we bundled into my folks' car and off we went to Benihana.

We walked into the restaurant and the scent of steak and sizzling onions transported me right back as we were shown to our long communal table. A woman who looked strangely familiar was sitting at the far end. It was Dawn, grinning madly and jumping up. "Happy birthday!" she cried. Everyone at adjoining tables looked our way. She looked around, abashed. "Inside voices, right?" she said more quietly.

As we sat down, Dawn pulled four sparkly party hats from her pink L.L. Bean bag. "Your mom called me and told me it was your birthday," she said, "and when she said you all were bringing back the old tradition of going to Benihana, I said, 'Well, then, I'll get the party hats.'"

My folks laughed and put them on as the people at the other end of our communal table gawped. I didn't move to put on my hat, so Dawn jumped up and strapped it onto my head. "You look so bummed," she said, laughing. "I've got to get a picture of your expression. You look exactly like my dog Stevie when I try to give him a bath." She turned again to rummage in her bag, displacing a Tupperware container of Cheerios, a packet of wipes, and two children's books. "Do you believe all this crap?" she said, pulling out a full-sized box of tissues. "I give up." She pulled back and looked at me. "You look like one of my babysitters, I'm telling you."

The elastic from the hat was too tight, so I pulled it to allow myself some air. "Whoops," I said. "The elastic snapped."

Dawn pulled off her own hat. "Here," she said, fastening it onto my head. "You can have mine." I couldn't help but laugh. Dawn grabbed a grease-filmed placard on the table that said "Specialty Drinks." "'An experience at every table,'" she read aloud. "Hey, Lily. Remember how we used to order that nonalcoholic drink when we were kids?" Our usual was a Roy Rogers, a sick-making concoction of ginger ale, orange juice, and grenadine, festooned with six plastic swords that stabbed unrecognizable fruit chunks, all of which seemed to be the same virulent red of the maraschino cherry.

"I think we should break with tradition this time, and get some actual alcoholic drinks," Dawn announced. She turned to the waiter. "I'll have the Cherry Blossom."

I grinned at her. "And I'll have the Tokyo Peach."

"Make it two Cherry Blossoms," said my mother.

My father raised his hand. "Scotch. Neat."

A waiter scurried over with menus, my parents fumbled for their reading glasses, and we studied the menus in silence. A few minutes ticked by. My father murmured something unintelligible, but otherwise no one said anything. Why was the stillness so oppressive? Menu reading didn't need to be interactive. My parents were as familiar to me as my grayish slippers at home, and Dawn could not have been a more benign presence, yet I was hunched tensely over the menu like a turkey buzzard. The ambient noise in the crowded room seemed to fade until there was no sound at all.

I scanned the menu, desperate to pick anything. Hibachi Chicken. Hibachi Shrimp. Hibachi Scallops. Hibachi Steak. Hibachi Calamari. Nothing had changed on the menu of Traditional Dishes, except now there was South Beach Hibachi, an attempt at being contemporary.

Mercifully, my mother spoke up. "Hmm," she said. We all

leaned toward her eagerly, hoping she would make a comment that we could build upon. "Everything looks so good."

We all nodded. "It sure does," said Dawn. This exchange opened the door for the usual things that people say when they're out to dinner and studying menus. *I've been good all week, so tonight I'm going to splurge. I think I'm going to get an app, because I'm not getting dessert. Has anyone had the Hibachi Steak? I'm starving, I had a really light lunch. Does anyone want to split an appetizer? I really should get a salad, but . . .*

As everyone relaxed, Dawn fell into a spirited discussion with my parents. Their conversation washed comfortingly over me as they exchanged local reports about the new bagel place in town, the poor turnout for this year's Fourth of July parade, and the brash young superintendent of Dawn's school district, whose new ideas were quite unpopular.

"Let me tell you what, we have cleared our calendar for voting day," my father boomed. "That superintendent thinks everyone in town has *beaucoup* bucks to throw at a school gym. He should just ask his dad for money."

That woke me up from staring trancelike at the gummy fish tank in the lobby.

"Dad, why are you still voting on school board issues? Didn't your kids move out years ago?"

He smirked. 'Well, some of them didn't." My mother swatted him as I drained the rest of my Tokyo Peach. "All school board issues have a price tag, believe me. Why wouldn't I want to have a say? These kids are going to be your boss someday. They don't need to be overindulged with a state-of-the-art gym, for the love of Pete."

A chef materialized at our table. "My name is Bill," he said, pointing to his name tag. "Have you been here before? Do you know how our menu works?"

"Oh, yes," my mother said, waving her hand. "We've been bringing these girls here for years."

Bill's eyes flicked over to Dawn and me, and I knew he was thinking, *Those two are looking at girlhood through a rearview mirror.*

My mother pointed at me. "And tonight it's her birthday!"

*Please, please don't ask how old I am,* I prayed, and then I realized that I had hit the age where it is not polite to ask how many candles you are blowing out.

Bill kept his eyes on my parents. "Do you know what you'd like?" We gave our orders. Shortly afterward Bill returned and the show began. He sliced, diced, and flung a cleaver around. Then he kicked into high gear and, with one quick movement, tossed some shrimp into the air; with the tip of his knife he bounced them onto my mother's plate.

Dawn and my parents clapped, but I examined the shrimp. Were they done cooking yet? They still looked a little gray.

Then Bill flipped pieces of steak, one by one, into a tidy pile onto my father's plate and clacked together his large wooden salt and pepper shakers to release a cloud of pepper dust over the meat.

"A little more," said my father, pointing at his Hibachi Steak.

"Thank you, Bill," my mother said quickly. "This is great." She had a deft way of making up for my father's brusqueness without having it sound like a rebuke. Because my dad felt that tipping was an outmoded practice, he made the waiter work for it. He never said please or thank you, and I was forever slipping more money onto his grudging 10 percent. I wasn't going to argue with him tonight, but our disagreements had ruined more than one dinner when I tried to explain that he wasn't punishing the restaurant by refusing to augment the waiter's salary, he was punishing the poor guy bringing the food.

Dawn took her purple drink umbrella and stuck it behind her ear. "Remember when we used to do this?" she cried. "We were so queer." Involuntarily I looked around in embarrassment. Thank God none of my New York friends could see this. Then again, why was I casing the place? Of course they weren't going to be at a chain restaurant on Route 22 on a Friday night.

Dawn brightened. "Oh! I almost forgot. I just got you a little something. Excuse the wrapping job. Kade insisted on doing it." She pulled out a crumpled package and handed it to me.

"Kade is a nice name," said my mother. "What's the origin? Is it a family name?"

"No," said Dawn. "My husband and I just liked the sound of it. His full name is Kaden."

My father's upper lip lifted ever so slightly, and my mother shot him a look of warning.

I examined the package. "Oh, Dawn," I said. "It's nice enough that you came to dinner. But thank you." I pretended to open it carefully so I could save the wrapping paper like my parents do.

"Just rip it open!" said my mother, signaling the waiter for another drink. By that point, she had tossed back a whole branch of Cherry Blossoms.

I pulled out a paperback book from the wrapping and read the title out loud. *I'm Divorced. What Now?*"

My mother and Dawn exchanged anxious glances. I could tell that they were unsure of what my reaction would be.

"What now?" I said heartily. "How about another drink?"

Everyone at the table cheered. I turned to Dawn. "Thank you," I said feelingly, giving her a hug. "I love it."

"I know this might not be your thing," she said apologetically, "but if you do read it, I can tell you that it definitely helped two of my friends. I know some people laugh at that stuff, but not me. Do you want to hear something funny? When I go to a bookstore, I head straight for the self-help section." She laughed. "I even read books for problems I don't have. The other day I was reading *Chicken Soup for the Teenage Soul,* even though my kids can barely say the word *teenager.* I don't think they know what a teenager is. I just feel good reading those books, somehow."

I flipped through it. "This will really help. Maybe there will be some advice on how to respond to the 'Are you married?' question at the reunion."

My mother perked up. "Oh! It's coming up soon, right? I guess you two are going together, huh?"

Dawn did not speak first and looked at me. I smiled at her. "That was the plan," I said. She grinned back.

A chorus of voices singing "Happy Birthday" interrupted us. It was Bill, carrying a platter of fried ice cream doused with chocolate syrup and blazing with sparklers. He led a ragtag group of waiters who clearly wished that they were somewhere else as they grimly sang along.

I grinned as the people at nearby tables joined the chorus and Dawn and my folks raucously filled in *dear Lily* for the waiters. You *can* go home again. My parents were alive and healthy, my childhood best friend was by my side, we were all together in this safe, familiar place. For the first time since Adam left me, I was completely filled with happiness.

As we left the restaurant and headed for the car, Dawn and I were wearing matching paper umbrellas in our hair and walking a little unsteadily. I thought back on my last birthday, which took place in a chaotic New York bar. A knot of my co-workers from *Tell Me Everything!* huddled together, but the rest of my friends didn't really know one another. Some were holdouts from college, others were PR people I had met through work, two were neighbors, one was my yoga instructor. They all stood around in individual units, despite my increasingly shrill efforts to introduce them.

Adam kept telling me (or, rather, shouting to me over the music) not to take it personally that my friends were politely shunning one another. But I did. Why couldn't they have made an effort for me? My friends in public relations were used to schmoozing, but obviously a yoga instructor wasn't worth their time. After the obligatory forty-five minutes, each one gave me a kiss good-bye with a volley of excuses about babysitters and deadlines and murmured promises that we would get together soon. *I'm right here,* I wanted to say as I watched them head for the exit, hurriedly pulling out their cell phones. *Can't we get together right now?* My drink consumption increased as the group diminished, and all that came from the evening was a raging hangover.

Instead, here I was in the backseat of my parents' car, drowsy and pleasantly full of Hibachi Chicken and looking out the window at the fat yellow moon as it followed us home. My dad's favorite oldies station played softly as he chatted up front with my mother. I blew kisses at Dawn as she drove away in her minivan, waving frantically from the front seat. When we were twelve, we told each other everything, without embarrassment or shame. We knew each other utterly. I hadn't had that kind of purity of friendship since.

I looked down at my present. I had never read a self-help book in my life. Dawn had written an inscription on the inside cover. *So glad that we reconnected! Lots of love, Dawn.* It was my only birthday gift, but it was much more thoughtful than the rounds of tequila shots I had received the year before. Sigmund Freud once said that true happiness was the deferred fulfillment of a childhood wish. When I was a kid, I ardently wished that Dawn and I would grow up and live in the same town and be best friends forever.

*chapter seventeen*

Only a few days remained before the reunion. After a fruit-
less search for a dress at the mall, I decided to take a morning train into the city to fetch my reliable black Prada dress
out of my storage unit. I phoned my friend Drew and asked
him if he wanted to meet for lunch, knowing that he could
always be counted on for last-minute get-togethers.

Drew was a friend from college whom I dated for exactly
one weekend before we decided that friendship was our best
course. He was the manager at Film Forum, the downtown
movie house that showed independent films from all over
the world and hosted events like "An Evening with Farley
Granger." His passion was silent films, and he was con-

stantly petitioning the board of directors to feature more of them. Drew, due to his surplus of time and love of conversation, was one of those friends who would willingly accompany you to get keys made or your driver's license renewed. He was waiting for me at the New Jersey Transit counter, a slight figure in a plaid thrift-store shirt and threadbare jeans. His lank longish hair hung over his thick nerd spectacles.

"Hey, babe," he said, wrapping his thin arms around me. He nervously smoked two packs of cigarettes a day, so getting close to him was like sitting directly behind the exhaust panel of a city bus. "Let's go get your stuff, and then we can eat."

We walked to the storage place off the West Side Highway as he told me about his latest paramour, a photographer whom he met in the lobby of the Film Forum. Her specialty was photographing insects in the midst of devouring each other, a sufficiently mordant occupation for Drew. She put competing species in a box and waited for one of them to get hungry. "Now the ASPCA is on her," said Drew. "After they did a write-up in the paper, she's been harassed a lot."

"Could this be serious, this thing with her?" I asked, already knowing the answer. He never said yes outright.

"I think so."

"That means it's not serious."

"Not true. Not true. That means I'm a reasonable adult. Look, she's smart, funny, motivated, and she loves old films. But she's busy, so I only see her once a week."

"If you were both really into it, you would want to see each other all the time."

He lit a cigarette. "Not necessarily. You've been out of the game for a while, Lillian. When you get older, your job really can take over your life. I mean, I'm still working on my film, too, so a lot of times, nights are out." For the past three years, Drew had been filming a documentary called *End of the Line*, a series of profiles on the sole remaining holdout in various New York professions—the last pinball-machine repairman, the last Checker Cab driver. "I just got a lead on the last squeegee man," said Drew. "He laid low during the Giuliani administration's crackdown. Now he's somewhere in Hunts Point. Next week I'm tracking him down."

I was unnerved by the city's jostling hordes as we walked along. Had I been in the suburbs too long? We walked past a heaving mass of pigeons, bunched together on the sidewalk. "There's probably a child under there," Drew remarked dryly, sparking up another cigarette. A half pack later we arrived at the storage place and I got my key from the attendant, whose eyes never left the Knicks game on his tiny TV. "I can see why some people live in these units," Drew said as we walked down a long corridor. "Look at this. It's ten feet by twenty. That's . . . okay, I can't do the math on square feet, but that's pretty big. I know a guy who keeps his collection of marionettes in here. It's ironic, really. You define yourself by your possessions, and then you can't even display them to let people know what you're about. Now he probably has people over and they think his apartment is boring, not knowing that he's this crazy puppet collector."

I delved through my dresses as he kept talking. "Maybe I could do a documentary on storage," he mused. Drew was always in midscheme. "I know there's a band called Mini Storage that rehearses in one of these things in another facility downtown. That would be kind of funny, right? And I read that one place in Chelsea is a center for African art, it's this big scene, and all these guys in dashikis gather together on the loading dock, trading and buying and making music and cooking food and stuff."

I pulled out a pair of shoes from a box and stuffed them into a bag. "Shouldn't you finish the film you're working on first?" I despaired of him ever finishing. One former cigarette girl he had interviewed had already died. "Come on, let's get out of here and go eat."

Drew announced that he wanted a grilled cheese, which might have been less a craving than a tacit admission that both of us were broke. "How about this place?" I said, pointing at a restaurant called Mulalley's Grille.

He shook his head. "You know my rule: I don't eat at places that have an *e* on the end of *grill.*"

"Oh. Right. Sorry. Why is that again?"

"If they're changing the spelling for no good reason, it means that they're trying to compensate for lackluster food."

Drew had a boundless trove of life rules, simple stratagems that he deemed necessary for happiness and that he was not shy in announcing. No "inspirational coach" movies, except on airplane flights longer than four hours. Never wait in line for breakfast; no exceptions. Baseball caps are for males under six years of age or over sixty-five. Do not date a woman who uses *journal* or *dialogue* as a verb. And no sandwiches at dinner ("There's a pathos to sandwiches at dinner. Lunch only").

After a few blocks we found a diner on Eighth Avenue and slid into a booth. As we studied the menus, he said, "I don't think I want a grilled cheese anymore. Maybe I'll get a hamburger. Burgers and steaks are the most popular last meals of death row prisoners, did you know that? Well, what if I get hit by a truck later on today? I should have a meal that most people would consider the ultimate."

"Jesus, Drew."

"And a milk shake, too, just in case."

"Just in case of what?"

"Just in case I get hit by a truck." A waitress took our order, and then Drew said casually, "So you probably heard about Adam."

My stomach plummeted to the floor and beyond, past the diner's foundations, past the city's network of sewer pipes and subway tunnels, past the soil and rocks and down, down to the bits of pottery and clay pipe fragments thrown out by Dutch settlers in the 1600s.

"No, I haven't," I said evenly. Drew was just as close to Adam as he was to me, and, unlike some others, had remained friends with each of us.

"He's moving in with Elyse, the woman he's been dating."

I shook my head. "I don't know who that is."

"Elyse Brooks. Does that sound familiar? She's the daughter of Marvin Brooks. The petrillionaire? No?"

I shook my head again, stupidly. "She's some sort of designer," Drew continued. "Purses or something. I met her a few times. She's very nice."

Meanwhile, I was still mindlessly checking the "married" box whenever I had to fill out forms. "The divorce was just final a few weeks ago."

He nodded. "I know. It's fast. I'm sorry. I guess he had been spending a lot of time at her place, and they figured that—"

I cut him off. "I don't need to know." I tried to regain my footing. "I haven't talked to him in a while. Maybe I'll give him a call. I've been trying to make the transition into friendship."

"I'm not friends with any of my exes. I don't think you can be real friends with someone you dated."

"You absolutely can. Often the basis of a relationship is friendship. The romance may dissolve but the base is there."

He shook his head. "I disagree." *I disagree* was Drew's favorite expression and arguing his most beloved hobby. "There are too many tensions that are hidden, just waiting to flare up." He dispensed of his burger in four bites. "I tried being friends with my last girlfriend," he said. "We did the lunch thing, exchanged dating horror stories, but then when I met someone promising and I told her about it, she burst into tears." He groped his shirt pocket for cigarettes before realizing he couldn't smoke in the diner. "There's too much history. If you've gone out for a long time, you've seen them puke, you've seen them cry with their nose running. You've seen parts of them at close range that only their doctors have looked at. It's too close. It's too much."

"But it seems odd to just erase your past," I said. "I don't mean keeping a stalker in your life, but what about that compatible person who has clearly moved on? The reason you were with them in the first place is that you liked being around them and shared at least some common ground. Just cutting someone off strikes me as a little cruel."

Drew folded his arms. "There are six and a half billion people in the world, which if you ask me is a pretty big pool of potential friends. I think some people are right for you at the time, and then you move on. Ideally, you're continually growing and changing, and not everybody is doing it alongside of you."

I shook my head. "I disagree."

We continued our argument as we walked all over Manhattan for the rest of the afternoon. It was extremely satisfying. Eventually he dropped me off at a subway downtown. "Can you make it to Penn Station on your own?" he said. "I know you're a suburban girl now."

"Funny," I said. "That's some A material."

When I got on the subway and sat down, a disheveled man at the other side of the car immediately perked up. His hard brown eyes eagerly sought mine, and as the train started moving he darted over and sat down next to me. "Hey, how are you, good," he said. "Can I ask you something?"

I didn't respond.

"I asked you a question," he said loudly, and I rose to get off the train and change cars. Had I forgotten how to fade into the background? Did he flap over to me because I looked vulnerable? Six weeks out of the city and I had neglected to bring reading material and, worse, was making eye contact with strangers.

As I boarded a New Jersey Transit train, I found that I was eager to get back to the suburbs. "You again," said the burly, mustachioed conductor who had taken my ticket in the morning. "Did you have a nice day in the city?"

"I did," I said shyly, biting back the impulse to tell him that I actually lived in the city.

"Well, I'm glad that you had fun, young lady," he said. I loved that the train conductors still wore hats.

I couldn't believe how relieved I was to be on the train homeward. How could that be, when the best day of my entire life took place in New York? It was a fall day three years ago that commenced with a trip to the Metropolitan Museum with my friend Jina to see relics from the lost city of Petra excavated from the Jordanian desert. Where else could you take a subway to see an actual lost city? Then we went for lunch at Saks, with a quick stop afterward in the shoe department, where we noticed a group of large men in ill-fitting Big and Tall suits who had crammed their bulky frames into the delicate faux Louis XV chairs grouped around the shoe displays.

"See the earpieces?" Jina said quietly. "Bodyguards. For whom, I wonder? Look sharp." We were looking discreetly around, elaborately casual, when we nearly bumped into a woman who was studying her sandaled foot in front of a mirror. It was Aretha Franklin—in town, I remembered from my morning paper, to perform at Radio City. Without taking her eyes off the mirror, she said, "What do you think, girls?"

She was wearing baggy knee-high stockings underneath the sandals, which were a vivid peacock blue and glittering with rhinestones.

"Don't look too closely at my hose," she said in her rich, rumbling voice.

"They're great!" we squeaked, trying unsuccessfully to keep it together.

That night, after meeting friends at a bar in Murray Hill, I had decided to walk home to my apartment when I noticed a crowd massing near the Queens Midtown Tunnel. My mouth fell open as a pair of enormous elephants plodded magnificently by, followed by a group of nonplussed zebras. Before the circus opened at Madison Square Garden, the animal handlers walked their charges through the tunnel and across Third Avenue, where I stood. I was so exhilarated that I couldn't sleep afterward.

How could the suburbs compare to a lost city, a Motown legend in the shoe department, a parade of circus animals on the street? Yet I couldn't wait to have some of my dad's pork chops in a cooking bag. And now that I had my black dress, and had reinvigorated my mojo by being in the city, I was ready for the reunion.

*chapter eighteen*

I sat in my parents' car at the arrivals area of Newark airport, my stomach percolating with nervous tension. I was
waiting for Kimmy, Lynn, and Sandy, who had coordinated
their flights so that I could pick them all up at once. We'd
booked two rooms at the Hamilton Park Hotel and Conference Center—Kimmy and Lynn in one, Sandy and me in the
other—but hadn't decided whether or not we were going to
Friday's "informal event" at Playmaker's bar on Route 22.
Most people were only attending Saturday night's shindig.

Did the car smell like the sesame bagel with butter I had
just eaten? I hastily rolled down the windows. I checked my
hair again in the rearview mirror. I couldn't believe that I

had forgotten my sunglasses, crucial for my insouciant, devil-may-care look. I squinted through the glass windows of Arrivals. Was that a shopping atrium? Maybe I could race into Sunglass Hut. Wasn't there a Sunglass Hut on every corner of Newark International? I put the car in park. I could probably run in quickly. There was time.

*Shoot.* There were Lynn and Sandy, laughing as they ran through the double doors, each lugging huge suitcases. Kimmy was walking coolly behind them with a small wheeled cart and a pricey but discreet leather tote in a perfect buttery shade of camel. We all squealed as we hugged. I hadn't squealed properly in years. "Hi, girls!" I cried, popping the trunk and instinctively taking Kimmy's bags first.

Lynn was slim as always, her blond hair a neat curtain, her posture correct. She had on expensive jeans, black boots, and a close-fitting black blazer, and had put on more makeup than she was obviously used to wearing as a wind-blown riding instructor. Kimmy was tan—a resort tan rather than a salon tan—and had on a creamy white sweater and the sort of menswear-style trousers that looked chic on her and made me look like a security guard. Where were the wrinkles from the plane? Her only jewelry was a pair of simple but hefty diamond studs, just as she had worn in high school. Her parents had allowed her to upgrade them at every graduation: eighth grade, high school, college.

"Hi, honey," she said casually, as if I lived next door and she had just seen me. I hugged her, enveloping myself in the familiar scent that clung lightly to the entire Marino family: the interior of a new BMW.

Sandy jumped in and grabbed the both of us. "Hiya, Chugs!" she shouted, using my hard-drinking nickname from high school. I had always chafed at that nickname, but begging her to stop only made her use it more.

"Hi, Jugs," I replied, using a nickname made obsolete after Sandy's breast reduction. Her reddish brown hair was frizzy from the plane ride, and her freckled face was split into a wide grin. She was wearing black leggings and an enormous red puffer coat to ward off the November chill. She carried a flowered pillow from her bed at home and a faded tote bag that looked vaguely familiar. "Do you recognize this fabric?" she asked, holding it up. "It's my skirt with the taxicabs all over it! I had it made into a tote bag! I couldn't give it up."

I shoved their luggage into the trunk and they piled into the car, Kimmy taking the front seat as she always did.

"I'm starving to death," Sandy announced from the back.

"Well, then, let's go to the Nauseous," I said. Everyone cheered.

"I'm getting the tuna melt," Sandy announced. "I wonder how it will taste when I'm sober."

Everyone began to talk at once, the pitch of our voices unconsciously rising the way it had when we were kids. "Lillian!" Lynn hollered over the din. "I brought something that's going to make you laugh. Do you have a tape player in this car?"

"Of course," I said. "Remember how cheap my father is? I drove this thing in college. It only has 160,000 miles on it. My dad claims that if you replace your oil every three thousand miles and check your transmission, your car will last forever."

"Then play this," she said, handing me a cassette. "It's a tape you made me for my seventeenth birthday. Look at the two sides. One says 'Before You Go Out,' and the other says 'When You Come Home.' See? One is to psych you up, the other is to calm you down after a big night. Now I pretty much just listen to the mellow side, because there is no going out."

I put it in and a muffled version of the Cure's "Love Cats" came on. I drove crazily to make the girls laugh. We roared into the parking lot of the Nautilus Diner, aka "the Nauseous," and walked to the entrance in a tight unit, talking simultaneously. I was nearly overcome with a surge of pure love for the three of them. It was so exhilarating to be enclosed within a posse. In New York I traveled everywhere on my own. Being part of this little group restored in me a long-dormant sense of security. It wasn't about me anymore; their personalities lifted the weight off of me. When I walked around New York by myself, all eyes relentlessly evaluated me, but when we moved together as a group, the only thing people saw was a group. It was so freeing. No wonder we traveled in a pack as teens.

We had a satisfyingly rowdy lunch. Everyone recklessly ordered fries—Sandy unapologetically adding cheese—and Lynn flirted with the pimply fourteen-year-old waiter. Kimmy insisted on picking up the tab. Then we headed to the hotel to unpack, singing to my mix tape as the years dropped away. I forgot that Sandy and Kimmy had kids, that Lynn was a teacher, that I was, as Vi termed it, a divorcée. We chattered about old boyfriends as if they were still young and single and paunch-free. I had an overwhelming urge to drive straight to the shore with them and guzzle a cheap warm beer from a sand-encrusted can.

We headed back to the hotel, piled into one room, and collapsed onto the double beds. I cleared my throat when there was a brief lull in the loud conversation. Time to get it over with. "Listen," I began haltingly, "I just want to tell you all about the Adam saga so that we can get it out of the way." I relayed the whole story as they nodded and reached over periodically to squeeze my knee, their chins puckered with concern. They asked dozens of questions. They analyzed my every answer as if it were complex foreign policy. I was floating in the intoxicating force field of their empathy.

"Enough of this," Sandy said suddenly. "Let's think of the positives here. For one, you'll always have a clean house." I had tweaked the truth, claiming that I had an apartment lined up and that my residency at my parents' house was ending in two weeks. "For another, you can have whatever you want in the fridge."

"No more sports programs droning in the background," Lynn put in.

Sandy stood up on the bed. "Oh. My. God. You're going to start dating again." Everyone yelled at once. She gestured at her stomach. "No one has seen this body but Ryan for fifteen years except the doctor that delivered my three kids." She appraised my stomach. "You're lucky you haven't had children yet, Lily. No stretch marks."

"Talk about stretch," said Lynn. "I can't laugh without peeing."

We fell right into our age-old tradition of self-denigration. Kimmy jumped up and ran to the mirror. "Look at this," she announced, pointing to her scalp. "Underneath this color, I'm totally gray. If you look really close, you can see it in my hair part. Can you see? It's a gray strip! God love Ramon, is all I have to say."

Sandy joined her at the mirror and inspected her hairline. "My hair fell out in chunks after I had kids and my friends kept saying it would grow back," she said. "Well, it didn't. I have a bald spot on the top of my head like my uncle Bernie."

Kimmy pulled up her shirt. "Remember what great tits I had? Look at what happens after you breast-feed four children. I'm like a man."

"What are you talking about?" Lynn demanded. "You're not even saggy."

"Well, that's because I got a lift. My father went to med school with one of the best plastic surgeons in the country, so I took a little trip out to UCLA Medical Center. I really wanted to get a double surgery and fix my stomach, but there was just too much recovery time."

She scrutinized the taut stretch of tanned flesh that was flatter than mine was in high school. "Ugh, kids just ruin you."

I didn't say a word. "Kimmy, are you kidding?" said the ever-reliable Lynn. "With that stomach, I would have thought you had adopted. Your tan is so even, you can't even see the stretch marks." Kimmy continued to gaze at her reflection with a critical eye as I asked the group whether we were going to the cocktail hour at Playmaker's.

"I can't imagine anyone we hung out with being at Playmaker's," said Lynn. "I think most people we know are coming in tomorrow."

"I say we go for an hour," I said. "We'll look at it as stopping by on our way to dinner."

Lynn wrinkled her nose. "I don't know. Playmaker's? I didn't go there in high school, so I'm not sure I want to go there now. I think it's just going to be the geeky kids."

"Guess what," I said. "They're not kids, and neither are we. And we're not exactly hip anymore."

"Come on, people," said Sandy. "Why travel all the way here to stay in? There's one kid I did a bunch of plays with—remember Jason Monachino, the lead in *The Music Man*? I want to see him. He said on the website that he was going to Playmaker's."

Kimmy looked over at me slyly. "I'll bet your old friend Dawn will be there. Remember her?"

"You know, she lives in Belleville," I said. "I see her around. She's actually pretty funny."

Sandy smiled politely. No one said anything.

"Okay, then," announced Kimmy, picking up a makeup brush. "One hour."

*chapter nineteen*

Bethel Memorial Alum Night started at five-thirty, so in order for us to casually roll into Playmaker's at eight as if by afterthought, we had dinner first. At eight-fifteen we were still touching up our makeup in the parking lot, but finally we strolled in and made our way to the bar, which was festooned with dozens of frantic signs. TUESDAY $5 BEER BUST!!! DON'T MISS FRIDAY NIGHTS AT PLAYMAKER'S WITH COMEDIANS DANNY DEISEL AND HEY MIKEY! WEDNESDAY HUMP DAY DOLLAR MARGARITAS!

Two codgers sat moodily at the bar. "Private event?" said the bartender. He pointed to a far corner of the room where a few dozen people stood around holding drinks. "Over there."

"Let's get out of here," Lynn muttered.

"Too late," I said, pasting on a smile. "We've been spotted."

I scanned the faces as we walked over: Kathy, our earnest class treasurer, squarish in a gray suit; a shy girl named Carol; Michelle, the former goth chick turned Texas mom; our Spanish teacher, Mrs. Furtado; and a sprinkling of people who, I realized with slight panic, I did not recognize at all.

"Hey, girls," said Kathy heartily, acting as the official ambassador for the evening. "Don't you all look pretty. Kimmy, my God, how do you do it? You must not have kids. I've got three at home that run me ragged."

*Don't say it.* "I have four," said Kimmy. We gave Kathy an awkward group hug and then looked around, smiling, as we clutched our drinks.

"Break it up," Sandy said out of the side of her mouth. "Let's mingle, for God's sake."

Michelle ran over, squealing, and hugged all of us. I had never hugged her before, and I could tell by the puzzled expression on Kimmy's face that she hadn't, either. *We're adults now,* I told myself. *So act like one. Gracious. Calm. Friendly.*

"Lillian!" Mrs. Furtado came toward me with outstretched arms.

"*Buenos dias,* Mrs. Furtado!" I cried. *Buenos dias, Señora Furtado, or, as you were occasionally known, Mrs. Fur Taco!*

"It's time you call me Shelly," she said grandly.

"I don't know if I can."

"Nonsense," she said. She had hardly aged, and now we had

caught up with her. "So I read in the updates that you're a television producer. Very impressive!"

I dipped my head modestly. "Thank you."

She leaned forward. "Listen, I don't know if your boss Vi has authors on her show? But I wrote a really great book that's coming out in two months. It's from the University of California Press, and it's, this is oversimplifying but it's sort of an atlas of Spanish religious practices, which I know sounds dry but it's quite fascinating, because . . ."

I had the uncomfortable realization that my Spanish teacher was pitching me. In the rare cases when we featured books on the show, it was a tame tell-all written by a movie star of waning wattage, or a book that highlighted a graying star's late-in-life hobby or cause: animal rights, Southern cooking, cruise travel.

". . . feel odd about asking you, but of course we have no publicity budget, it's just a small university press, and I always think of you fondly, I mean if you recall, I wrote that recommendation for you when you were applying to colleges, and . . ."

*And now it's payback time.* I fished in my purse for a business card and handed it to her. I'd tell Vi that Mrs. Furtado was my teacher and that's how she would introduce her. I could already hear her saying, *As you all know, we're like a family on this show, and this nice lady here just happens to be the former high school teacher of my executive producer.* I could spare fifteen minutes at the end of the show for my Spanish teacher, who struggled in vain to interest us in Cervantes. She once took the class to an authentic Mexican restaurant in Morristown in an attempt to spark the interest of thirty bratty suburban kids who disdained the unfamiliar food because it didn't have a shiny coating of orange microwaved cheese like Taco Bell.

I nodded. "I'm sure we can do it."

"Oh, Lillian," she said, giving me another hug. Elated, I moved on to a few other classmates and chatted with them. This was a useful dress rehearsal for tomorrow night. As I struggled to remember the name of one beefy guy who was telling me about his software business, I spied my former biology lab partner, Ankur Saxena. He was standing off to the side with a small blond woman. They both wore rimless glasses. Ankur, always slight, had filled out nicely and had a prosperous, authoritative look, with his neatly trimmed beard and perfectly erect posture. The last I heard, he was getting his Ph.D. in . . . economics?

"Ankur!" I was suddenly so glad to see him. Why had I not kept in touch?

"Hello, Lillian," he said. He was less effusive than I was, but then he had always been fairly reserved. "This is my wife, Jane."

"Hello, Jane," I said warmly, taking her hand. Ankur told me that he was a professor of economics at Columbia, where he had met Jane. They had two children and were trying for a third.

"Ankur was my long-suffering lab partner for two years," I told Jane as I cooed over the photo of their kids that Ankur retrieved from his wallet. "He used to crack me up in class." Neither replied, so I went on. "He was always so modest, so I don't know if he told you how well liked he was at school." I was exaggerating. Ankur Saxena didn't inspire any dislike, which was a feat in itself in high school, but I figured that every man wants to look good in front of his wife, so I slathered on the praise. "Everyone respected him because he did so well academically, but he also knew how to have fun," I continued. "Do you know what his nickname was? Did he ever tell you?"

She looked at him quizzically. "No," she said.

"It was 'Sexy,'" I announced. Now she would laugh and we could form an alliance, gently teasing him together. "Remember graduation, Ankur?" As he made his way to the podium to collect his degree, I had started the chant: *Sex-EE, Sex-EE, Sex-EE,* which reached a wild crescendo as he faced us all and waved. I had cheered the loudest for the friend that I had proudly cultivated outside of my insular little group.

Ankur did not laugh. "Right. Yes, I remember," he said evenly. He was swaying a little and I realized he was drunk. "Made a fool with thirty of my relatives watching. You know, Lillian, for my parents, it was a serious occasion. After graduation, I wasn't going to go get bombed at someone's beach house like you. I had to go back to my house and explain that what you all were doing wasn't an insult."

His wife laughed nervously and tugged at his sleeve. "Ank. Let's lighten up a little."

He clumsily batted away her hand. "I just want to be called by my real name."

"Right, right, of course," I said quickly.

He laughed. "Why do you look so surprised? To see that I repudiate the attentions of a pretty and popular girl? I didn't *want* to be friends with all of you. That's what you never understood."

Lynn stole up behind me. "Let's go, right now," she murmured. "We did an hour." She marshaled us out, playing the bad guy as I mumbled apologies to Ankur and his wife.

"That was rough," said Kimmy, shuddering. "Was it me, or was everyone a little freaky? That was like being at a medieval fair." We all walked quickly to the car and then, giggling, broke into a run.

"You know what's so odd to me?" shouted Lynn from the backseat as we roared out of the parking lot. "Some people surrounded me and then they wouldn't talk. They just sort of waited for me to say something."

"Forget about that, let's discuss Todd Bevan," said Sandy. "How cute was he? He really cleaned up. Remember how he used to throw chairs in class? He was smart to wear his fireman's T-shirt. Everyone loves a fireman." She looked at me. "Why so quiet?"

I shook my head. "I'm just rattled by that little scene with Ankur." I repeated what he said and was rewarded with a torrent of indignant comments. Who the hell did he think he was? Seriously! What, had he been saving up for this for twenty years? He was always a little off, wasn't he, Lillian? Fuck him! Not your problem!

But his comments replayed in my head for the rest of the night, even after we flopped on the beds and ordered ice cream sundaes from room service and Sandy tossed a pile of bad celebrity magazines on the bed and Lynn pulled her favorite nail polish out of her suitcase to give us manicures. I knew without looking that it was Ballet Slipper Pink, just as I knew that Kimmy would eat peaches and plums raw but couldn't stand them if they were cooked, and that Sandy was deathly afraid of driving over bridges. I felt I knew them intimately, but could that be the case when I was barely acquainted with their husbands and children? Was your fifteen-year-old self your truest self? Did I need to be closely involved in the second half of my friends' lives to entirely know them?

I sat up on the bed. "Do you feel the same inside as you did when you were a teenager?" I asked them.

"Exactly the same," Sandy answered immediately. "I look in the mirror and sometimes I'm shocked. And when I do things that are parental, like scold one of my kids and tell them not to play with the straw in their drink, I feel like I'm acting. Like I really don't care if my daughter plays with the straw in her drink, whereas I felt like my mother genuinely worried that the neighbors would think I was an .animal."

She lay on her stomach and put her chin in her hands. "I still feel that playfulness that I did when I was fifteen, definitely," she said. "I'm still attracted to sparkly things, like a crow. That's my fifteen-year-old self. All my return address labels still have *Peanuts* characters on them. God, do you believe how serious everyone was tonight? I'm astounded by how much people lost their sense of humor. It's like it's not permitted anymore when you're an adult. I was so afraid of my personality changing after I had kids."

"You didn't change at all," said Lynn.

"I think I'm the same, but I don't think everybody is." Sandy considered. "Although I wouldn't relive that time period for anything."

*I would.*

"I like being this age. I'm more confident now. I'm not pretending that I know things, I feel like I really do know them, and I feel easy in my own skin. Back then, everything was a little too raw."

"I liked feeling everything so intensely," I said hesitantly. "I haven't had that sort of pure feeling since."

Sandy looked dreamily at the room's dirty stucco ceiling. "I do miss making out," she said. "Ryan and I don't do that very much. And I'll tell you something, Ryan's not the best kisser in the world. He's a little sloppy. You think you can teach someone that stuff, but you really can't." She sighed good-humoredly. "I married him anyway, but when I think of a really good kisser, it's this guy named Duncan that I went out with for a week in college. I didn't even like him that much. In fact, I sort of hated him. He was this big, preppy, husky guy, he looked like a banker even in sophomore year, and he was really cocky. Ugh, he was so smarmy. But holy crap, could he kiss."

I thought of what Ginny had said about women's erotic memories.

"I miss nothing," said Kimmy as she did yoga poses on the bed. "I loathed being a kid. I couldn't wait to get older. I hated being subjugated—not being able to eat when I wanted, not being able to drive myself places. I was so frustrated at the perception that children were a different species than adults." She did a downward dog on the floor. "I certainly didn't feel that way, and I remember being in a constant state of rage at the injustice of it all. I felt I had the same sort of sensibility, the same kind of intelligence as an adult did."

"I felt like you did, too," said Sandy. "I never thought of you as a kid, even when you were one."

Kimmy nodded. "When I was older and started to travel to countries where I didn't speak the language, I remember thinking, 'This is exactly what it's like to be a child, when other people know their way around, and can communicate better, but you know that you're just as competent and smart.'"

I turned to Sandy. "Do you feel like we know each other well, even though we haven't seen one another these last few years?"

She nodded. "I do. Want to test me? Right now you're paying attention to our conversation, but in the back of your brain, you're brooding about Ankur's comment and wondering if you should fix it tomorrow night by talking to him."

I jumped up. "You're right. I was thinking of telling him that I—"

Lynn interrupted. "Just let it go. He wanted to say his piece."

"But he misunderstood me. We were friends and he acted like I had chosen him against his will, like he was a pet or something."

Lynn sighed. "But Lillian, you sort of did choose him like a pet. You palled around together in class, but did you ever go to his house? You never saw him on weekends, or brought him to parties. There was a definite line."

"I guess he was more like the friend that you have in the office, where you hang around Mondays through Fridays but you don't know their home number," I said, hating how shallow I sounded.

"Who cares?" said Kimmy. "It was a long time ago. Besides, Ankur isn't the only thing you're obsessing about." Lynn and Sandy exchanged smirks. "So are you planning on hooking up with Christian tomorrow? When I brought him up at dinner I noticed that someone was pretty flustered." They all hooted as my face went crimson.

"I may have something like that in mind," I admitted. "I won't lie."

Sandy shook her head. "I can't imagine hooking up with someone. God, it's been . . . what, fifteen years? I'd have to buy new underwear. And the elastic in mine is finally stretched out the way I like it."

"Lillian," said Lynn. "I'll bet he still looks hot. He was so athletic. And his whole family had good hair."

"Yes, but it's the mother's side of the family that determines baldness, right?" I said. "I never met the grandparents."

Kimmy deftly executed an elephant-trunk pose. "Listen," she said. "Have a fun night with him, fool around—"

"Tell us everything," Lynn put in.

"And then go back to New York, start dating again, and meet someone nice."

I smiled enigmatically. Christian would not be some fling.

*chapter twenty*

Later that night, when Kimmy and Lynn had retired to their room and Sandy was snoring softly in her bed next to me, I lay awake thinking of Kimmy. The sight of her yoga flexing hurtled me back to one summer in high school, when she and I attended a weeklong soccer camp at Dartmouth, the closest I would ever get to those particular hallowed halls.

Because it was July, we were able, thrillingly, to stay in an actual dorm. For weeks we had excitedly made plans to live like real college students, buying food for the mini-fridge and flip-flops for the shower. Kimmy's older brother had schooled us on exactly what to bring and had even helped us steal a milk crate from the deli. We weren't exactly sure what the crate was supposed to store, but according to him, every dorm room had one, so we wanted one, too.

Every day after soccer practice, we would walk home to Kimmy's house, carefully honing the lies that we were going to tell the college boys we met. We crafted elaborate biographies, rehearsed over and over: We were students who had just completed our freshman year at Duke, but Dartmouth was offering dorm space to us—this revealed our utter naïveté—while we considered transferring schools. I was from Charlottesville, Virginia, and lived on a horse farm, while Kimmy hailed from D.C. and lived in a townhouse in Georgetown. We both had boyfriends but made it clear to them that we wanted to be free for the summer. (That way, if we didn't like our potential suitors, a "reunion" with our boyfriends offered a convenient out.)

We bought decorations for our temporary dorm-room walls that we thought were sufficiently collegiate and would impress older guys—a Bob Marley poster that said "Smile Jamaica," a still of a deranged Jack Nicholson poking his head through a chain-locked door in *The Shining*, an ad for Corona beer (exotic to us because it was drunk with a lime). Kimmy's brother had grudgingly supplied a few tattered album covers to display—Flesh for Lulu, Ministry, and Tom Waits. Mrs. Marino, getting caught up in the festivities, drove us to Bloomingdale's and had us pick out matching Marimekko bedspreads. We carefully avoided babyish florals, finally selecting a grown-up pattern in an understated dark red.

On the big day, Dr. and Mrs. Marino drove us to Dartmouth, stopping first in New Haven so Dr. Marino could take us to the pizza place that he loved to frequent when he attended Yale. When we arrived at the dorm room, we took our milk crates and hurried the two of them off, Mrs. Marino crying and Dr. Marino slipping Kimmy a one-hundred-dollar bill. "And you have the Amex, right?" Dr.

Marino said absently. "Just don't go crazy. And buy your brother a sweatshirt."

We busily unpacked and ornamented the room, turning on our boom box and locating the college radio station, as Kimmy's brother had instructed. Then my heart thudded in excitement as Kimmy grabbed the keys. "Let's walk around," she said. We left our door open a crack to announce our arrival, in case any guys happened by. We explored the entire campus, me surreptitiously studying every face that we passed, Kimmy cool and inscrutable in her perfectly faded Girbaud jeans and white Mia flats. Then again, she had once visited her brother at Princeton, so she knew exactly what to expect. Nothing fazed Kimmy—not ordering at a posh restaurant, not her first trip to Paris with her family. She knew how to charge things at her parents' country club and how to carry on conversations with her older brother's friends. She knew what outfits to wear to graduations and weddings. Dartmouth was certainly no cause for alarm.

We passed the campus store and she pulled me inside. "We'll need some things to wear," she said. She grabbed a basket and started digging through a pile of sweatshirts with concentration.

I held one up. "Kimmy. Kimmy. Look at this T-shirt. It says 'Coed Naked Lacrosse.'"

"No," she said.

"Stupid," I agreed, and put it back. She loaded up the basket with Dartmouth sweatshirts, sweatpants, shirts, socks, a tennis visor, and Dartmouth notebooks to use the following year in high school. Then we topped the pile with some junk food—our new favorite drink, Capri Sun, which came in a silver bag, Marathon candy bars, and Kimmy's favorite gum, Freshen-up in cinnamon, which she called "come gum" because each fat capsule contained a blob of viscous goo in the middle.

"Thanks, Dad," Kimmy said as she paid. I laughed conspiratorially even as I was a little horrified at how much merchandise she unthinkingly bought. The chubby clerk who rang it all up was only a few years older than us, and new at the job.

"Oops," said the clerk apologetically. "I have to deduct this. I rang it up twice by mistake. It'll just take a minute."

Kimmy looked freezingly at her and didn't say anything. I wanted to smile sympathetically but was afraid Kimmy would see me. That was the queasy feeling she often elicited in me. My part of our covenant was that I would roll my eyes along with her when she encountered a hectoring father or a slow waiter, no matter how much it made me cringe, but in exchange I was permitted to move comfortably through her world. As a shy person I siphoned her confidence, and if I had to act haughty occasionally, I was willing to make that trade.

What I loved about Kimmy was that she pointedly ignored the fact that my father owned a small hardware store so I could ill afford the designer clothes she wore. She would casually hand me some castoffs, some with the tags still attached, and say, "These always looked better on you." Or she'd buy a sweater and say, "We'll share this." Occasionally she would have her mother pick up two of the same item for us. My father would have been mortified if he knew that her parents bought clothes for me.

I wished that I felt the same way, but I didn't experience a particle of guilt, nor did I feel bad that Kimmy never bothered to come to my house after school. I was happy to go to her house, which had the first Betamax in the neighborhood and an older brother with an extensive album collection and a freezer full of Pepperidge Farm blueberry turnovers that would have been gone at my house in five minutes but languished for months at the Marinos'. Mrs. Marino collected Lladró figurines, which she displayed in a lighted glass case in the living room. I vowed that when I got older, I, too, would collect Lladrós.

The dumpling-shaped Mrs. Marino was so cowed by her glamorous daughter that she—like everyone else—sought to be Kimmy's friend. She called me her second daughter. When I phoned the Marino home, she made a point of chatting with me for a minute before handing the phone to Kimmy. She cheered me on at field hockey games. Every year she took Kimmy and me out to a special dinner for my birthday. I felt more comfortable around Mrs. Marino than I did with my own mother, so much so that when Kimmy told me one year that she was going to get her parents to invite me along on their annual vacation in Palm Beach, I assumed the biggest problem I'd have would be convincing my own folks to allow me to go away for a whole week.

Kimmy had regaled me many times about the Breakers, the opulent monument to the preppy good life—the hotel staffers who would come out to your beach cabana to spray your face with chilled mineral water, the ten tennis courts, the croquet games on the wide green lawn. It sounded like heaven. "I just have to ask them and it's done," she said. "My brother won't care. He plays golf with my dad the whole time anyway."

The weekend after Kimmy told me about the trip, I begged my parents to let me go with the Marinos. Forty-eight hours later, after gales of angry, hysterical tears, they agreed, as long as I paid my airfare with the confirmation money my grandparents had given me a few years earlier. When I triumphantly called Kimmy to tell her that at last I had won them over, she said that her parents had just told her the vacation was family only. Her matter-of-fact tone conveyed that she had calmly accepted their verdict without argument. I had deluded myself into thinking that Mrs. Marino would surely want her "second daughter" along on vacation.

We brought the bags of Dartmouth merchandise back to the dorm room, passing on the way a gang of preppy boys with their Lacoste collars up, all carelessly blond and a little cruel-looking. "Look at the one in front," I said quietly. "Doesn't he look exactly like Blane in *Pretty in Pink*?"

"Totally," she said.

I pointed at a banner that hung from a dorm room. "'Free Steve Biko,'" I read aloud. "Who's Steve Biko?"

Kimmy didn't answer and we wandered over to a restaurant called Lou's.

"What should we do now?" I said after we got the bill. "Maybe we should check out the student center. It's Friday night; maybe some kids are hanging out there."

She shrugged. "Let's go back and take showers," she said.

After we duly toted our buckets with shampoo bottles in them to the showers, we returned to the room. Kimmy put on a pair of underwear and then pulled a cream silk teddy out of her luggage and shimmied it on. She sat down at the desk, which had a mirror propped up against it, and slowly, methodically pulled a brush through her hair.

I was used to this behavior from our sleepovers, in which Kimmy would brush her hair as she talked to us, her eyes never leaving the mirror. I just didn't expect it here. I slowly got dressed, sneaking a look at Kimmy's caramel body and how it contrasted with the milky glow of the lingerie and the pale slice of bikini mark that peeped from underneath her thin straps. Her breasts were perfect and seemed to hover near her chin, while my recent and insignificant acquisitions had already earned the nickname "East Westies" from my teammates because they pointed in different directions.

I sat on the bed and waited for her to announce what we were going to do next. "If you're not into going out," I ventured, "maybe we could just go get some ice cream and watch some TV."

She shook her head. "I'm on a diet," she said mildly as she flexed a brown arm and turned it in various directions.

I waited on the bed for another half an hour, pretending to read a magazine, but she didn't move. Sometimes we would talk about soccer, or her various crushes, or her attempts to lose weight. Other times she seemed perfectly content to brush her hair in the silence. I wouldn't dream of challenging her, so I sat on the bed and watched her as she watched herself or lounged fetchingly on the bed. I kept wondering if she was hoping that a college guy would stumble in and catch her in her teddy, but after a while I realized that it wasn't about me, or a boy walking in. It was about her.

After a few hours, we turned out the light and went to bed. I wondered if she was intimidated by the older kids and too shy to initiate a meeting, burdened with being the leader of our two-girl posse. But as time went on and Kimmy spent each night in her silk teddy, I had the creeping suspicion that it was actually her idea of a good time. Hell, if I had slim brown ankles like hers, I'd be admiring the way they looked in my expensive white scrunch socks, too.

My mother had never warmed to Kimmy, despite my pleas that she get to know her. Granted, during the few times that Kimmy had been to our house in the evenings, she had always been slightly taken aback by the sight of my mother, weary and rumpled after a day of work, eating a bowl of cereal for dinner at the kitchen table without bothering to change out of her suit first. My mother immediately detected Kimmy's carefully concealed aversion.

"I don't dislike her," my mother said once. "I just feel like she isn't necessarily the kindest person. I see some of the things she says and does, and I feel like karma will get her someday." But karma never did catch up to Kimmy Marino. She glided through Trinity College, picking up a shopping-mall mogul along the way, produced four beautiful boys, and moved confidently among various environments scented with orange blossoms, Italian leather, lavender, and gin and tonics. Some people do just fine.

*chapter twenty-one*

The next day I spent an absurd two hours perfecting my casually natural look for the Bethel Rams homecoming game, but when we arrived, there was no sign of Christian. *Where are you?* I halfheartedly watched the Bethel Rams get pounded by the Chatham Gladiators as I scanned each face in the bleachers. Then we went back to our hotel room to spend another two hours on our more formal look. Somehow, we were all ready at exactly five o'clock, when the cocktail hour commenced.

I was idly putting on another coat of mascara when I remembered with a start that I was supposed to go to the reunion with Dawn. In the day's excitement I had completely forgotten our plans. "I'm making a quick call!" I yelled to Sandy over our getting-ready music and ducked into the hall.

I dialed her number. She had probably left already. I secretly hoped that she had. Her machine picked up. *Thank you, Jesus.*

"Hey, Dawn!" I said brightly. "Lily here, how are you? Listen, I know you wanted to go together tonight, but I got a late start and methinks you already left." *"Methinks"? Who says that?* And I was talking way too fast. I took a deep breath to slow down. "Anyway, guess I'll just see you there, okay?" I clicked the phone shut. *Done.*

I burst back into the room. "I'm not going downstairs yet," I told Sandy. "Let's wait until five-thirty or we're going to stand around with the caterers." We sat on the beds, momentarily quiet. I smoothed my black dress and readjusted my stilettos. Was I wearing too much makeup?

Sandy jumped up. "This is stupid," she announced. "Let's just go downstairs. Forget being cool! I need a drink."

She banged on Lynn and Kimmy's door and herded us all into an elevator. My heart began to race sickeningly as the door opened onto the kelly-green carpet of the Event Ballroom.

"You guys," I said, panting, bending over as they formed a concerned circle around me. "I think I need to sit down."

"You're having an anxiety attack," Lynn diagnosed. "I used to get them before I did riding competitions. Take a deep breath."

I looked into their familiar faces and my heart slowed. "I'm okay," I said finally. I desperately wanted to get away from the ominously blinking lights of the elevator bank, a direct doorway to my past that could randomly disgorge anyone.

"There's a name-tag table," said Kimmy, taking charge. Tags with identifying senior-year photos were neatly laid out, along with a crude box with a hole cut in the middle and a pile of three-by-five cards. CLASSMATES, GET OUT THE VOTE! a hand-lettered sign read. CAST YOUR BALLOT HERE!!!! VOTE FOR: MOST CHANGED, LEAST CHANGED, MOST LIKELY TO HAVE MIDLIFE CRISIS, LONGEST TRIP TO GET HERE, ETC.!!!!

We affixed our tags and went straight to the bar for white-wine spritzers. "No red wine all night," ordered Sandy. "It'll dye your teeth." She looked down at her senior-year photo. "Do you believe I got a perm, with my curly hair? And of course when it got flat on top, I went to Jo-Ann's Hair 'Em and permed the perm." Her eyes widened. "Look," she whispered. "I think that's Brian Miller, but I'm not entirely sure." Mildew? Was he with Christian? I looked his way with elaborate casualness, smiling vaguely.

"Let's go talk to him," said Sandy, dragging me over just as she did in high school. "Hey, Mildew!" she hollered.

He looked shorter than I remembered, and was wearing the same khakis and oxford shirt of his preppy youth. He was balding from the top down, but the growth at the bottom was still lush, and a little too long as it curled over his collar. His green eyes were still beautiful in his slightly puffy face.

He smiled. "What's up?" he said mildly, as if we had just seen him last week and not two decades ago. I briefly hesitated. Did I give him a kiss? I had never kissed Mildew in my life. Did you shake hands, or hug? I made an emergency decision to kiss every class-mate on the cheek, even if I had never touched him or her in my life. We were all grown-ups.

I asked Mildew a few halting questions and relaxed a little as he droned on about his adult day-care empire. *Christ, was he always this dull?* "These are really high-end units," he was saying. "It's an un-derserved market, and as baby boomers age, they're used to the good life, so this facility is really state-of-the-art. There's a large garden in the back where residents can grow vegetables and flowers, a hair salon, lunch prepared by a gourmet chef, a spiritual hour . . ."

"What's a spiritual hour?" I asked.

"You know, meditation and what have you. We try to be nondenominational. And we have a computer room with twenty computers, all brand new, as well as executive vans for transportation, and . . ."

This was a person who once attended a party wearing only his socks, a guy who earned his nickname by happily living in his mother's dank basement, where he hung a tapestry over the one grimy window to block out the feeble light. He brought in a bumper-pool table and a water bed and, for the crowning touch, enlisted Christian and Michael Garrett to help him construct a full bar next to the washing machine. Now he appeared to be easing into a sales pitch. Was he ever going to ask me a question? Was he even remotely curious about anything that I had done?

Mercifully, other classmates approached me and for the next half an hour a festival of exclamations ensued. *Hiiiii! You look amazing! Good, good, I live in Rahway, you know where that is, near Linden? How many kids do you have? Three? Well, then, you have your hands full, am I right?*

I looked over at the lobby and blanched. Dawn was walking hesitantly in with her husband, whom she had said she was leaving at home. There was something about her ill-fitting blue taffeta dress that twisted my heart. I flushed with shame at the insincere message I had left on her machine.

I hurried over to her. "Hi, Dawn," I said. I hugged her but she stayed rigid. "This must be Dave." He was a husky man with a pleasant face and deep dimples. He shook my hand. "I left you a message a while ago, trying to catch you," I rushed on. "It's been completely chaotic today, and I guess we just missed each other."

She nodded. "Right. I left a couple of messages with your parents. Let's just talk about it later, okay? I want to have fun tonight."

"Okay," I said, relieved. "I really am sorry." We made stilted small talk until she was surrounded by a noisy group of math club kids, one of whom, it was rumored, had rented a white stretch limo for his arrival.

I made my way to the bar for another white-wine spritzer as various classmates called my name and motioned me over. I realized that the last time I had been in a room in which every person knew me was at my wedding. Some classmates were defined in my head by a single incident. *Hey, there, John, who threw up on my new Tretorns at a Violent Femmes concert! Hi, Amy, dogged by an absurd but persistent rumor that you once had an erotic encounter with a frozen hot dog at a party!*

I shouted my drink order to the beleaguered bartender and gathered my thoughts.

"Hey," said the person next to me. It was a guy named Andy whose last name, I was almost positive, started with a *V*. Andy had hung out in the art crowd, although if memory served, he wasn't necessarily arty. What I mostly remembered is that he used to spend Friday nights going to midnight showings of *Pink Floyd The Wall* and that he had a small port-wine stain on his arm. He always sat in the back row of every class and actually pulled off a fair amount of legitimately funny jokes. His specialty was whale and dolphin noises.

"Remember me? Andy Wells. Your home ec partner from, what was it, sophomore year? Mrs. Wenstrom? I hope it doesn't offend when I tell you that you were a lousy cook." He was angular and pale, with brown hair that flopped over his eyes—in a sloppy rather than hip way. I glanced involuntarily to his arm and confirmed that he still had the port-wine stain on the skinny wrist that poked out from his brown suit.

"So, what are you up to?" I asked as I monitored the elevators. Was that Ankur? No. I had rehearsed my conciliatory speech to him, but no sign of him yet.

"Do you want the embellished story that I've told six times so far, or the straight-up story?"

"Give me the straight-up story."

"I live in Red Hook, in Brooklyn, and I'm a freelance animator, so I go to places like VH1 and work on some project for six weeks. Then I spend another two weeks in a coffee place, worrying about where my next gig is coming from." He took a deep breath. "I was once married and it lasted for eight months, so I suppose that's all I need to say about that. I don't know why it's still hard to say. It was a while ago. Plus half the people I've talked to tonight are divorced."

"I'm divorced," I volunteered. I halfheartedly provided my update, keeping my eyes on the door. At this point, my patter was so polished that I actually believed an apartment was waiting for me back in Manhattan.

"I'm going to tell you something," he suddenly said.

"All right, then." I looked at him expectantly. He didn't say anything and I cleared my throat. "Maybe you're making the announcement later?"

He laughed. "No, no. I just wanted to say that, I mean this is probably the whisky talking"—he held up his glass and rattled the cubes of his drink—"but I had the most raging crush on you back in the day."

I looked away from the elevators and faced him. "You did?"

He sighed. "I knew it," he said. "You had no idea." He looked down at his drink. "God," he muttered.

"I love that you did," I said. "I wish I had known." *Why did I say that? How would that have changed anything?*

"You seemed different to me than all of your friends," he said. "You were the only teenage girl I knew who used to like old movies. And medical museums. Remember how we rallied Mr. Seymour to take a class trip to Philadelphia to see the Mutter Museum and those twins who were joined at the head? To me, you were just kind of an oddball. Which I liked. In fact, I still have a book you loaned me."

I couldn't recall any specific encounters with Andy aside from an ongoing series of comics that we would draw in history class, passing them back and forth, starring Mr. Seymour, aka "Mr. Semen," in various compromising positions.

"It was *Franny and Zooey.*"

I laughed. "Oh, I remember. I believe I was congratulating myself on how edgy I was."

"I'm embarrassed to say that I named my cat Bloomberg."

I laughed. "Did you really? That's so high school. I love it." I took a gulp of my drink and smashed my teeth on the glass.

"Whoa, there," he said. "Are you okay?"

I put my drink down. "Yes, yes, I'm fine. Although losing my teeth is one of my biggest fears. You want to know something that haunts me a lot? It's going to sound insane."

"I love insane."

"When I'm crossing the street in New York, I have this deep-seated fear that someone on a bike is going to crash into me and I'm going to fall forward on my face as my bloody teeth fly everywhere."

He thought for a moment. "Is this based on anything? Did you have some sort of playground accident once?"

"No. It's just my own imagination. Now you tell me one of your irrational fears so I'm not self-conscious."

He frowned in concentration. "All right," he finally answered. "I always wonder: What if I'm home in my apartment in Brooklyn, and I order takeout, as many bachelors do, and I start choking on a Chinese spare rib? You can't make any noise, because you're choking, and you're alone, anyway." He stroked his chin absently, hypnotized by his vision of horror. "I suppose you could knock on your neighbor's door as you're gasping for breath, but if they look through the peephole and you have a peculiar expression on your face, they're not going to open the door," he said. "And, you know, knocking without explaining—that's odd. You're pounding on someone's door, and you're just sort of grunting. It's disturbing. Who can blame them for not opening the door? Then you slowly sink to the floor and die in the hallway, surrounded by piles of supermarket flyers and bags of recycling."

"Right," I said, nodding. "That's not completely irrational. I mean, there's no drill for choking, so you're completely unprepared if it happens. It either"—I looked toward the elevator and abruptly stopped.

*Christian.*

*chapter twenty-two*

He didn't see me and I quickly looked away. *Holy shit he looks great he looks so great, what do I do, do I keep talking to John, I mean Andy?*

Andy leaned forward. "What?" he said. "What's your deal? Are you okay?"

"Excuse me," I mumbled. "Ladies' room." I grabbed my drink and speed-walked to the restroom.

I stared at my reflection and tried to breathe. *Get a grip,* I told myself. *You're thirty-eight years old.*

A bathroom stall opened and Dawn emerged. "Dawn," I said urgently, searching in my bag for my lipstick. "You're not going to believe this. Christian's here. He looks amazing. I don't know what to do."

"Wow," she said. "This is what you want to talk to me about right now? Did you already forget our awkward meeting earlier? Or how about the fact that we were supposed to come together? I've got to tell you, it's real fun coming to your reunion with your husband. As a matter of fact, I have to get back to babysitting him. You're on your own."

I put on my lipstick and smoothed down my hair, half listening. "You're still upset?" I said, my eyes on my reflection. "What, because we didn't walk in together? Jeez. Now who's acting like high school?"

She looked at me mutely and walked out.

I gave my hair one last swipe, gulped the remainder of my drink, and took a shaky breath.

I returned to the bar but Andy had left. I ordered another drink, and there he was, it was Christian, walking toward me with a slow smile. Kimmy, Lynn, and Sandy had their eyes trained on me like sharpshooters from various points in the room. He was wearing a slim black suit and a simple white shirt, open at the neck. His dark hair, still thick, was cut short and messy, and his face had faint creases around the eyes that gave him, as Vi termed it, "a little seasoning." When I had used my own mental age-enhancing equipment, I had thinned his hairline and dulled his eyes. It was inconceivable that he should look better than he did in high school.

Then he was right in front of me, grinning. Instantly I focused on the crooked tooth to the right of his front incisor, the one I hoped he would never get fixed. It was him. He was here.

"Well, well," he said, measuring me with a lingering glance.

"Lillian Curtis. If I had known you were going to look like this, I would have married you right out of high school."

He leaned over and put his arm behind me on the bar. It was almost touching me. I could nearly feel its warmth.

"So, Christian," I began in a high voice that I tried in vain to lower.

"So, Lily," he said softly, as the room swayed.

I steadied myself. "Are you living here now, or are you planning on returning to—London, is it?"

He smiled again and my stomach turned over. "Lily," he said. "Come on. You didn't check up on me before tonight? I checked up on you."

"Oh? What do you know?"

"That you're a TV producer and you got divorced from some guy named Adam."

I laughed. "Okay, I guess I might have heard that you work for an agency in London, and that you moved to New York. Where they also have an office, yes? And you were engaged to someone with an exotic name." I pretended to think. "Suki?"

His smile vanished. "Saskia," he said. "*Engaged* is a strong word. But yeah, it's over."

I looked at him expectantly.

He took a sip of his drink and looked around the room. "You know," he said, shrugging. "It ended the way these things usually end."

*What way? Infidelity? Money problems? She wanted children and he didn't?*

He shrugged. "But nothing is ever really over, is it?"

Was he talking about Saskia? Or me?

He took a sip of his drink. "So, where are you living?" His amused gaze was fully focused on me again.

"I'm in the process of moving right now," I said. "So I'm at my parents' house until an apartment opens up. And you?"

"You remember how my folks had a place at the shore, in Sea Girt?" Oh, I remembered. Whenever they weren't using it, Christian held parties for a select few. As his girlfriend, I was co-host, enjoying the power of being present before the others pulled up the driveway. "Well, I'm squatting there for the time being. Eventually I'll move into the city, but might as well live rent-free for a while, right?" I struggled to keep my eyes on his face as I heard Vi's voice in my head: *Use your eyes to fascinate a man. Keep your head still, follow him with your gaze, and try not to blink. Every actress worth her salt did her close-ups without blinking. Mark my words, you will bewitch him!*

"And you're an ad man?" I said in what I hoped was a playful tone. The ice cubes in my drink were clinking, and I realized it was because my hands were trembling slightly. I put my glass on the bar.

"No, I'm a branding strategist." He scanned my blank face for comprehension. "Say that Sony creates a video game, and they need to clearly convey the look of it, and the attitude, and what it's trying to say. Well, then, they call us. You can brand or rebrand anything. We've done bands, sports gear, charity campaigns, all sorts of stuff. Or we reinvigorate some old brand that nobody cares about anymore, like Cadillac, or this British luggage company we just did that's two hundred years old."

I was hanging on to the conversation by the barest thread because I was now watching his mouth as he talked. "What's the name of the company?"

"Have you heard of Edj? That's E-D-J." He smirked. "We tend to use guerilla tactics sometimes, so we can't seem to stop getting in trouble. Which is a good thing. Anyway, they sent me to the New York office, I don't know for how long."

Michael Garrett lurched over and the room stopped spinning. "Hey, man," he boomed to Christian. He moved in for the frattish handshake that starts high as if you're throwing a baseball and ends with a low clapping of palms. Michael, my former third-string crush, was still trim, but his skin was leathery and dappled with brown spots from years of baking in the sun, and he had a hungry, haunted look. Or maybe he was sun-dazed. He owned a fleet of boats on Cape Cod and took groups out for sportfishing expeditions. Instead of wearing a suit as Christian was, he sported a Hawaiian shirt to convey that he had opted out of the rat race and was going the Jimmy Buffett route.

"Hey, Lily," he said, giving me a grudging kiss on the cheek. His demeanor was slightly frosty, as it had been in high school when I monopolized too much of Christian's time. Twenty years later and still threatened. Dope. How could I have ever had a crush on this guy? No wedding ring, I noticed.

Michael ignored me and homed in on Christian. "Hey, later we're going up to my room. I've got some great weed from a client of mine. He's a doctor and he prescribes it for cancer patients. That medical shit is so much more potent, it will blow your freakin' mind."

Christian held my gaze for a brief second that said *Too bad about Michael.*

"Yeah, sounds good, we'll see," said Christian. Michael gave me a look of triumph.

"So what are you up to, Michael?" I asked.

"Well, you know I run sportfishing trips. I've got eight boats. Sometimes we do bachelorette parties." He reached into his pocket and handed me a business card. All night long, people had been passing me their cards. If I ever needed my pool cleaned, my house sold, and my computer updated, I was covered. "I got divorced last year," he added.

"I'm divorced, too," I said, but he kept going.

"Now I'm doing the online dating. You know, at first I resisted, but you can't believe the good-looking girls that send photos." He whistled. "Wow, look at Pam Sardi. Still hot." He made his way over to her, and we were alone again. Christian's arm had not moved. *Arm behind me almost around me not moving arm.*

"So, are you going to go get baked in Michael's room?"

He rolled his eyes. "I think he's baked enough." He looked at me. "Listen, I'm taking you home later, right?" I made a quick calculation: If I stayed in the hotel room with Sandy, I'd never be alone with Christian. Change of plans.

I nodded. "Yes."

*It's happening. It keeps moving forward and it's happening.*

During the next hour, Christian remained at my side as knots of classmates approached us. I needed to go to the bathroom but refused, so afraid was I that he would drift away. Finally I could stand it no longer and raced to the john. When I returned, he was still in the same spot at the bar.

Our class president, Hugh Futterman, walked briskly through the crowd, urging everyone to go to their seats for dinner. Lynn, Kimmy, and Sandy materialized, and we quickly commandeered a table.

"What the hell is going on with you two?" Lynn said in a low voice.

"I'm not sure," I said.

The moment we sat down, a swarm of bored teen catering employees thunked down glass plates of salad in front of us.

Kimmy stopped a waiter. "Um, can I have the dressing on the side? There's so much of it that you can't even see the lettuce. I thought it was soup at first."

"Sorry," said the teen. "The salads are, like, put together ahead of time and then we just take them out of the fridge."

"Good evening, class of 1988, and welcome," Hugh intoned. "The dictionary defines *reunion* as a gathering of friends, relatives, or associates after separation."

Where would bad speechwriters be if they couldn't lead off the proceedings with a dictionary definition?

"But this is so much more than just a simple gathering. 1988 was the year we left to make our way in the world. It was the year of endings, but also of beginnings."

As he droned, a PowerPoint presentation flashed behind him on a large screen of photos from our senior year culled from the yearbook committee. Hugh's words were drowned by the crowd commentary when each new photo appeared. Kurt Sebalius wearing a lilac bandanna as a headband, a look that had captivated me at the time. Pam Sardi in a FRANKIE SAY RELAX T-shirt. Why was it that the popular group got the majority of the slides, even when the person who put it together—Kathleen, the class treasurer, in this case—wasn't popular?

I caught my breath. A photo appeared of Christian and me at our lockers, him unsmiling, me beaming. It must have been late spring, because I was wearing a pink Forenza tube skirt with a huge faded jean jacket, sleeves rolled up to the elbow, while he had on a green military jacket with the sleeves ripped off. He had just gotten his right ear pierced (the right ear, as suburban kids everywhere knew, indicated that you were straight). I looked quickly at Christian, two tables over, and met his gaze. My whole body felt tingly and numb, as if the anesthesia was kicking in. *Okay, now, close your eyes and count backward from ten.*

"What's Hugh up to, anyway?" Lynn whispered to me.

"Didn't you read the website? He raises ferrets and he's a Civil War reenactor."

The swarm of teens reappeared to swap our salad for plates of congealed beef slices that curled at the edges and a desiccated squiggle of mashed potato. "Let's get room service later," said Kimmy, throwing down her fork. "I can't eat this shit."

"Listen up, everybody," Hugh said as his mic screeched. "If you haven't yet voted on your classmates, please visit the table where we have set up a ballot box. You'll get a kick out of some of the categories, like Most Changed. Thank you, Kathleen, for coming up with this idea." Polite applause. "We'll announce the winners after dessert."

I snuck a few furtive looks at Christian. It was just like being in class, when he was right in front of me and I could gaze at him whenever I wanted. He was looking at the podium, so I watched his right hand, which held his wineglass. He had the most beautiful hands, substantial and masculine but still graceful. Hands were so important. He looked over and I quickly glanced down at my potato squiggle.

After dinner, DJ Noyz, aka Craig DiMartino, a Paramus computer programmer by day, got the party started with "Blister in the Sun" as people crammed onto the miniscule dance floor. Sandy was the only one of us girls who liked to dance. Kurt Sebalius was flinging her around the floor, and she was laughing helplessly. Her hair had completely escaped her tight bun and flew in all directions. Christian was also at the bar, perhaps three people away. I knew exactly where he was located at all times.

I was chatting with Hugh when I saw Charlotta Janssen approach Christian. She was tall and slight, with long, honey-colored hair that hung in a loose ponytail. She wore a simple slate-gray dress cut in a deep *V* in the front, exposing her fragile collarbone. She looked like a delicate woodland wildflower, a snowdrop among the showier suburban geraniums and impatiens. I had practically memorized her Classmate News entry. *Moved to San Francisco and opened an art gallery . . . Travel all over the world . . . Saw Christian Somers in Paris, he is doing great.*

They chatted, her smiling and repeatedly pushing a stray piece of honey-colored hair behind her ear in a way that I found supremely irritating.

I took a deep draft of my drink.

Sandy flopped next to me at the bar, damp with sweat. "Kurt can really dance," she said, panting. "Who knew?" She gathered us together. "Bathroom break!" she announced.

We made our way to the bathroom in our comforting pack, inviting inquisitive stares just as we used to.

Sandy blundered into a stall and started peeing without fully shutting the door.

"Sandy! Close the door, for Christ's sake," Lynn said, loudly banging it shut. "What if someone else was in here?" All of us were drunk.

Kimmy applied lipstick. "Lily, you're hooking up with Christian. It's so obvious. Everyone's talking about it."

That pleased me, being talked about.

Sandy banged out of the bathroom stall. "*Chicas!*" she hollered.

"C'mere. I have something to tell you all." We gathered in a circle and she put her arms around us. "Love you guys. Love you!" We linked together in a sloppy group hug, swaying slightly. "B-double-f, double-a," she said. "That's what my kids say. It means 'best friends forever and always.'" Sentimental tears moistened my eyes, but I tamped them back so my mascara wouldn't run.

We rolled out of the bathroom in a gratifying unit, and my goodwill evaporated when I saw that Christian was still talking to Charlotta. How many times was she going to tuck her goddamn hair behind her ear? It was so contrived, one of those silly girl moves.

"Don't get riled up," Kimmy said quietly. "And if you're out with him later, do not bring her up. Come on, now. Take a deep *pranayama* breath."

I obeyed her, although it made me dizzy. Or maybe it was the thousand white-wine spritzers I had tipped back.

Hugh took the podium again. "It's time for our awards ceremony," he announced, as everyone shushed one another in an exaggerated way, followed by gales of laughter and more shushing. "The people have spoken and we have tallied the votes. No voter apathy here, ha ha. Our first award of the evening, for Most Changed, goes to Michelle Brennan." She was the goth chick who had transformed into a Dallas housewife. She took the stage, grinning and waving, to scattered applause.

"Thank you, Michelle. Next up is Most Successful. It's no surprise that it's Greg Garcia." Greg was the math nerd who had rented the white stretch limo for his arrival. He was now some sort of tech tycoon. He did exaggeratedly deep bows at the podium as he accepted his hastily written certificate.

"And now for the Least Changed, or what we might call the Fountain of Youth award. It's a tie: Christian Somers and Lillian

Curtis, come on up!" I tried to look nonchalant, but I was smiling like a pageant winner. Christian looked slightly abashed, but as we both strolled up to the podium the room erupted in wild cheers.

*"Whoo!"* Sandy hollered. *"Whoooo!"* She gave a piercing wolf whistle.

I looked around the room at the kaleidoscope of benevolent, grinning faces. We were the king and queen of the prom. *Freeze this moment,* I told myself, just as I had twenty years ago.

Later, after the last business cards were exchanged and DJ Noyz packed up his computer equipment to head back to Paramus, I told Kimmy, Lynn, and Sandy that I wasn't going back to the hotel. Christian had offered to drive me home before he headed down to his parents' shore house.

"I'll come back in the morning and wake you all up," I said. "Then we'll hit the brunch buffet."

"I'm going to pass out in about five minutes," said Sandy. "You won't miss anything."

Lynn squeezed my hand. "Good luck," she whispered. They encircled me for another dramatic, lurching hug and sent me off.

During the ride home, Christian and I talked to fill the silence, but neither of us could focus on the conversation. I only snapped back to consciousness when we reached the driveway. Christian turned off the car ignition and looked at me in the silence.

*It's happening. It's moving forward and it's happening.*

He leaned forward and began to kiss me, and the world tilted upward. I was kissing him back and it was natural and easy and for the next half hour I was utterly unaware of anything around me. He had become an even better kisser since our teen years, and I tried not to imagine the many, many women who had brought him to that point.

The only thought I could coherently form was *This is it.* I had re-captured that elusive feeling I longed for, that had hung suspended, maddeningly out of my grasp, when I would hear a certain song that took me back. I had almost been able to grab it sometimes, but not quite. I was too old; too much had happened. But no: Tonight I was free and eighteen and had a roomful of people clapping for me, not for anything I did but simply for remaining a person who deserved admiration. I was kissing someone whom I never thought I would see again. He stepped out of my past, handsome and whole, and I was levitating with happiness.

Then my mind was empty again and I drifted in a contented haze until my parents' porch light abruptly snapped on.

Christian pulled away. "Is that your father?"

I fumbled for my purse. "I should go."

"Listen, what are you doing next weekend? Come to the shore."

I was visited by another feeling I hadn't had for years: I was a child playing hide-and-seek, hiding behind a curtain and on the verge of being found, so faint with excitement that I thought my insides were going to explode. "Sure," I said. My father turned the light on and off. "Let me give you my number."

He grinned. "555-2084."

I floated up the driveway. My father was waiting in his pajamas with his arms folded, but I didn't care. I could handle him. I could handle anything.

*chapter twenty-three*

Blearily I opened my eyes and tried to focus in the direction of my alarm clock before I realized that I was at Christian's house. He was sleeping next to me in bed. He didn't make a sound, nor did he stir. I was careful not to wake him, because I wanted to see his place in the daylight.

I blinked and eased myself up slowly. It was crucial that I had time to gather my thoughts and review the prior evening. I had driven down to Sea Girt in a fever of anticipation with my car windows cracked to let in the cold, briny air, waving to my mother as I pulled out of the driveway. How different our lives were: When my mom was thirty-eight, she had two young teenage daughters and was putting in long hours at work to pay for our college educations. Now I was thirty-eight and speeding down to the shore to spend a decadent weekend with a new guy.

Once I stopped to get coffee at a Go-Mart to draw out the journey and prolong the feeling of excitement. When I was a teenager, I had driven this route countless times at eighty miles an hour, fearful that I would miss something at a keg party, but this time I knew Christian wasn't going anywhere. He was waiting for me, and we had all weekend.

He met me at the door with a lingering kiss and a glass of wine. "I want to take you to my favorite place for dinner," he said. "Captain Bob's Sea Catch. It's a shack, but it's right on the beach. A mile from here. I thought we could walk. Is it too cold? I'll get you one of my sweaters."

I stood in the hallway while he disappeared into a bedroom. His parents hadn't changed the décor of the place one whit since the eighties: the photo collages of family vacations, the giant cognac snifter filled with matches from various beachside restaurants, the bookshelves crammed with yellowed paperbacks and warped board games missing half of their pieces, the animal figurines made of shells with glued-on google eyes.

We walked through the quiet neighborhood. I loved the lonely, slightly wild feel of shore towns in the off-season. As we walked we looked through the windows of the gracious old houses and wondered aloud about who lived inside. The night grew chillier and I pulled on the brown V-neck he had given me and took surreptitious sniffs of the sleeve. It smelled like a musty beach house, but somehow I couldn't stop breathing it in.

The shack made a defiantly cheerful spot on the dark windy

beach, bright with music and good-natured locals. We ordered a leisurely feast of crabs and beer, while Christian filled me in on some of his neighbors. We were even joined for a while by the macho Captain Bob himself, wearing a shirt unbuttoned to the waist to reveal a leathery stretch of chest pricked with wiry white hairs.

When the crabs arrived I asked Christian about his family. I pretended not to know that Geordie was a hedge-fund manager who lived in Morristown and had three kids. Marc was an architect who commuted to the city from Summit.

"He has two kids," said Christian, pouring another beer. "And my folks are retired, so they live for the grandkids. That's all they talk about. They're always on me to have kids. Especially my mother. The woman is relentless. You would think five would be enough, but I guess grandchildren are like crack."

"So did you ever plan on having kids?" I asked casually.

He shook his head. "Not really. I guess I wouldn't rule them out. I always had too much to do. In the past year I've been to Tokyo three times. That's kind of hard if you have a kid."

"Why did you go to Tokyo?"

He shrugged. "This Japanese soda company wanted to capture some of the American market. Didn't work out."

I loved the staccato way he spoke. "Do you ever get tired of all the traveling?"

He laughed. "Never. They put me up in nice places. I fly to a city, jump into a new culture, and learn all I can. I meet new people, get free stuff. There's no downside, really."

"What about your family? Don't you miss them?"

He picked open a crab and pushed it toward me. "Sure, I do. But they'll always be there. And my folks have their hands full with Geordie and Marc."

Many beers later, our walk back to the house was unsteady. As was my vow not to have sex with Christian for at least the weekend.

As I lay motionless in bed, I surveyed his parents' bedroom—the polyester floral bedspread, the wicker chairs, the glass lamps filled with dusty seashells. Christian had taken over the room and blotted out his mother's vacation-home décor with his things, although there was still a prescription bottle for his father's acid reflux medication on the wicker bedside table. His mother's vanity table had turned into his makeshift office, which he had covered with a laptop computer, a stack of notebooks, and a flurry of Post-it notes. A jumble of luggage was piled in the corner, exploding with pants and socks and CDs and books. I squinted at a book title, trying to read it from across the room.

The silence was broken by the jangle of the phone on the bedside table next to Christian. He grunted and felt for the receiver.

"Yeah?" he mumbled. I could hear a man's calm voice as Christian sat up and stretched. "Yeah, you told me about that. I know. Get the oil tank refilled." More talking. "I'll call, Dad. It's the weekend. It's closed. They just send the bill to you, right? Uh-huh. Right, winterize the windows. I saw the note."

I watched his face, waiting for him to look at me and roll his eyes or smile. "I'm not turning off the phone yet, I told you. I can't just use the cell phone. It doesn't always work down here. Listen, I've got to go. No, no, just tell Mom I'll talk to her later. Okay. Bye."

He hung up and rolled over to give me a kiss. "Are you as hungover as I am?" He groaned and then got up and put on some track pants. His muscled stomach was as trim as it had been when he was a teenager. "I'm going to go for a run. I pass a bagel place on the way back. Do you want me to get you something?"

I smiled. "Why don't I make you breakfast?"

He put on his sneakers. "I don't know what's in there, but my mom does like to cook. Check the freezer. They put everything in there because of the bugs." I wanted him to kiss me again, but he was in running mode.

He left and I put on my clothes and crept downstairs, shivering. I opened the fridge and saw eggs and milk. The eggs were only a few days expired. The pantry was full, even if some of the boxes were a little old. Where were the cookbooks? I looked for a phone to call Vi for a recipe. I knew that she would also want the details, and I was dying to tell somebody.

"Good morning," Vi sang.

"Vi? Is that you? You never answer your phone."

"I sent Mrs. P out for papayas, so it's just me and the dogs. I'm in a tropical mood! It's so dreary today. Where are you?"

I clutched the phone harder as a thrill passed through me. "I'm at Christian's," I whispered.

"Lillian! It's awfully early. Tell me you didn't spend the night."

"I did."

"Remember what I told you? If a man can't be bothered to wait for two weeks, he's not worth having."

"We didn't do it," I lied. "Listen, I'll tell you the details later, but I wanted to get a recipe from you. I have twenty minutes to make breakfast and not much to work with. I'm at a beach house."

"Have you got eggs? Milk? That sort of thing?"

"Yes."

"How about bourbon?"

I searched the pantry and produced a dusty bottle. "Yes."

"Then I have the perfect thing: Man-Catcher French Toast, from my cookbook. It has about ten thousand calories, but as you know, mine is not a cookbook for dieters."

From 1965's *Lights, Camera, Cook!*
*Vi Barbour Shares Fifty Mouthwatering Recipes from*
*the World's Most Glamorous Gals That Will Make You*
*the Leading Lady of Your Next Dinner Party!*:

I have made no secret that I am very liberated, but I do love to cook. When I have company I serve dishes that my guests will dig into with relish, like a juicy steak with scads of mushroom gravy and fresh rolls dripping with butter. And my guests would be sorely disappointed if I did not serve my signature Cherry Fantasia for dessert!

Does comfort food bring you happiness? You'd better believe it! As my girdle will attest, I have a weakness for good food. Ever since I was knee high to a French bread loaf, my favorite scent has been vanilla extract. I spoil those around me with a groaning sideboard of specialty dishes. Food is love, so lavish it on friends and family!

"Ooh, I love your French toast," I said. "Will you read me that one?"

"Surely. I call it a man-catcher, but it looks as though you've already caught one."

"We'll see. When I'm safely at my folks' house, I'll call you, I promise."

She read me the recipe and then said, "While I have you on the phone, I'm going to be frank. It's time you came back to work. How about giving me a date?"

I thought for a moment. "When will your patience run out?"

"I would say about three weeks."

"Done. I should go, Vi. Thank you for this."

I had the French toast cooking when Christian returned holding two cups of coffee. He put them on the table, quickly crossed the room, and enfolded me in a sweaty hug.

The rest of the weekend slipped by in a euphoric haze. We took out his dad's motorboat and had lunch in the middle of the ocean, huddled in blankets and sweaters as the cold waves lapped the sides of the boat. We often sat in comfortable silence, a relief after Adam's endless analytical chatter. We took naps, brought beers to the beach to watch the sun set, and then made the trek back to Captain Bob's, where I was pleased that the cap'n greeted me this time by name.

On Sunday evening, after we had finished a spaghetti-and-meatball dinner and lay reading the paper, I said hesitantly, "I suppose I should get back tomorrow." I sighed, sneaking a glance at him. "Back to reality," I said, skirting around the fact that my "reality" involved sleeping in my childhood bedroom.

Christian continued to read the paper. "Maybe you could drop me at the train station," he said. "I have to go to the office tomorrow. We're starting a new campaign, and I don't really know too much about it."

"Sure," I said cheerfully.

The next morning I left him at the train with a lingering kiss. "See you soon," he said as he got out of the car, lean and sophisticated in head-to-toe black. His clothing was close cut from his stint in Europe, so he looked different from all the other rumpled men on the platform and drew all eyes as he walked. A hot bolt of possessiveness ran through me. I waited for Christian to turn and wave, but he saw someone he knew and fell into a conversation. Hating myself, I honked the horn and watched, satisfied, as he put up his hand.

*chapter twenty-four*

The next morning I awoke in my own bed and stretched luxuriously. For almost a minute, I groggily thought I had woken up to an ordinary day in my old room. I could hear my father humming as he made breakfast. Then memories of the weekend with Christian flooded in and I blushed, although I was alone. That delicious moment of recognition, that secret slide show you play over and over!

I heard my father's heavy tread on the stairs. He rapped on the door as I wiped the grin from my face and tried to make just-waking-up sounds to hide my embarrassment.

"Well, look who's here," he said. He could never quite pull off a lighthearted teasing tone.

"Hi, Dad," I said in a purposely scratchy voice.

"Are you joining your mother and me for breakfast?" When he didn't ask me about the weekend, I knew that his discomfort level matched mine.

"You know, Dad, I really need to get a run in. You guys go ahead."

He left and I shimmied into some running clothes. I didn't feel like eating.

The two of them were seated at the breakfast table reading the paper when I padded downstairs. "Listen to this," my father was saying. "You're not going to believe this loser." He adjusted his reading glasses and cleared his throat. "So this guy lives in a suburb outside of Toronto with his mother. He's thirty-five." He looked at me hastily. "That's not the loser part, Lillian, just so you know. Anyhow, he gets pulled over on a Friday night as he's riding home from a bar and gets a ticket for drunk driving. And you know what he was driving?"

My mother and I waited. "His mother's *motorized wheelchair.*" He cackled. "Ah, Christ. What a world. That means that he also drove the wheelchair *to* the bar."

I quickly poured some orange juice, and it slopped over the side of the glass. Sponge. Where was the sponge? I had the car keys. One more second and I could escape. My mother cleared her throat.

"I'm glad to see you decided to return," she said. "You know, Lily, you're a grown woman. Obviously. But when you're living in our house, just have the courtesy of letting us know your whereabouts."

"I told you I was going to Christian's." I tried to keep from sounding surly. Couldn't my parents just get off my back for once?

"That was Thursday. It's Monday. We didn't know how many to cook for, first of all, and then we left the front-porch light on all weekend and it burned out and now your father has to replace the bulb."

My father stared at the paper without blinking. He was clearly just going to wait this little confrontation out.

"Sorry, Mom. I'll definitely call you next time."

My father looked up sharply. "Next time?"

I looked at the clock. "It's now nine-twenty, and I'll be going to the park for forty-five minutes."

"Ha, ha, Lillian," said my mother, swatting me.

I ran out of the house, giddy again, got into the car, and sped to the high school. As I pulled into the parking lot, I saw a lone figure on the track. I recognized that red running suit.

Whenever an image of Dawn's quavering chin in the women's room popped into my head after the reunion, I had shoved it out. I contemplated pulling away, but I knew she had seen my car. I was not ready to deal with this. I just wanted to run around the track in a trance and think about Christian.

I walked slowly over to the field. Should I wait for Dawn? Should I start running slowly to see if she talked to me? As I stood there, she rounded the corner, keeping her eyes on a point in the distance.

"Dawn . . ." I began, but she passed me. I didn't know what else to do, so I loped onto the track, maintaining a distance of ten yards behind her. Around the track we went this way—one lap, two laps. At three laps, I had just decided to leave when I noticed that she had stopped running. She walked over to the bleachers, panting, and sat down.

I tentatively approached and she looked up and met my eyes.

"Dawn, listen, I want to apologize—"

She looked at me with pure hostility and the words stopped in my throat.

"You know what?" she said. "I'm thirty-eight years old, and I thought I was done with this. I'm married. I'm a mother. High school was a long time ago. And I justified a lot of what happened back then by telling myself that we were young and that's how kids are—they're cruel, they alienate each other. It's a survival game. You're mean to one so that another accepts you. I see it with my own kids."

"I know I should have—"

She cut me off. "If you're really sorry, you'll just listen to me. I have to get this out. Before the reunion, I sat waiting for your call like I was sixteen, while my husband kept saying, 'I don't understand why you just don't call her.' But of course I couldn't. Even now, that's not the way it works. And then at the reunion, you passed right over me. And when I was crying in the bathroom, do you think I didn't notice how desperate you were to get away from me?"

She smiled tightly. "I mean, I understand. I was kind of horrified to be crying, too. But that's the point, Lillian. I don't like the person you turned me into. Or the person I always was that you brought me back to." She sat for a moment and I forced myself not to talk.

"I spent years after high school trying to build up my confidence and forget certain things," she said slowly. "I was really looking forward to the reunion, because I was a different person. But then when you snubbed me, I went back to that time period where I accepted that sort of treatment. And then for the rest of the night, I just couldn't shake that feeling. I wasn't myself." She sighed. "I ended up leaving early. We still had a few hours with the babysitter, so we went to Friendly's. Dave got me a hot fudge sundae and I ended up telling him all about my pathetic high school years."

"You weren't pathetic," I faltered.

She smiled to herself and shook her head. All of her hostility had suddenly vanished. "You still don't get it. I wasn't saying that I was pathetic, I was saying that high school was pathetic." She stood up and grabbed her car keys.

"I'm going to make this easy for you, Lillian," she said. "You don't have to apologize anymore. I'm going to find somewhere else to run, but when we see each other, I'll say hi to you. Don't worry, it won't be awkward. I just don't think we're healthy for each other. Let's just leave it at that."

She walked to her car without looking back. I watched her, brushing away tears with the sleeve of my tracksuit. My heart twisted when I thought of the night at Benihana, but my sadness was mingled with undeniable relief that I didn't have to deal with her anymore, didn't have to think about her anymore. There was only room in my head for one person.

*chapter twenty-five*

Christian didn't call Tuesday. Or Wednesday. By the time Thursday rolled around, I was reduced to eating two granola bars a day and compulsively checking my e-mail every few minutes. I had gotten a quick note from Kimmy and Sandy, both along the lines of *Running the kids to soccer practice, talk soon, miss you, love you.* Funny how quickly it all dissolved.

The only message I had received all day was from Andy, my classmate with the port-wine stain. As I opened it, I reminded myself that I needed to stop identifying him in that way. It was a very small port-wine stain.

*Hi Lily,*

    *Your old friend Andy here, the one who is afraid of choking on a Chinese spare rib and dying a lonely death in a dark hallway as my neighbor watches through a peephole. Remember? Yes, I'm the one who told you within the first five minutes that I'm frequently jobless and hanging around coffee shops. (I'm actually at a coffee shop now but lest you think I'm completely degenerate, I start a gig next week, one that I'm pretty excited about.)*

    *I didn't see you for the rest of the reunion, but later, I did see Raymond "Heinie" Heinemeyer trying to get raunchy on the dance floor with your friend Kimmy. I'm sure it's an image she'll never forget. I know I won't.*

    *In our brief and weirdly dark conversation, you mentioned that you were changing apartments in the city. Maybe I could show you around Red Hook sometime. It's a little rough around the edges but that's the charm, and you can get much more space than you can in Manhattan.*

    *Well, there's a homeless man who has been edging closer to me and now he's reading this over my shoulder, so I should probably go.*

    *WBS (that's "write back soon" if you don't remember),*

*Andy*

He was pretty funny. Weekends were reserved for Christian, but I did need an apartment. And I had nothing to do. "Sounds great," I wrote back. "How about this week? What day is good? WBS."

Then I did my customary trolling of the New York papers for tidbits about Adam. He was ridiculously easy to track because he and his new girlfriend never seemed to spend a single night at home. *Aha.* A photo in the New York *Daily News:*

Spotted . . . Elyse Brooks, handbag designer and daughter of
hedge-fund honcho Marvin Brooks, with Realtor boyfriend
Adam Sheffield, at last week's Guggenheim gala.

I rolled my eyes. Adam, who wore a wrinkled suit at our own
wedding, was in a tux, while Elyse wore a dark, low-cut dress, her
glossy hair blown stick-straight. Drew had told me that Adam was
thriving at his new job because Elyse's rich friends threw him a lot of
business.

Elyse had wrapped both arms around Adam, and they were grinning. I looked more closely. No, Adam was beaming like a kid on
Christmas morning.

"He's happy," I said softly.

He deserved happiness. He wasn't a bad person. We were not the
right match. For the first time, I felt no animosity toward either of
them.

I shut down the computer and made myself leave the house. I
did a double run on the track to make the day pass, but when I came
back in the afternoon, there was still no word from Christian. I took
a long shower, stopping to turn off the water when I thought I heard
the phone. Nothing. An errand-filled weekend with my parents
loomed, and I listlessly debated taking up Drew's invitation to go
into the city to see his latest Film Forum opus.

I was about to phone him when my mother called me down for
dinner.

"You haven't had much of an appetite lately," she said, handing
me place mats to set the table. "But I have a feeling you're going to
eat tonight when you see what we made. We went all out! Your father
splurged at Costco."

"Look at this," he said, holding up a platter. "Restaurant quality." My father's "splurge" was steak that had been trimmed and
pre-marinated, which boosted the price a dollar per pound. This
time, he proudly announced, he had gotten Costco's herb-and-
garlic-marinated filet mignon.

My father examined the small pile of meat on the platter. "I
bought a pound and a half," he said worriedly. "It shrank a little. But
that just means the flavor's more condensed." He took out a serrated
knife from the utensil drawer and tried to slice it, but it was so tough
that he had to dig out the electric carving knife from the back of the
pantry to cut it into thin slices, fanning it out on the platter so it
looked more abundant.

*Ding* went the microwave, and he took out a jar of gravy and
dumped it over the meat. The gravy made a sucking sound as it
slurped out of the jar.

"*Walla*," he announced. "Who says you need to go to a steak-
house?"

My father asked me to finish the mashed potatoes. "The water's
boiling already," he said. "Just read the directions." The potatoes
were another Costco specialty. They came in a pack of eight
envelopes—two plain, two roasted garlic, two "fresh" herb, and two
with the intriguing title of "Loaded," which meant that the dried potato flakes were blended with more dried flakes of sour cream,
cheese, bacon, and chives.

"What kind of potato mood are you in, Dad?" I called to him as
he put the meat platter down on the coffee table in the TV room.

"Are you kidding?" he called back. "We're having filet! Loaded,
of course."

I opened the bag (*Homemade Taste in Four Minutes!*) and peered
inside. The potatoes looked like grayish-white fake snow, dotted

with a few specks of green, brown, and yellow. I fished out a tiny brown fleck and sniffed it. It smelled a little like a dog treat. I put it in my mouth to see if it tasted like bacon. It had a smoky yet chemical flavor, not unlike the way the air tastes when you pass a factory on the New Jersey Turnpike. Then I dumped the potato flakes into a saucepan of water, covered it, and let it sit, as directed, until it thickened up. *Walla.*

Just as we took our places at the coffee table, the phone rang. I leapt to get it, remembering that my folks had a policy never to answer the phone during dinner.

"Hello?" I said breathlessly, taking a risk that I'd be chatting with an elderly member of one of my parents' volunteer groups.

"Hey." It was Christian. "What are you doing this weekend?"

*Get across that you weren't waiting for him,* I told myself. "I'm not sure," I said in what I hoped was a casual tone. "I was thinking of going into the city, to a film festival that my friend does. This time it's French gangster movies from the forties. Maybe you could come with me."

"Or you could come down here."

My heart jumped into my throat. "Well, the festival goes all week, so I guess I could go later," I said. Who was I kidding?

"Great. See you tomorrow? In time for dinner."

"Okay!" I chirped. "Until then."

"Bye."

I weaved back to the coffee table, sat down, and started eating the steak in big bites.

My mother put down her fork. "Let me guess," she said. "That was Christian."

"Yes, and I'm going to his house for the weekend. I'll be back Monday and I'll definitely call you this time."

My father blotted some gravy with a dinner roll. "Who is this person?" he said. "This is the kid you went out with in high school?"

"Yes, I told you. You remember Christian. He works at a re-branding agency called EDJ. They're based in London, but they have a New York office, and he moved here."

My mother frowned. "So he has a place in the city and at the shore?"

"No, just the shore. He's staying at his parents' house until he gets situated."

My parents exchanged looks. "So you're both living at your parents' houses?" said my father.

"It takes a while to find a place in the city, Dad."

"What did his father do?" asked my mother.

"He's an accountant, but he's retired," I said, careful to keep the irritation out of my voice. "Why is it that parents always want to know what other parents do for a living?"

"So Christian's some sort of ad executive?"

"No, he's a marketing and branding consultant. He creates new visual identities for companies that want their products to be cool."

My mother frowned. "Is that a full-time job? It doesn't sound full-time."

"Oh, it definitely is. It definitely is."

My father belched lightly. "Has he ever been married? Any kids or any of that?"

"No. He was engaged but they called it off."

"Why?" they both asked.

I waved my hand vaguely. "For the usual reasons that these things get called off. It didn't work out. He said they both weren't happy, and they talked about it a lot, and decided to split."

My father glowered. "'Am I happy?' 'Are you happy?'" he imitated in a high voice. "Your generation, I swear to Christ I never heard so much self-analysis. Everyone sitting around and asking themselves over and over and over if they're happy. Is my job the be-all and end-all? Is my wife my soul mate? Am I *fulfilled*? Am I *satisfied*? Our generation didn't do that, and you know what? I think we're happier."

I looked at my father and sighed. "You know what, Dad? You may be right."

That threw him. He looked suspiciously at me but said nothing further.

"Now," I said. "Are we done with twenty questions about Christian? I have to pack."

"Twenty questions with no answers," barked my father. He picked up an old newspaper and scanned it, frowning. "Sharon, what's for dessert?"

I passed on the fat-free pudding cups and made my escape to go pack.

*chapter twenty-six*

I pulled into Christian's driveway, and a thrill raced through me as I saw that he was sitting on the porch waiting for me. He was wearing battered jeans, a fisherman's sweater, and a navy blue ski cap. His face, lightly tanned from being out-doors, offset his gray-blue eyes even more vividly. He looked relaxed and confident and masculine sitting on the porch holding a cup of coffee to keep his hands warm. All that was missing was a fluffy golden retriever at his side.

"I see you came prepared," he said, eyeing my thick sweater. "I had your spare sweater here just in case." My V-neck from last week was folded on the porch. Without saying anything, we started our walk to Bob's.

We had a routine, and it was only a couple of weeks. He had brought me a sweater.

As we walked, I asked him the questions I had forbidden myself from bringing up during our first two weekends, and he filled in some of the tantalizing blanks. After college, he taught diving for a while in Nantucket before he met a girl and followed her to Los Angeles. He fell into advertising when one of his roommates got him a low-level job at his agency. People were always doing things for Christian. After he broke up with his girlfriend, he joined a friend on a trip to Paris and ended up staying for a year, where he assisted a photographer he had met at a party.

He eventually moved to London, where he got a job at EDJ and met Saskia. After their breakup, he needed a change so he volunteered to helm projects from their New York office. "I had had enough of London, anyway," he said. "Too expensive." Now he worked for EDJ three days a week on a freelance basis (to my chagrin, my parents were right; it wasn't a full-time job).

"I make what I need," Christian said. "I do it just enough that it stays interesting to me."

He didn't ask, but I supplied my truncated biography, too. When I ended with my divorce, his only question was "So what was wrong with Adam? How did he lose you?"

I flashed on Adam telling me that he was bored to death of us. "I guess I just outgrew him," I said smoothly.

After dinner, we walked back to his house. As he turned the key in the door, I gloried in the familiar musty smell of the living room. "Sorry for the mess," he said, flicking on a light. Empty bottles of wine and stuffed ashtrays littered the room. "I had a little get-together last night."

In the kitchen, the sink was piled with wineglasses, some, I noted fretfully, with lipstick marks. He sat down at the kitchen table. "You want some wine? I'll have to wash some of these glasses." I got up to do it myself. I had never once gone to bed with dirty dishes in the sink.

As I scrubbed the glasses with an ancient sponge, I noticed a Post-it on the cabinet reminding him to winterize the windows. "Did you winterize the windows yet?" I said, trying to joke. "That sort of thing drives parents crazy."

He shook his head. "I wish they'd get the hell off my back."

"Are you looking for an apartment in the city? Adam could definitely get you a deal. We're still on good terms."

"I don't know," he said. "I'm keeping my options open."

I flashed back to our senior year in high school. Early on a Friday night I had waited anxiously for Christian to call me. Six o'clock had passed, and then seven o'clock. Finally in desperation I phoned him to find out if his plans included me. *I'm keeping my options open,* he had said.

I sat down on the couch. "You're not really the type that makes plans, are you? I remember that wasn't your thing in school, either."

"No," he said, sitting next to me. When he sat that close I had trouble concentrating, but I pressed on, emboldened by the two Navy Grogs I had drunk during dinner at Captain Bob's.

"I guess I just want to know what motivates you. You've always seemed a little restless to me, and I don't quite know what's behind it."

He sat back on the couch, amused. "Why do women always ask these kinds of questions? Um. I don't know. I don't know what motivates me." He thought for a moment. "Okay. I guess one motivator is that I like each week to be different. I would kill myself if I lived in the same town forever, like Geordie does. I'm always kind of churning. I'm never really content. But I don't think that's necessarily a bad thing."

I waited for him to say more, and after a few long seconds he went on. "At work there's always a new campaign, and sometimes when I was in London they used to send me to different cities to spy on the college kids. Report back the trends. That was cool. Berlin, Paris, Kraków—I went all over, and I'd bring my little notebook, sit in a square. Or when we did a campaign for this snowboarding gear, I went to Chile, to the Valle Nevado. You have to take a helicopter to get there." He looked at me and sighed.

"But I can see by your face that I haven't answered your question in the way that you want. I don't know. I guess I seek stimulation. Or so I've been accused by certain women." He laughed. "I think people are way too concerned with how they're perceived. I never think about externals. I just take it all in."

I couldn't resist a few more questions, which he answered with tolerant humor. Did he ever feel insecure? Of course, especially at the beginning of a new job. Has he ever had his heart broken? Yes. Saskia. She dumped me, pretty much. Did he ever think about me after high school? A slow smile. Sometimes.

Then his arms were around me. "Question time is over," he said.

On Saturday we arose early and took a day trip to Philadelphia so Christian could document its underground art scene for EDJ. Christian's boss had read that it was becoming a haven for displaced artists who had been priced out of New York.

We walked for miles through the city as Christian photographed street paintings and posters and galleries. Then we met up with a friend of a friend of Christian's, a twenty-two-year-old artist named Coyote who "painted" with different shades of human hair, who led us to a guy who wouldn't give Christian his name who ran illegal underground clubs in various houses. I smiled indulgently at Christian as he and the guy chattered excitedly about new scenes, new neighborhoods, emerging trends.

The nameless guy gave us the address of a barbershop downtown that had been around for decades and was the neighborhood community center. Christian wanted to discreetly snap pictures of it from across the street. EDJ was harvesting ideas for a campaign to revive a once hip sneaker company.

"I have to find places that look especially authentic," Christian said as he snapped away. "I know, it's ridiculous. But this is what they pay me for."

While he went to a skateboarding store to talk to the pierced kids who worked there, I walked to the Museum of Art and wandered its peaceful halls.

On the train ride home, I was exhausted, while Christian was completely energized. "Isn't chasing trends sort of a never-ending job?" I asked him.

"Yes, but the hunt is part of the fun," he said, looking through the photos in his digital camera. "Some of this stuff is pretty hidden, so it's like you're a detective."

"But you're chasing something that you'll never find," I persisted. "Because there's always that itch for the new, you never get to the end. You can never sit back and relax and just enjoy what you like."

"Well, yes," he said, kissing me. "Exactly."

On Sunday we saw a matinée at the tiny movie house in town, where I was unable to follow the film's plot—something about World War II espionage—because I kept thinking, *He's here, right next to me, in the dark.* My eyes stayed purposefully forward, on the screen, but I was acutely aware of every sip of soda, every infinitesimal shift in his seat. Halfway through the movie he cleared his throat and I marveled at his deep voice, the polite concision of his cough, its laudatory lack of phlegm.

I prayed he wouldn't want to discuss the movie afterward, but thankfully all he said when the lights came up was, "Ready to go?"

Back at his parents' house, we made linguini with clam sauce, and as the pasta was boiling in the pot and I was setting the table, the phone rang. I could hear a man's faint voice. "Hey, what's going on," Christian said in the hearty voice that guys use for other guys. He leaned against the wall. "Hold on a second." He put his hand over the receiver and looked at me.

"You're leaving tomorrow morning, right?" he said. I nodded. Why did that sting? Three days was plenty. He turned back. "Yeah, I could do that. I'll pick you up. Is she working? Okay. Later." Who was *she*? Was he picking her up, too? I didn't ask. My stomach thrummed.

The next day I was up at dawn and decided to leave early to regain some of my waning power. I invented an early phone meeting that I had to conduct with Vi, which Christian accepted without protest. Then I brooded as I drove home on the turnpike.

He had folded me into his life, but when I had mentioned the Film Forum again, he laughed and said, "Oh, you're having me meet the friends already?" The remark was half in jest, but his point had been made. But then at Captain Bob's, he had said that his friend was running in a race the following weekend on Long Beach Island. "You'll love the scene afterward, everyone's drunk by ten in the morning," he said. So clearly it was a given that I would be there. Well, not *clearly*. It seemed he just didn't like to make plans in advance.

I steered the wheel with my left hand so I could freely gnaw on the cuticle of my right thumb. The turnpike exit signs whizzed past my unseeing eyes. Why couldn't I just enjoy the moment? It's not like I wanted him to sob out a declaration of love or whisper that he missed me after we had been apart for a few days. What did I want? Why was I upset?

Maybe it was that he was in control of our budding relationship. He was never nervous that I wasn't going to see him. He assumed—correctly—that when he wanted to see me, he could. He controlled the plans, he arranged the setting. When he mentioned his friend's race, why could I not say to him, " 'So I guess that means that I'll be seeing you next weekend?' " Yet I held back.

This situation was no different than it had been in high school, when Christian irrefutably drove the bus. But because no being is more indecisive and flighty than a teenage girl, it was a relief to conform to what he wanted. Christian never made a misstep, whereas I had made so many. And at seventeen, I was used to being ruled anyway, by my parents, my teachers, the tyrannical girls at school, my boss at Donna's Dog Wash II.

And part of the magic of being with Christian in high school was the deliciousness of filling in the blanks—thinking of him while I was doing my homework or before I went to sleep at night. It was a game, a way to constantly be with him. He didn't like to talk on the phone beyond making plans. I didn't see him on weeknights, or after school when he had practice, or on Sundays when he played street hockey with his friends. And so I invented a heightened persona for him, in which my fevered daydreams colored in his inadequacies.

But now that I was an adult, conjuring up those daydreams was almost impossible. When you're younger, concealment is alluring—

is he hiding a secret pain? Silence can be translated into depth. My older eyes saw his stonewalling as something else. At our age, Christian should have been eager to fill in the blanks for me. He, not my daydreams, should be moving the story forward.

He enjoyed spending time with me, but so far, he seemed uninterested in my life. This, also, was nothing new. When I was a teen, I wasn't insulted when he held himself apart from me. I tacitly agreed that my life was mundane. My family was pedestrian, my house was shabby, we never went anywhere for vacations except to Florida and once to Hershey Park. But now his incuriousness, his contention that he already knew me, seemed like an emotional shortcut.

Then again, I didn't necessarily want to answer questions about myself. I was glad not to have to talk about the divorce, or the current shambles that was my life. He probably picked up on my reticence and was being tactful. Well, I was going to meet him halfway. We were adults and I was going to take a chance and invite him into my life—meet a friend or two, swing by and say hello to my folks. Nothing too taxing. I vowed to bring it up the minute he called me.

*chapter twenty-seven*

In the meantime I took the train into the city to meet Andy so that he could show me around Red Hook, the Brooklyn waterfront area where he lived. Like a tourist, I took a cab to meet him because there was no direct subway service to it. He was standing out in front of his apartment complex, wearing an old navy peacoat that he said was once his grandfather's and a worn pair of brown cords.

As we walked up the stairs to his apartment, he showed me the courtyard and explained that the building had housed dockworkers in the twenties. His place was small but clean, and every available surface was covered with his artwork.

"Let me give you the house tour," he said. He spread his arms. "Well, we're done."

In the kitchen area he had set out cheese and crackers. "I have wine, too," he said. "And go ahead and make jokes about my port-wine stain, by the way. I do. It's nature's tattoo. I was ahead of the curve, really. I'm an early adopter. It's in the shape of Bangladesh, if you'll notice."

Then we took a walk to the edge of the harbor, past a row of warehouses and a few artists' studios. A raw wind whipped off of the water, and I snuggled deeper into my coat. "I like to walk along here in the early evening," he said, "because the trucks have gone from the warehouses and the streets are empty. All the big flat buildings are like empty canvases. There's not a lot of visual clutter and it's just quiet."

He turned into the entrance of a park that sat on the edge of the harbor. In the distance the majestic green figure of the Statue of Liberty rose out of the bay. We were the only people at the water's edge.

"I can't believe you found a pocket of New York that's so utterly still," I said.

He nodded. "It's easy to forget that New York is a port town," he said. He looked down at the dark green waves. "I love the sea smell and all these weird objects that wash up, buoys and life jackets and even an actual creature sometimes. See, isn't that a jellyfish?" He pointed. "Never mind. It's a plastic bag. I did see a crab, once. He kept snapping his claws at a floating beer can. Maybe he was trying to obey New York's recycling laws. I always think I'm going to see a body, which makes me feel a combination of excitement and dread. I guess it's probably better in theory than reality."

We watched a few tugboats chug by and then a red and black cargo ship. "There are a lot of ships that go by with strange flags of origin," he said. "A lot of them have Liberian registry, which is kind of a scam. They call it a 'flag of convenience'; it's like offshore banking. They register it in Liberia to save on income tax and wages. Plus there's less regulation."

He took me to another part of the harbor and pointed at a sunken ship whose rotting masts jutted out of the swirling water. "Doesn't that give you a spooky feeling?" he said.

"It does," I agreed. Then we wandered down some side streets. The neighborhood was a mix of worn houses done up in a nautical theme, public housing, and nineteenth-century warehouses, some of them converted into apartments. "There's kind of a weird community here," Andy said, nodding at a large guy who walked a pit bull. "Fewer people live out here, so you kind of have to make a commitment. There's no subway around. I mean, it's changing a lot. There's strange little workshops and businesses, like there's one I'll take you by, a few streets over, that provides antique cars to movies—little marginal places that you didn't even know were businesses."

We stopped at a bakery to warm ourselves, and he bought me a cupcake and a hot chocolate. Then he continued the tour, which wound through art galleries, an antiques shop, and a former sailor's bar called Sunny's. We followed some old trolley tracks that curved through the cobblestone streets and wound up at another waterside park.

"I love it here," I announced. "I can't believe I've lived in New York for so many years and I've never been to Red Hook."

"I'm telling you, there are still decently priced apartments to be had," Andy said. "There are art festivals out the wazoo; in fact there's one in two weeks that I'm going to be showing in."

"Well, then, why don't I come back?"

He grinned. "Why don't you? It's on a Saturday and we could go watch the soccer teams play at this field near my apartment. It's just a bunch of regular guys who play, but some of them are really good. The best part is the food carts that spring up around the games. A lot of the players are Colombian, and the trucks sell the best tacos and papusas you've ever eaten."

"What's a papusa?"

"They're from El Salvador, and they're sort of like empanadas. They serve them with pickled cabbage slaw. You know what? There's a storefront place around here someplace that sells them. Want to try one?"

I nodded. This was my favorite kind of day, wandering from one discovery to the next. He stood for a second. "Just let me think of where it is." He hit his forehead. "Think. Think!"

The phone in my purse buzzed, and I jumped. "You keep thinking," I said hurriedly to Andy and answered with a carefree laugh in my voice.

It was Christian. "Hey," he said. "I know this is last-minute, but a few of my friends are descending on me later tonight and I wanted you to meet everybody. I don't suppose you want to drive down."

I calculated. It was three-thirty. If I took the train home and then drove to Sea Girt, I could get there by seven.

"Sure," I said. He didn't ask where I was, and I didn't tell him. "See you soon."

I snapped the phone shut.

"Is everything okay?" asked Andy. "I remembered where the place is, and—"

"I think I may have to go to that place another day," I said. "I should get back. I have plans tonight."

His eyes hardened. "Right," he said.

I rushed back to New Jersey, and two hours later, I was driving on the turnpike, bound for Christian's party.

*chapter twenty-eight*

I had been a hit at Christian's get-together—cracking jokes, keeping glasses refilled, winning his friends over with bright questions and commentary. But the party had taken place on Tuesday, and I returned home the next morning. By Friday he hadn't called. I had nothing to do but fixate on the phone, which seemed to ring every ten minutes for my parents. It was my last two weeks at home before I returned to the city after Christmas. I had asked Adam to try and find a place for me in Red Hook, but in the end he had secured a relatively cheap apartment in Washington Heights, which, he informed me, was now called "WaHi." I found a hard-up moving company to move me in between Christmas and New Year's, and

I'd start work on the second of January. ("All right, my patience has run out," Vi told me on the phone. "Your midlife crisis is over. I'm seventy-four and I've never had a crisis—early, mid, or late.")

The weekend loomed. Dawn was avoiding me. My folks' plans were dully parental—a library benefit dinner, a community house-tour organization meeting, a Sunday trip to the fabric store for some sort of holiday project. I didn't feel like going into the city alone. Well, maybe I'd do a double feature at the gigantic spotless movie theater on Route 22. I'd make a bag of microwave popcorn and stow it in my purse the way my mother did. Or I could wander through the mall. Why wouldn't Christian call me? Were two visits in one week too much? I had to talk to somebody.

I walked briskly over to my mother's catalog basket and rooted out the J. Crew catalog. I needed a new cardigan, anyway. I dialed the customer-service number and asked for Trish, smoothly explaining that she had been my representative when I ordered last week. What if she had quit? A cold tremor ran through me as a supervisor put me on hold.

At length I heard her cheery voice. "Welcome-to-J.-Crew-this-is-Trish-how-may-I-help-you?"

Suddenly I wanted to hang up. What the hell was I doing? Why would she even remember me?

"Hello?"

I cleared my throat. "Oh, hi, Trish. This is Lillian Curtis. I placed an order with you before my high school reunion?"

"Oh, sure! How are you, hon? How did it go?"

"It was so much fun, better than I could have ever hoped. Listen, I have an order to place. I don't want to talk your ear off. I know you must think I'm a weirdo." I let the statement hang there.

"I've had weirder, believe me. You can't believe what some men say on the phone. Followed by no order!" She let out the phlegmy laugh of a moderate smoker.

"How are you doing?" I asked.

"Well, I've got some good news, too. I've been promoted. I am now a client specialist. We do personal shopping, help coordinate your work wardrobe, preorder limited-edition items . . ."

I was losing her. She was lapsing into the robotic cadence of a telemarketer.

". . . locate hard-to-find specialty items, or petite, tall, or ex-tended sizes."

"What are extended sizes?"

She stopped and became human again. "You know, I'm not sure, to be perfectly honest. I think it's a new term for 'plus size.' I'm still in training. So now you can always ask for me. Just say I'm your spe-cialist." She laughed. "So, did you meet your big high school love? His name was Chris, or something."

I was touched. "Christian. I can't believe you remembered. It was fantastic. We've been together ever since."

"Well, how about that." There was an expectant silence.

"Oh. Uh, I would like to order the Italian cashmere sweater."

"Crewneck? V-neck? Cardigan? Boatneck?"

"The cardigan. Small."

"How about the color? We have a sale on a couple of the ones that aren't going too quickly. Yellow Corn, Burnished Olive, Weathered Olive—no, wait, Weathered isn't on sale, just Burnished, along with Warm Sage . . . I think that's it. Oh, also Cool Meadow."

"What's Cool Meadow?"

"It's like a light green. Like a tree frog, sort of. You know those pictures of tree frogs?"

"I think I'll take Night Sky in small. If I get it by next week, I can wear it when I see Christian next weekend. If he calls, that is."

"You're not going to see him this weekend? It's Friday, right? I lose track of days, sometimes."

"It is. He hasn't called, so I guess he has plans."

"Why don't you just call him and see?"

I chewed my thumbnail. "I don't know."

"Wow, you really did go back to high school. Time is short, don't you think? Who has time to play games? When I deal with people now, I'm very direct. And if we don't mesh, then it's good-bye. Call him up."

"I don't know why I'm hesitating. I know it sounds like I'm a teen again."

"Listen, you want to talk about wasted time? I wish when I was younger I had listened to that voice you hear in your gut."

I ignored her mixed metaphors.

"That voice is your conscience, and when you're younger, you make a habit out of ignoring it. So I guess I would say to listen to that voice. I wish I had listened when it told me not to marry my first husband, Randy, who spent half of his paycheck on scratch-off tickets and the other half on going out with his buddies. If you want to see him, call him. But I say, don't wait around for any man."

"Thank you, Trish. You're the best client specialist I've ever had."

"Good luck. And your sweater will arrive in five to seven business days."

I dialed up Christian before I lost my nerve. He answered on the first ring.

"It's me, Lillian."

"Well, hello," he said in a low voice that made me flush. "What's up?"

When you're dating someone, *What's up?* can be deadly. It never means *Let's have a nice long chat* or *Come on over, I'm dying to see you.* It means *Please state your reason for calling.*

"I . . . I just wanted to invite you to lunch on Sunday with Vi," I said. "We're meeting in the city, and I thought you might want to come. She's a hoot." I'd never used the word *hoot* in my life.

He paused. "A hoot, huh?"

"She's really a character. And she's a big celebrity among the gray-hairs. Believe me, if you were thirty years older, you'd be very nervous. And she's dying to meet you."

He laughed softly. "What does she know about me?"

On safer ground, I became coy. "Just the basics." I took a deep breath. "Anyway, will you come?"

"Sure. I have to pick up something at the office anyway, so I can go there afterward."

I gave him the location of the restaurant and the time and hung up, elated.

*chapter twenty-nine*

I met Vi at Sardi's, her favorite restaurant in New York. She was waiting for me out front, fifteen minutes early, as usual. Today she had on a turquoise bouclé suit with a skirt—never pants for "luncheon"—matching turquoise shoes with a low square heel ("I'm a city girl and I need to walk"), and a necklace of fake pearls as big as strawberries.

Vi had been coming to Sardi's for a half-century. "They always make me feel like a visiting head of state here," she said, pushing open the door.

A manager flew over. "Ms. Barbour!" he cried, kissing her on both cheeks.

"Hi, Max," she said. "You remember my producer, Lillian."

"Yes, yes, of course," he said silkily. He guided us to Vi's regular table under the picture of her caricature as she received hosannas from the waitstaff and the tuxedoed bartender. "How are you, Lillian? There is another joining you, yes?"

We settled in as Vi waved to a woman at a table in the corner. "She was in *The Fantasticks* for years and years," she whispered. "I'm usually good with names, but for the life of me, I can't remember. What the heck was her name? Well, it'll come to me."

"Don't you worry, Vi," I said. "I forget everyone's name." I looked around happily. I loved coming to Sardi's, with its maroon walls and menu that featured classic "Sardi's traditions."

Vi studied the caricatures. "I get so tickled that I'm right next to Lucille Ball," she said. "And diagonal to Robert Mitchum. He was so handsome when he was a young guy, but he really hit his stride when he was in his forties and fifties. Most men look better when they get a little seasoning." She craned her neck to read the name on a new drawing that had recently been hung on the wall. "Tony Danza," she said. "Who on earth is that?"

"He was in a few popular television shows, like *Taxi*," I said.

"Yes, but why is he hanging next to Gregory Peck?" She motioned for the waiter and he hurried over. "This Tony Danza, why is he on the wall?"

"I believe he did *The Producers* on Broadway, Ms. Barbour."

She nodded. "Oh. Well, that makes sense."

"We typically add forty or fifty new portraits every year, so as you can see, we've put up Donny Osmond, Jason Biggs—"

"Jason Biggs?" she demanded. "Never heard of him. Oh, I can't keep up." She studied the menu. "I know we're still waiting on Christian, but I love to think about what I'm going to have, don't you? So many choices!" She leaned in closer. "So—before he gets here—are you serious with this young man?"

I nodded. "I think so."

"Well, I'm glad that you started to date again. Some women get self-conscious when they're past the first blush of youth, but I think anything is possible if you have a sense of how special you are. Women who are truly happy with themselves have that sparkle, that glow, that's irresistible to others! Don't you think? I had a friend who was as plain as a can of paint, but whenever I saw her at parties, she was surrounded by a crowd of men. It wasn't the way she looked, it was the way she acted—she just loved life, and people were drawn to her. She was enthusiastic, and gay—oh, I don't mean *gay* in the contemporary term, she was just . . ."

She looked up, and I felt a fluttering in my stomach at the sight of Christian striding toward our table with a smile. He was wearing a charcoal suit with a bright hot-pink striped shirt. I watched Vi's eyes as she took him in, and I knew she was thinking, *Mmm, handsome.* Then her penciled eyebrows drew down slightly, and I knew she was thinking, *Where's the tie?*

"Well," Vi trilled, as he gave her a kiss on the cheek. "Aren't you a sight for sore eyes? Lillian, you didn't tell me how handsome he was. Well, yes, you did."

He sat down. "I've heard a lot about you, too, Vi." A waiter appeared, and he ordered a martini. "Sorry I'm late," he said. "I had to drop off a proposal for this new video-game campaign. They want to use graffiti, and I think it's a bad idea." He sighed. "I work for a bunch of twenty-two-year-olds. They rule this business."

Vi put down her menu. "Lillian tells me you're a branding expert."

He waved his hand. "Yes. It's sort of complicated. I shouldn't talk business at lunch anyway."

Vi brightened. "Let's talk food, then. I see here there's onion soup au gratin and spinach cannelloni au gratin. Guess what? I'm ordering both! I'm getting double au gratin!"

Christian smiled politely.

"Save room for dessert, kids. Lillian, can we have the baked Alaska for two?"

I squeezed her arm. "As usual."

Vi twinkled at Christian. "They have a really spectacular signature dessert, it's called Floating Island. It's floating in the most heavenly vanilla sauce! It was popular years ago. You must try it."

He shook his head. "I don't eat dessert."

"Well, we do," I said heartily. "Right, Vi?"

She put down her menu. "So you recently lived in London, Christian? I once had a flat there when I was doing theater. It was in the swanky part of town, too—Knightsbridge."

He smiled. "No kidding."

The waiter took our orders, and then Vi once again fastened onto Christian. "So I'm probably closer to your parents' age. What does your father do? Or maybe he's retired."

"He is. He used to be an accountant."

"How is he enjoying retirement?"

"Now he's doing the taxes of everyone in his extended family, so I don't even think he knows he's retired."

"And your mother?"

"She stayed at home with us, which was really nice when we were growing up. And she does a lot of volunteering." He caught himself. "Not lately. She's been sick."

Vi and I both leaned forward. "The poor dear," she clucked. "I hope she's holding up all right."

"Well, she's lost a lot of weight, but she's getting back on track."

Vi's eyes flicked to mine and read that I had no idea Christian's mother was sick.

He suddenly stood up. "Will you two excuse me for a moment?" he said. "There's someone over there I haven't talked to since I left for London. I'll just be a minute." He took his martini with him.

Vi looked at me. "He seems like a nice enough man. A shame about his mother. Is it cancer?"

"You know that I don't know, Vi."

"How well do you really know this person? You've been together a month, and he's never mentioned this? Either he's not close to his mother, or he's not close to you."

"Well, maybe he doesn't want to scare me off. Or maybe it makes him too sad to talk about. I'm sure he planned on telling me."

Christian didn't make the impression on Vi that I had hoped he would. When our food arrived, he hurried back to the table, but he had been gone a tad too long. For the rest of the meal, he answered Vi's questions, made polite small talk, and even had a few bites of our baked Alaska. But one of Vi's favorite pastimes was talking about herself, and he never asked her a thing. After lunch, he insisted on paying, gave us both a kiss, and went quickly back to his office.

As Vi and I were gathering our things, a waiter appeared, grandly carrying a tray with a Floating Island on it. "The chef made this especially for you, Ms. Barbour," he said, putting it down with a flourish. "We know that this is your second-favorite dessert. You cannot go quite yet."

"Well, all right," she said with mock exasperation, reaching for a spoon. "Now I'll have to walk an extra turn around the block. Do you know that my daughter wants me to join a health club? I know they're the big rage now, but strenuous exercise is downright dangerous. It can cause a heart attack! I told her that I prefer to just add a little zing to my daily activities. When I empty the dishwasher, for example, I'll do a few extra stretches."

"Doesn't Mrs. P empty the dishwasher?"

"Not on her day off."

I waited for her to say something about Christian.

"Lillian," she began. I smiled. "You didn't think you'd get away without hearing my opinion, did you? You know that I tell it like it is. I can see why you are besotted. He's charming; he's wonderful to look at. He's certainly not Adam. Adam was too eager to please. But I worry that you're putting your entire heart into this. More than he is, I gather. You didn't even know his mother was ill. And you know, he didn't ask me anything about myself."

"Which must have driven you bonkers, Vi."

"Well, yes, but it's also not very polite. What struck me more is that he didn't ask me anything about *you*. I'm a wealth of information about all things Lillian, and you two are just getting to know each other. I had prepared a couple of amusing stories, but he didn't show any interest. Does he know your feelings about garbagemen, for instance?"

I shook my head. "No," I admitted. I always maintained that in New York City, firemen received all the adulation—and to a lesser extent, policemen—but our sanitation workers were cruelly ignored. New York's Strongest, who spent the day enduring the blatting of impatient horns from drivers who were forced to wait half a minute while they haul away our trash. My father claimed that sanitation men "had it easy" because they could collect a full pension after twenty years on the job. Easy? Rat bites, maggots, hypodermic needles? Every time I saw a sanitation worker (not "garbageman," thank you) I commended the startled man for his good work. My friends thought it was strange that on holidays I sent cards and food baskets to sanitation headquarters, but Vi had enthusiastically taken up the cause, leaving stocked picnics for them in a Styrofoam cooler at the end of her driveway.

"And I was just waiting to tell Christian about your sensitivity to smells," she added. Like a mole, I had a hypersensitive nose that regularly conveyed more information than I wanted about a person. On one elevator ride, I could discern a smoker who had one cup of coffee followed by an ineffective breath mint who had showered the night before using herbal shampoo after an Italian dinner washed down by two to three glasses of red wine. I took a deep sniff of the air next to her. "Aqua Net. Dove soap. Chanel lipstick, which smells a little like rose," I diagnosed. "And Youth-Dew, but your suit smells faintly of L'Air du Temps, crossed with"—I sniffed. "Did you wear this suit to an Indian restaurant?"

She thought for a moment. "I did!" she said delightedly. "What a special talent you have." Only Vi could view an offputting eccentricity as a "special talent."

She leaned closer and squeezed my arm. "But back to this Christian. I'm just worried because the last time we talked, you were tossing around phrases like 'the one that got away' and 'the real thing.' You know I'm not one to hold back, and I must tell you, I think you're throwing yourself into this romance to distract yourself, to hide away from the world."

I started to protest and she cut me off. "I know it can be frightening to face the future. But let me tell you something: Do you know that the years after Morty died have been the best of my life? And when I went to his funeral, I wanted to leap into the grave with him. But after I grieved, I began to date. I made new friends and started doing a great deal of volunteer work. As you know, I lost him to lung cancer, and so I made special visits to cancer wards. What I treasure most isn't the awards that I receive—although I won't lie, I love to get them! But more than that, I love to be of help to people. That's the key to happiness."

She dug her spoon into the Floating Island. "I'm at the age now where newspaper reporters ask me if I think about death. I know they're hoping I'll say something profound, but the only thing I ever tell them is that I don't want it to happen! I am positively greedy for more life, and I want you to be, too." She sighed. "Maybe I'm wrong about this young man, honey. I hope that I am, although at my ripe old age, I have pretty good instincts. He just seems so . . . so . . ."—she waved her spoon—"so muted."

She wasn't entirely wrong. And next to her Roman candle of a personality, he had seemed particularly withholding.

"Just don't pin all your hopes on him," she said. "Can't you just have fun, and take this as a lark?"

I put my spoon down. "I don't think so," I said, struggling to keep my voice even.

The tension was broken by two women in their sixties who were edging toward the table. One held a napkin and a pen. "Oh, Miss Barbour," the taller one quavered. "We never miss your show. The people you have on, those are the real stars. Not like today."

The other one elbowed forward. "You look beautiful," she declared. "I love your hair. Do you do it every day?"

Vi laughed. "Do you know that this is the first question I'm always asked? Even with all my achievements! I get it done by my girl twice a week." She signed the napkin with a flourish. "And the second question I usually get is, 'Vi, how do you keep your skin so youthful?' I'm very candid about the eye-lift I had five years ago. I am in show business, after all."

The women glowed in the warmth of Vi's confidential circle. "It looks extremely natural," the shorter one said loyally.

After the women left, Vi stood with me outside the restaurant as her driver idled on the street. "I've said my piece," she said, hugging me. "Oh, Lillian, are you cross with me?"

And suddenly, as I felt the fragile shoulder blades beneath her turquoise suit, I was not.

*chapter thirty*

I made a final trip to CVS to get some things for my new apartment. There was a CVS on every corner in the city, but the stores there were cramped and the clerks more beleaguered. I enjoyed the space and the friendliness of your suburban variety of CVS. I needed some hangers and a new laundry bag—Adam had taken custody of ours—and a fresh supply of CVS mustache bleach.

As I filled my cart, I hummed along to the Phil Collins tune playing softly in the background. I had always hated Phil, but suddenly he sounded good to me. Was it actually decent music, or was it simply nostalgia? Or because I had a

crush, did the whole world, including Phil Collins, seem more ap-
pealing?

I had just stopped to inspect the cheap nail polishes when I
glanced up and saw the top of a familiar head in the bandage aisle. It
was Dawn. Wasn't there a CVS closer to her house? I slowly put my
basket down. If I walked out casually with my eyes forward, it would
be plausible that I hadn't spotted her. I arranged my face into a preoccupied *Oh, I forgot something* expression and headed decisively for
the exit.

Halfway to the doors, I stopped. What was I doing? I could handle this. I had planned to call her, especially because I found that I
really did miss her. If I smoothed things over now, we could spend
the next week together and perhaps even go to the historical home in
Morristown that we had planned to tour. There was a kitchen garden
that we wanted to see, and for an extra ten dollars you could have tea
in the parlor, which was done up for the holidays. Dawn loved those
sorts of activities as much as I did. She wouldn't smirk at the period
dress of the guides and would happily watch an hourlong candle-
dipping demonstration.

I smiled and walked over to her. She was heaping boxes of Loony
Tunes bandages into her basket with a concentrated expression and
jumped when she saw me.

"Oh, hi," she said. She did not smile. She wasn't going to make
this easy. A vein in my left eyelid began to twitch crazily, and I hoped
she wouldn't notice.

She looked down at the bandages. "I probably go through a box
of these things a day," she said. "Sometimes I think my kids just
make up injuries because they like to wear them."

"Listen, Dawn," I said. "I'm glad I ran into you. I've been meaning to call you. I've been so upset since I saw you at the track, and I want you to know that I understood everything you said."

She stared at me, not speaking.

I took a deep breath. "I really miss you, and I'm only here for a few more days and then I go back to New York. I was hoping we could do all the fun things together that we planned. Remember the Thayer House Mansion? We could go have tea, and I think there's a textile exhibit, and . . ."

She stood motionless, her lips pursed.

"Dawn," I went on, my voice rising. "I really am sorry. I know I hurt your feelings, but I want to make it up to you. I can be a good friend to you, the kind that you want."

She looked momentarily stricken. I knew then that I had broken her down, and my breath came more easily.

I went on. "What are you doing now? Let's go have coffee at that place you like, and we can talk."

She stared at me evenly. "You know, Lily," she said in a tired voice that was almost a monotone, "it took me a long time to separate myself from the girl that I was in high school. And I really liked who I was becoming. And somehow you managed to undo it in one night."

A bright red spot appeared on each of her cheeks. "We've had fun together, but somehow I've always had this feeling that you thought you were doing me a favor," she said. "You're quick to remind me that you're from the city, painting this hip picture of yourself, but in reality, you're not happy, and I am. You think you hide how you feel, that little bit of contempt, but I watch your face when I talk about the kids, or my husband, or what I do all day. Well, guess what? I like living in the suburbs. This isn't a compromise for me. I even like my minivan."

"I don't look down on you," I said.

"You did then and you do now," she said, distractedly pushing some hair out of her eyes. "And the great thing about being an adult is that I don't have to participate anymore. In school, you're with the same people for twelve years and you have to find a way to make it work. Well, I don't have to do that now."

I stared at her, incredulous, tears gathering in my throat. Biddable Dawn, with her #1 MOM key chain, was dismissing me. She looked at me sympathetically. "I'm sorry, Lily. I know deep down that you care. I really hope that you'll be happy."

I tried to speak but only managed a weak croak as the tears rose from my throat to my eyes. Her words stung because they were true.

I fumbled in my purse for my keys and turned to walk quickly to the car.

*chapter thirty-one*

Ginny was back, this time for a pre-Christmas visit. She always spent the actual holiday with Raymond's family, so she usually came home for a long weekend beforehand and left the kids with him.

I sat in the kitchen and pretended to busy myself as I listened to their latest phone conversation. "Well, I told you not to buy whole-bean, didn't I?" she said. "Are you sure the grinder's broken? No. No, it's a valid question. Sometimes you get impatient and you declare something is on the fritz when with a little investigation . . ."

Ginny glanced at me and pressed the receiver close to her ear, but Raymond's angry voice was still audible.

"I resent that," she said calmly. "I resent that. You're transferring your aggression to me when you should be frustrated that you didn't get the coffee ground yourself when we were at Whole Foods." Angry voice. "Right. You know, I'll be honest, I actually don't taste a difference when you grind it right before we drink it." Pause. "Well, yes, I know. But it's really time-intensive, and I just think that in the future we should save ourselves a lot of frustration and get it ground at the store." She frowned and tried to motion me out of the room, but I stayed.

"Well, maybe you can use the blender to grind it. I think there's a grind setting. Or try the food processor, that might be better."

I just couldn't imagine her and Raymond having sex, and I was cursed with being able to imagine, in living color, sex between any two people on earth. But I could easily imagine them filling their days with these sorts of conversations.

"And please remind Irina that both kids have Creative Play class today."

"Creative Play?" I whispered as she narrowed her eyes at me. "You need an organized class for that?"

"It's at three. Yes. Thank you." Ginny and Raymond were elaborately polite with each other, but there was a touch of antipathy behind their clipped pleases and thank-yous.

She hung up and turned to me. "I really amuse you, don't I?" she said.

I nodded. "You do."

My parents walked briskly downstairs to get breakfast before heading out to Community Cleanup Day.

"What a treat to have you here again, honey," said my mother, hugging Ginny.

"I cut out something for you from the paper," my father told her.

"Something about your town that I thought you'd be interested in. Madison's growing real quick, the article says."

Ginny nodded as she carefully sliced a bagel. "The private biotech sector is really expanding. It's probably about that. The university has been seeding a lot of biotech start-ups, so those jobs have been booming."

My father blinked a few times. He didn't know enough about the biotech industry to make a pronouncement. Ginny glanced at him and quickly said, "I notice there has been a lot of construction around here, too. When I drove in I couldn't believe how torn up the road was near Boonton."

"They're putting in another superstore," he said. "It's called a Super Stop and Shop. What happens if you just want to get a goddamn carton of milk? They're no fools, they put the milk in the back, and then you need a sherpa guide to get you out of there." Now he was on familiar territory. "Bigger supermarkets, bigger cars, bigger food to put in giant refrigerators. You know the DiMartolos who are putting that addition on their house? I'm walking by one morning and I got to talking to the contractor. Good guy. I say, 'What's going on?' He tells me they're putting in a laundry room on both floors so they don't have to walk down the stairs." His mouth drew down in disgust. "No wonder everyone has big fat backsides in this country."

My mother grabbed her purse from the front closet and gave us a kiss. "Listen, girls," she said. "We'll be back late this afternoon and then we'll have an early dinner together." She gulped some coffee and looked at her watch. "It'll be just the four of us, like old times."

They bustled out and Ginny and I took our coffee into the living room. She nestled into the couch. "So tell me all about Christian," she said. "I've heard little bits on the phone, but I want the whole story."

Glowingly, I told her everything for the next hour while she nodded and refilled her coffee twice. I had just spent another weekend at his parents' house and had met a few more of his friends. When I finished she looked out the window. At length she said carefully, "You know, you sound just like you did when you were a teenager."

I smiled. "Well, I probably have that same kind of excitement that I did when we were kids. You remember that feeling."

"Yes, we talked about it." She hesitated. "But I'm picking up on the bad parts of being that age. The insecurity, the nervousness. I'm wondering if you're not seeing him through your teenage eyes, rather than seeing him for what he is now." Her clear eyes searched my face. "I'm a little worried about you," she said. "I think you're regressing. It's more than spending all that time holed up in your room, or eavesdropping on my phone conversations."

"I only did that once."

"You drive like a teenager now, racing as fast as you can to a red light and then stomping on the brakes. You're getting surly with the folks." She shook her head. "I don't know."

I shrugged, determined not to let her know that I was bothered. "What's wrong with taking a break? What's wrong with revisiting the happiest time in my life? Why wouldn't you want to return to a more innocent time?"

She flapped her hand impatiently. "No time period was ever innocent, and certainly not the eighties. That's the biggest fallacy in the world. I hate the whole marketing of decades, anyway. They're just artificial constructs." She regarded me. "And it wasn't an innocent time for you. You seemed pretty miserable to me, and you were a popular girl. I recall lots of crying in your room at night. You struggled with your grades, you were constantly warring with your friends."

She sat forward. "In fact, now that I'm thinking about it, you really only liked your last year of high school. I wrote a paper related to this, it's what I called the 'peak-and-end effect.' When people are asked to reflect on some episode, say high school, they tend to focus more heavily on a peak experience during that episode, like the senior prom, or on how that episode ended. They tend to be foggy on the rest of the moments. I remember one study looked at people who had gotten colonoscopies. One group got shorter procedures, the other group got longer procedures, but with less pain at the end. Overall, both procedures actually involved the same amount of pain, but guess what?"

I stared at her until I realized that she actually wanted me to say "What?"

"What?" I said.

"People thought they felt more pain during the *shorter* procedure. Why? Because the longer procedure had a more comfortable ending. We really tend to remember endings at the expense of everything else. Everyone knows how *Casablanca* ended, but how did it begin?"

I knew she wasn't asking me because she was immersed in lecture mode. Not that I could have answered, anyway. Didn't it open with a German officer meeting another officer at the airport? Or maybe it was a French officer. Or a French officer meeting a German officer.

"I just feel like you're using your present needs to fill in blanks in the past," she was saying. "Memory is like a shuffled deck of cards, and you just sort of . . . no, no, that's not the right analogy." She sighed impatiently. "Planning the future is essential to living. I just read this study of—"

I inspected my nails. "Ginny," I interrupted coolly, "do you know how exhausting it is when you cite studies in what should be a normal conversation?"

"I'm just saying that by re-creating the past, you're only creating a fragmented picture. And by failing to understand how tenuous your grasp of the past is, you misinterpret what the future is going to be, so you misinterpret the sources of your potential happiness. And this Christian, who doesn't sound much like a grown-up, by the way—rootless, impulsive, resistant to any sort of commitment including picking up the phone—I suspect that what really made you happy was the longing for him rather than the actual man himself. In fact, one of my colleagues calls this—"

I flopped down on the couch, trying to distract her. "Ginny, please, with the studies," I moaned.

But she would not be deterred. "What is so scary about the future?" She looked at me. "You know what? I think the first step is taking an accurate look at the past." She clapped her hands. "I know. Where's your journal? Let's have a look. Let's see it with adult eyes. I assume enough time has passed that you're okay with my reading it?"

"Please," I said. "Like you haven't read it before."

She smiled. "I did, once. But I'm telling you the truth when I say that I felt too guilty to read it again."

In the meantime I could still quote from the notebook that contained Ginny's scribblings. It was less diary entries than dreadful poetry that I memorized and recited to my friends. One stanza in particular was a guaranteed crowd-pleaser:

> *A faded brown rose am I*
> *I am a bride's boquet [sic]*
> *Tossed aside after the rice has long been thrown*
> *Pain is a consolation; such a fragile thread we hang by*

*The sorrow in my heart is a hundred flowers screaming*
*In dumb repose you cannot hear*

Sheepishly, I thought of my friends howling. There was something earnest about Ginny that I should have left alone.

"So," she said, standing up. "Where is it? I'm not trying to torture you. I think you have a completely distorted view of your past. Prove me wrong."

I remained seated. "I don't know where it is," I confessed. "I haven't read it in fifteen years, probably. It was always under my mattress."

She folded her arms. "Where could it be?" she muttered. She jumped up and went to my bedroom, me trailing behind her. "Is it okay if I look?" she asked.

I nodded. I was actually eager for her to find it.

She tore through my closet, my bedside table, my dresser, getting distracted a few times by the artifacts. "What is this?" she asked, puzzled, examining a laminated card. "'License to fart,'" she read slowly.

"It was from Spencer Gifts," I explained. "See the front? It was issued by the Mayor of Gas Town. Sandy gave it to me."

She tossed it back into the drawer. "I don't know why you hold on to this stuff."

We ransacked the room. Nothing. Ginny thought for a minute and said, "I know. I know where it is. It's in the attic."

"No, I've looked up there already," I said. But she was already in the hallway, pulling down the creaky ladder that led upstairs. I followed her, inflamed by the same sense of dramatic purpose that we had as kids, when Ginny would urgently announce, "We're collecting all the caterpillars in the yard, right now, let's go," and off we'd rush with buckets as if we were being timed.

She disappeared up the stairs while I helpfully volunteered to hold the ladder. "I'm not going to think about the spiders," she called. Silence. "Here are some boxes, filled with . . . it looks like stuffed animals. These are all my things, I think." The ceiling creaked as she moved around. "Here's another box. This is . . . yes, this is my stuff, too."

For twenty minutes I sat, waiting, as I heard the sound of rummaging and boxes being moved. Then: "Lily," she said sharply. "Is it a black and red notebook?"

I stood rigid as excitement flooded me. "Yes! Bring it down."

She carefully stepped down the ladder. "It was in one of my boxes, for some reason," she said, handing the dusty notebook over. "Ugh, I'm going to wash my hands."

I impatiently opened it up as she disappeared into the bathroom. Written on the first page was "Ginny, go ahead and read this if you dare. I'm sure it's much more interesting than your sucky life." Hastily I flipped past it as she returned.

"Now," she said, sitting on my bed. "Let's look at this lost artifact." I sat next to her and read the second page aloud:

Today is my sixteenth birthday. I got a ton of presents, I was psyched! I got Atari (and a *Space Invaders* cartridge) a bottle of Babe perfume, a subscription to *Seventeen*, and a pot of Indian Earth which I have been wanting forever.

"I bought you the Indian Earth," Ginny said. "Remember, it was that powder that dyed your face orange? It came in a fake earthenware pot."

"And you were supposed to apply it on your entire face, but I just put it on my cheeks, so that I had two orange spots."

Ginny laughed. "I saved up my babysitting money to get you that." Again I was overwhelmed by an urge to cry.

She crossed her legs and grabbed a pillow, slumber-party-style. "Skip ahead," she urged.

I flipped through a few pages, past my painstaking transcription of "Spring" by Edna St. Vincent Millay ("Not only under the ground are the brains of men / eaten by maggots"), past my blackly underlined quotes from self-pitying Smiths lyrics ("Now I know how Joan of Arc felt").

Then I picked a random page and read:

Another totally beat weekend. I drank an entire bottle of Boone's Farm at Vanessa's party and I was the most wasted I've ever been. I puked in my bed and had to clean it up early in the morning before the parents were up. And I hate Cheryl, she found out I told Lynn what she said about her. Of course I denied it but now Cheryl keeps calling my house and when I answer, she whispers, *Liar.* You can hear laughing in the background and then they hang up. I'm scared to go to school now because Cheryl is in three of my classes but I already took all of my sick days.

"You threw up in your bed?" Ginny said.

I nodded, pained. I had forgotten about that. "More than once, actually."

"Cheryl was an unhappy girl. I think she was conflicted about her sexuality. Keep going," she said. I flipped to another page:

I hate all of the boys in our sucky grade. I talk to them and stuff, but they're all a bunch of conceited fags. All weekend they just hung out with each other. I ask you, is that normal? And I'm sick of my untrusting, slimy parents.

I just got back from Jack Meyer's pool party and I hate myself. Deep hatred. Kurt and Cheryl and Craig and Sarah are all getting together after the party somewhere but I guess it's private. I have no real friends at all. I never get enough nerve to talk to anyone. Face it, I am a loser. I noticed it in school, too. What's the use. I am stupid, fat (118 pounds), too quiet, my nose is huge, I really suck royally at just about everything. I'm such a leech, and a scunge, people avoid me. I hate hate hate myself.

All I do is wait around for things to get better and they don't. The only guy that calls me is Doug Muller, who takes track and wears Wranglers. My mother is such a tense, obnoxious shrew, screaming at me about the most pointless, shitty things. She says she is going to "change my attitude." Oooh! I wish my mother was sent to jail. All she causes me is aggravation. I would love to punch her. I can't wait to leave this house forever and this scum-hole of a town. I feel like if I died, no one would even care.

"Good Lord," said Ginny, laughing uncomfortably. "This sounds like Charles Manson's diary. Like you're going to kill people and stack them like cordwood. Every other word is *hate*."

"Yes, but when you're a teenager, you're never going to write 'Boy, am I happy. It's a beautiful day!'" Still, my stomach began to ache when I remembered that night at the party and my forlorn walk home.

I paged to another entry, the writing sloppy and smeared. "I was drunk here," I said. "This must have been after a party."

So it's like 2 in the morning and the party is almost over and who starts talking to me but Chuck Monohan!!!! I've never talked to him in my life! He came in with the seniors but they mostly left after a while. We were both soo blasted, I had a bottle of Andre and then Sandy was pouring shots of "To Kill Ya" down my throat. So then I'm in Chuck's car (he said he drove drunk well because he paid attention more) and we end up in his driveway and we're making out! The funny thing was when I got up to leave he kept trying to trip me!

Ginny took the journal from my hands and read the rest. "'Finally we both fell'—no, he tripped you and you fell—'and he was pulling at my clothes, he's so strong, it was funny, and then I think we did "everything but."'"

My whole body had gone cold. My hazy recollection of the whole incident had been a triumphant make-out session with a football star. But then I had a brief, sickening flash of Chuck looming over me with unseeing eyes, holding me down and pulling off my clothes, his drunken dead weight pushing the breath out of me as he mechanically humped me on the gravel driveway. "I love you," he muttered thickly, and I realized he didn't know who I was. When he finished with a groan, he rolled off me and I sat up shakily, pulling down my shirt and pulling up my underwear.

Ginny kept reading. "'Then I got sick and he said I should walk home to sober up, which was a good idea.'" She looked up, wonderingly. "He wouldn't even take you home."

She continued: "'Now I have bruises and cuts all over me, wait until I show Kimmy and those guys. P.S. He just called, I don't know how he got my number, and he said this was between us and Shauna can never find out! I can't believe he called, what a nice guy!'"

Ginny and I looked at each other, stricken. "Even in your diary," she said slowly, "which you thought no one else would read, you're glossing over an ugly situation. I feel sorry for that sixteen-year-old girl. You were so excited that a big football star was paying attention to you that you couldn't even see he was essentially just holding you down and masturbating on you."

I hugged myself. "I can't believe I would have forgotten that."

She looked at me pityingly. "I can." She picked up the journal and read another entry.

I hate that bitch Jennifer. We were all in Science today and it was a substitute teacher and the guys were all trying to pull her pants down and she was screaming and pretending like it bothered her. It so didn't. Mildew yanked them almost off and you could see her underwear.

Ginny and I looked at each other. With my adult memory I recalled Jennifer's panicked face. She wasn't squealing in delight, she was near tears, but I was still poisonously jealous of her because she was receiving the attention that eluded me. I suddenly remembered with nauseating clarity that in that moment I wanted more than anything to trade places with her, to be in the middle of that pack of leering boys.

Ginny shook her head. "Any attention was good attention. That's how you saw it." She ran her hands through her hair. "God. I'm dreading the day when Jordan becomes a teenager. You know, Mom used to constantly tell us how smart we were, how we could do anything. She was so big on those feminist messages of empowerment. And none of it matters because you have that pathological need for reassurance, in whatever form it takes."

I grabbed the journal and flipped through the pages—some spotted with tears, others written in angry, traced-over block letters. Many passages had been scratched out later to cover embarrassment. Only a few pages expressed any form of happiness or even mild contentment. "I can't believe that my memories are so different from all of this," I said, my voice breaking. "I feel sick."

Ginny hugged me. "I wish I had known about some of this stuff. I wish we had talked more. Maybe I could have helped, somehow."

"You did help," I said. Her face shimmered glassily as my eyes filled with tears. "I'm really sorry, Ginny." I was sobbing.

"What? Why?"

"I have to tell you something. I read the poetry from your diary and sometimes I would recite it to my friends." I cried harder.

Ginny stopped smoothing my hair and laughed. "This has been torturing you? Please. My poetry was pretty ghastly. You had every right to make fun of it."

"I feel like an embarrassment to you," I went on, gulping. "My life is such a mess right now, and I guess I just felt like going back was easier, somehow."

She hugged me again. "Don't be one of those people who peaked at eighteen. Take a page from your friend Vi. She's, what—seventy-five?—and the last time I talked to her I got the 'best is yet to come' speech."

Later that night when I was in bed, I opened my journal again and read the entire account, my heart beating queasily with the realization that I had forgotten fully half of the events of my teenage years. More likely I had buried them. The deviously inventive cruelty of teenage girls, the thuggish obliviousness of the boys! Each passage unlocked another memory that had been happy when I had originally tucked it away and had since rotted between the pages.

Other entries flooded me with shame:

So Dawn's having one of her stupid Valentine's Day parties again. Isn't she a little old for this shit? A) there are no boys there, which was fun in eighth grade but come on, and B) it's in her basement, which smells like a cat box and C) I haven't even talked to her in like a year. She passed me an invite at lunch in front of everybody and when she turned around I pretended to crumple it up. Well then she turned back around and totally saw me.

And on the last page, I had written this:

It's Friday night and all my friends are out. Christian was supposed to come get me two hours ago and he's not here yet. Is he at the party already? Doesn't he realize I'm not there? I shouldn't have blown off Kimmy. And my parents keep asking where he is. We've been going out six months and he still won't come in and meet them, he just beeps the horn in the driveway. Dad said he's going to let the air out of his tires next time and he'll be forced to come in. Well, it's only ten o'clock, maybe he'll still call. Oops gotta go, there's the phone.

P.S. It was for my parents.

*chapter thirty-two*

The next day I girded myself to make two phone calls. The first was to Vi. "Oh, dear," she said worriedly. "Don't tell me you're not coming back on Monday."

I swallowed. "Of course I am. But I have to tell you something that's extremely difficult." I took a breath. "I think I'm going to have to start looking for another job."

She didn't speak.

"I feel as though I need to do something different, and I realized that I've been at the job for so long because I'm so attached to you, and—"

She interrupted me. "Lillian. I've been waiting for this. Mind you, I've been dreading it, but I welcome it, too. It pains me to say it, but I think you're ready to move on." Her voice broke. "I'm glad. It means you're feeling more optimistic about life. And I think Frank could replace you. Not that you can be replaced."

"I want to stay friends," I said miserably. "Like we always have been."

"Why, Lillian," she said with surprise. "We will always be the best of friends. Just try to separate us, Buster." Vi often addressed an imaginary adversary who had the gall to try and hold her down. "What's that Cole Porter song from *Du Barry Was a Lady*? She began to sing. " 'If you're ever in a jam, here I am!' Remember? 'If you ever need a pal, I'm your gal!' Gene Kelly was marvelous in that. In the meantime, where will you be looking for a job?"

"I don't know," I admitted.

"Well, what is your dream job? Don't think about it, just tell me the answer."

"Lots of things, I guess. Being a producer on the Food Network, or the Travel Channel." I thought for a minute. "I would love to work on *Sesame Street*, or really, anything done by the Sesame Workshop, but then again, everyone in the United States of America wants those jobs."

She frowned. "How do I put this delicately? You're not exactly what I would call a kid person, Lillian."

"I am, too. Anyway, this is different." I ticked off the reasons. "They've won over a hundred Emmys, they have shows in Israel and Jordan and India; people who have worked there say you have un-limited creative license—"

"So send out résumés! And I will make some calls. I think Irv Cohen's grandson is a producer on *Sesame Street*. I know everyone—or at least, everyone's ancestors."

"Thank you, Vi," I said feelingly.

The next call was more difficult. After three false starts, I dialed Christian's number. His voice was heavy with sleep even though it was nearly lunchtime.

"Hi, Christian."

"Oh, hey, how are you?" he said. He seemed glad to hear from me. "I meant to call you. Are you coming down this weekend?"

"No, I can't. Remember I told you I was moving into my new apartment? I can't wait. I'm sure my parents can't either. I think they have Costco champagne chilling in the fridge for the big moment when I'm out." In actuality all three of us got a little choked up when my mother slowly packed away my ratty orange afghan for the next visit.

"Oh, right. Yeah. Well, maybe another weekend. Fortunately my folks never come down here, so at this point I think I have squatter's rights. So what else is going on?"

"Well, I'm looking for another job. Vi's actually been great about it. She's calling around for me."

He didn't say anything. I heard him turn on a television.

"Well, give me a call when you're settled," he said after a minute.

I knew then that what Ginny said was true: My dreams that fluttered and wheeled around him were more exciting than he was. I had been doing the same thing I had done as a teenager, removing myself from my own life so I became an onlooker rather than a participant, endlessly chronicling and cataloguing.

I could have spent a perfectly pleasant year with Christian, perpetually Hanging Out, but suddenly I would rather have been alone.

"This next month will be pretty busy," I said.

"Oh." He sounded surprised. Then again, I would never know for sure what that "oh" meant, or what anything meant.

"Good-bye, Christian," I said, and put down the phone.

Then, before I could change my mind, I began to dismantle my bedroom. Down came the Soloflex and Squeeze *Singles* posters, the photo collage that Sandy had made me, the prom pictures and the Robert Doisneau print. I dragged in a contractor bag from the basement and tossed in the old bottles of Anaïs Anaïs and Pavlova and Benetton Colors. They didn't smell the same as they once did; they had turned from sweetness to rot.

I then put my old clothes from Esprit and Ocean Pacific into a bag for Goodwill. Some eighties-obsessed teen would snatch up those Gloria Vanderbilt and Sergio Valente jeans. With the last of my nerve, I gathered all of the artifacts from my dresser, dumped them into a big box, and had my father put it in the attic, with much sweating and cursing.

After I had completely emptied my bedroom, I brought my mother upstairs for the unveiling. "*Walla*, as Dad says," I said grandly, opening the door. "Your future guest room."

"Oh, honey," my mother said mistily.

"It's time," I said, as we looked around the bare room.

She nodded. "It's time."

*chapter thirty-three*

Two months later, Vi sat quietly in the waiting room of Sesame Workshop, her large white handbag on her lap. True to her word, she had secured an interview for me at *Sesame Street* with the show's executive producer, a seasoned, Emmy-harvesting hotshot still known to Vi as "Irv Cohen's little grandson." She insisted on accompanying me to the interview, and when I emerged from the producer's office she leapt up eagerly.

"How did it go?" she whispered. "You were in there for an hour and a half!"

"I'm trying to keep it together," I said in a low voice as we made for the elevator. "But I think it went really well. He liked my ideas. I was worried that I brought too many, but he said most people don't bring enough."

She nodded. "That's my girl."

When the elevator doors had shut, I nearly collapsed on her birdlike shoulders. "Oh, Vi!" I said. "We really connected, and it was supposed to last for twenty minutes at most. He said he would let me know next week but that I shouldn't worry. That's good, right?"

"That is *very* good," she said, grabbing both of my hands. "Shall I blow in another call to Irv?"

"No," I said, laughing. "You've done enough."

"Let's see. Where are we?" she said distractedly. "The Upper West Side, right? We just have enough time to go to Sardi's! It will be decorated for the holidays! We don't have to be back at the studio until two. Shall we have a festive lunch?"

As we walked out the door, chattering excitedly, we passed a man who looked slightly familiar.

"Lillian," he said, and I jumped. It was Andy Wells. I realized it was him at the same moment it occurred to me that after our Red Hook jaunt, I never followed up on his e-mail messages that said, *Where are you? Everything okay?*

"What brings you here?" he asked.

"Oh," I said, startled. "I just had a job interview." I hastily looked over at Vi. "Andy, this is Vi Barbour, my boss—my friend. Vi, this is Andy. We went to high school together."

"How do you do," said Vi, looking at him with the bright curiosity of a robin.

"How do you do," he said, shaking her hand. "I love your show. After I talked to Lillian at our reunion I started recording it, and now I'm completely addicted."

"Well, then, you just brought our demographic down about ten years," Vi returned.

"I especially liked the show with the veteran newscasters," he said. "I think it was last Tuesday. And also the one with the star of all those World War II movies, what was his name . . ."

"You really do watch the show!" Vi said delightedly. "George McCord. Do you know, he just asked me on a date? His wife died a year ago."

"Well, I think you should go for it, if I may be so bold," said Andy. "He still looks great, don't you think?"

"I do. I think he looks so much better now that he shaved his head. He was holding on to those three hairs for too long."

Andy nodded. "He has a nice-shaped head, so it works. You have to have the right head."

I looked at Vi. "You're going on a date with George?"

She shrugged gaily. "Sure. Why not?"

"So, Andy," I said quickly, to fill a looming silence. "Do you work here?"

"Yes, doing animation. Freelance, but it's six months at least, so that's good. I found out that I got the job on the day you came to Red Hook. I was going to tell you all about it, but then you got a phone call. Remember, where you jumped directly into a cab and left me standing on the street?"

Vi reached in her bag. "I'm going to return some phone calls," she said, and edged away.

"I'm sorry, Andy," I said. "I had such a great time that day, too. I was moving back into the city and I meant to e-mail you after I got settled."

"Ah." He raised his eyebrows.

"Well, I was also caught up in . . ."

"Going out with Christian Somers," he finished.

I smiled. "It's over. It was a bit of a mistake. I guess I needed to go back one more time."

He nodded, trying to comprehend. "Like a monkey in an experiment. You needed more food pellets. Maybe you just had to gorge yourself on pellets."

"Yes," I said, even though I wasn't entirely sure what he was saying. "So listen, why don't we go out for a coffee sometime? Just something casual." He shook his head.

"I don't think so," he said. "But thanks."

*Keep going,* I urged myself. *Push through your shyness. Stop being safe. Be a grown-up. Try again.*

"Let me make up for my rudeness and buy you one coffee," I persisted. "How about tomorrow afternoon? One cup and you can be on your way."

I glanced over at Vi, who was pretending to talk on her cell phone, which she barely knew how to use. It might have even been upside down.

Andy stared at the sidewalk. "I really have to go," he said hesitantly.

"Yet you haven't moved," I pointed out.

His eyes stayed on the sidewalk but I saw a faint smile.

"True," he said.


From Vi's 1985 autobiography,
*Who Says There Are No Second Acts?:*

If I wanted to, I could live among my memories. In my study at home, I have boxes of awards, heaps of photos, and many letters and gifts from fans. But I keep them tucked well out of sight. Do you know why? Because I prefer to be a part of the world, that's why. If you think that your life is over, it *will* be over.

Some of my girlfriends feel that the best time of their lives took place when they were young. This is nonsense, and what's more, it is positively dangerous. The "Good Old Days" weren't always that good! You must tell yourself that the best times are *right this minute.* Every day I wake up and think, "What shall I do today?" Maybe I'll meet someone who will become a life-long pal. I might try an exciting new ethnic dish, or wear my hairdo a different way. Perhaps I'll book a Caribbean cruise. Why, there is something new waiting for you every day! Isn't life marvelous? You'd better believe it is!

*about the author*

JANCEE DUNN grew up in Chatham, New Jersey. From 1989 to 2003, she was a staff writer at *Rolling Stone*, where she wrote twenty cover stories, among them profiles of Madonna and Brad Pitt. She has written for many different publications such as *GQ* (where she wrote a monthly sex advice column for five years), *Vogue*, and *The New York Times*. From 1996 to 2001, she was a veejay for MTV2, MTV's all-music station; the following year she was an entertainment correspondent for *Good Morning America*. She writes frequently for *O, The Oprah Magazine*, including a monthly ethics column called "*Now* What Do I Do?" Her memoir, *But Enough About Me*, which detailed her life as a chronically nervous celebrity interviewer, was published by HarperCollins in 2006.

Dunn lives in Brooklyn, New York, in a converted church with her husband, the writer Tom Vanderbilt, whose book *Traffic* will be published by Knopf in summer 2008.